ALSO BY JAN BURKE

Kidnapped

Bloodlines

Nine

Flight

Bones

Liar

Hocus

Remember Me, Irene

Dear Irene,

Sweet Dreams, Irene

Goodnight, Irene

THE
MESSENGER

A NOVEL

JAN BURKE

SIMON & SCHUSTER
New York   London   Toronto   Sydney

Simon & Schuster
1230 Avenue of the Americas
New York, NY 10020

First Simon & Schuster hardcover edition January 2009

SIMON & SCHUSTER and colophon are registered trademarks of Simon & Schuster, Inc.

For information about special discounts for bulk purchases, please contact Simon & Schuster Special Sales at 1-800-456-6798 or business@simonandschuster.com.

Designed by Jill Putorti

Manufactured in the United States of America

10   9   8   7   6   5   4   3   2   1

Library of Congress Cataloging-in-Publication Data
Burke, Jan.
The messenger / Jan Burke.
    p. cm.
1. Supernatural—Fiction. I. Title.
PS3552.U72326M47 2008
813'.54—dc22   2008030683

ISBN-13: 978-0-7432-7387-9
ISBN-10:   0-7432-7387-7

To my nieces and nephews,
with thanks for all the good they bring to our present day
and will bring to our futures

THE
MESSENGER

1

Come to me.

Frightened, Eduardo Leblanc shook his head within the diving helmet, the way a dog would shake water from its fur—trying to rid himself of the voice inside his skull.

Far below the surface of the Caribbean Sea, he had lost contact with the salvage ship, the *Declan*. The communication unit on his diving helmet had malfunctioned. He had been listening to an exchange between Krantz—the crew's marine archeologist, the only other diver down on this shift—and the ship. Suddenly the comm unit cut out, and Eduardo heard nothing other than the exhaust of bubbles from his helmet and the usual soft noises of his equipment.

He looked over at Krantz. Krantz was in charge here, supervising the underwater recovery work they were doing on the *Morgan Bray*, an American merchant ship that had sunk in 1815. The light for video equipment on the archeologist's helmet was on, as was Eduardo's. As far as Eduardo could tell, both cameras were still running. Through the faceplate of Krantz's mask, Eduardo could see he was still speaking to the ship, or at least narrating what his camera was seeing.

Come to me, and all will be well.

This was the second time Eduardo had heard the voice. The same thing had happened on his first dive in these waters, two days ago. The communications device cut out. He heard the voice. He felt afraid, and then—then the fear changed. Now Eduardo's fear once again began to give way to a sense of anticipation. He looked anxiously between Krantz and a small mound of sand a few feet away, one among many that undoubtedly covered artifacts from the *Morgan Bray*.

He checked the connector for the communications cable hookup on his air hat—the model was one of the finest available to commercial divers—to ensure that nothing was loose. As he expected, all attachments were secure, although nothing he did brought the transmissions back. He looked back at the mound.

This morning, as he readied for this dive, he told himself that he had only imagined the strange sensations he felt two days ago, and that certainly the voice he had heard was not real. He blamed the experience on a lack of sleep, thought of it as a hallucination—they were not unknown in this profession. The voice was inside his head, and not being heard over the system, or anywhere outside his own skull.

Now he heard it again, and turned back to the mound of sand among the scattered wreckage, feeling quite sure that this was the place the voice wanted him to be. With every passing moment, he felt better about his decision to heed its call. The nearer he came to the mound, the greater his sense of calm contentment. Why had he ever worried about the voice?

The comm unit suddenly came back online, and the archeologist, who had never treated Eduardo as anything but a mule in a diving suit, asked, in a tone of suspicion, what he was doing so far away from where he was supposed to be working.

The voice fed him his lines.

Tell him, "My talking apparatus failed again."

Eduardo heard himself effortlessly translate this odd phrase to his own wording. "My comm unit went out again," he said.

Krantz frowned. "That's dangerous—"

Tell him, "It seems to be working now."

"It seems to be working now," he heard himself echo.

Keep him happy, do your work. Come back to me when it is one hour before the time to begin your ascent. I am about to make you wealthy and more powerful than you have ever been in your life.

This now seemed entirely reasonable to Eduardo. He moved away from the mound and he and the archeologist continued their survey work, Krantz ordering him about as usual, until it was an hour before the time for the next team to take a shift. When the next prompting of the voice commanded him to stop what he was doing and walk back to the mound, Eduardo obeyed without hesitation.

"Eduardo!" Krantz said impatiently.

Eduardo looked back at him. A blank look came over Krantz's face, then he turned and went back to work on recovering what appeared to be a ship's bell.

He won't bother you now, the voice said. *Listen carefully, Eduardo, and I'll ensure he never bothers you again.*

Eduardo's radio went out again.

Eduardo decided that the breakdown of the comm unit wasn't such a bad thing. It was really great not hearing the ship give him orders. Being bossed around was no more fun underwater than it was on the surface.

Later he would wonder why he failed to perceive that the voice in the sea was far more commanding than any of his supervisors' voices. Right now, it didn't seem so much to be ordering him as coaxing him.

Do you want what I offer? Riches beyond imagination? Knowledge and power?

In Eduardo's mind, visions arose. He suddenly saw himself surrounded by beautiful women, pictured himself driving up to a mansion in a luxury car. He saw himself being treated differently, not as a menial laborer, dismissed as a young fool, but as an important person, someone others made way for, someone they admired.

Do you want these things? Truly want them? Do you have the courage to take what is before you, or will you live your whole life regretting that you failed to take this opportunity? I offer you the ability to move in the first circles of society. A life of leisure. The wealth to buy jewels, horses, land—to dress in nothing but the finest clothing. Do you want these, and other pleasures you dare not even dream of now? Say yes, Eduardo. Say yes.

Eduardo vaguely noted that the voice's accent was British. He frowned. Working in the Caribbean, Eduardo had been around plenty of Englishmen, and this voice didn't sound like any Englishman he had ever met before. Even the accent didn't explain how strange his words were, or why it was that when the voice said "horses," Eduardo thought of race cars.

"Who are you?" Eduardo asked. "Are you the devil?"

Eduardo heard a soft laugh. *No, I'm not the devil. Think of me as someone who was cheated, and needs your help to regain what is rightfully his own. I am willing to reward you handsomely for your help.*

Eduardo felt a little easier, hearing that. But he asked, "If you're not the devil, then who are you? What's your name?"

If you insist on a name—I have most recently been known as Adrian, Lord Varre.

Immediately the thought came to Eduardo that he must never call this being Adrian. He must address him as "my lord."

Indeed! Now say, "Yes, my lord, I agree to become your servant."

Eduardo hesitated. If this was all a hallucination, then what harm would it do to follow it through, as one would in a dream? And if not— he suddenly imagined one of the other divers saying yes to the voice, someone else getting all the wealth. His wealth. His race cars.

Riches, Eduardo. Think of going back home and showing them how well you've done for yourself.

It did not occur to Eduardo to ask how the voice knew this secret wish of his.

"Yes, my lord, I agree to become your servant," he said.

He waited for lightning to strike, even here on the floor of the sea. He braced himself, expecting Satan to appear before him, to tell him that he was going straight to hell. Instead, he heard only the soft sounds of the sea and his own equipment. Gradually, he was filled with a sense of well-being. Everything would be fine. He had nothing to worry about.

Excellent. Now, you must recover an object. I will help to ensure that no one knows you have taken it.

A few hours ago, he would have immediately pointed out all the reasons why it was impossible for him to do such a thing. Now he listened carefully as the voice gave him instructions. Eduardo could no more resist reaching to uncover the object beneath the mound of sand than he could resist his own heartbeat.

The object proved to be a small metal chest, crisscrossed with thick, rusty bands of iron and bearing two heavy locks. He felt excitement, sure that whoever had carried the casket aboard the *Morgan Bray* had stored something extremely valuable within it—jewels, most likely.

No, I'm afraid you won't find anything but ashes within, so for the time being this chest must remain sealed. Place it in the canvas bag attached to your belt.

Eduardo did as he was commanded. A sensation of pure bliss came to him. He felt overwhelmed by it, his mind reeling, disconnecting from his surroundings as if he were drugged.

Now, I'm going to call some of my friends to help us. You must not be afraid—whatever slight harm they do to you will not be painful, and will merely ensure that others are distracted. For your part, you must help the other man to ascend to the surface.

Eduardo blinked, and the dazed sensation dropped away. He was startled as the comm unit suddenly started working again—a shipmate calling frantically, "Do you read me?"

"Yes," Eduardo answered, "just came back online. I've been having trouble with my comm unit."

"Krantz told us that, but—"

"Yes, his is working."

"No, it's not! Not for the last few minutes. I've just been getting static. Are you guys okay?"

"I'm fine. Let me check on Krantz—he's not facing me."

When he reached Krantz, the other diver seemed to come out of a daze. By now the captain had come online.

"Begin your ascent," he ordered them. "I don't want you working down there until we get this communications problem straightened out."

So they began their careful rise toward the surface, halting as needed to avoid decompression problems.

"Can you hear me?" the captain asked when they had nearly started their last stage of the ascent.

"Yes, sir," Eduardo answered when there was no response from Krantz.

"I guess Krantz's equipment is out again. We've lost the cameras, too."

"We're almost ready to surface, sir," Eduardo said.

"Get Krantz's attention."

Eduardo reached out to the other diver and saw that although Krantz was breathing and his eyes were open, he seemed unaware of his surroundings.

"I think he may be in trouble, sir." Eduardo described Krantz's condition.

"Hang on to him," the captain said. "Bring him up as soon as you can safely do so. I'll have Doc waiting for you."

Don't be afraid, the voice said. *You're about to have a little company. You must leave my friends unharmed. They're just going to help us with a distraction.*

"Company?" Eduardo said.

"Say again?" the captain said.

But now Eduardo had seen large gray and white shapes swimming strongly toward them.

"We've got company," he managed to say, although his mouth was dry. It took all his will to resist pulling out his speargun.

"Say again?" the captain repeated.

"Tiger sharks. Two of them circling us now."

They came close, close enough for Eduardo to see their small eyes, their wide snouts. Both were well over twice his own size. He guessed the largest one to be about fourteen feet in length.

There was a long pause, then the captain said, "Stay calm. You know they may just be curious. Let go of Krantz if you need to defend yourself—we can pull him up." He heard the captain giving orders to other men.

He reached the surface without harm, and was just about to hand Krantz off to the waiting crew when the sharks struck. One bit hard into

Krantz's calf, causing Krantz to come out of his stupor with a scream. A moment later, Eduardo cried out in pain as well, feeling sharp teeth stab into his shoulder. The bite released, and a new wave of agony shot through him as strong hands hauled him up from the water.

Chaos reigned on deck. He nearly passed out as the crew worked to remove his equipment. It was soon seen that Krantz's injury was far worse, and while one crew member held a pressure bandage to Eduardo's wound, the doctor went to work to help the archeologist. He felt himself go into a state of oblivion, comprehending nothing but pain, and when his thoughts began to clear, the first of them was directed at the voice: *You tricked me.*

He waited for a response, even wondered if he had indeed hallucinated the whole thing, but then a reply came to him.

Tricked you? Not at all. Your wound will heal. For reasons you will come to understand later, it would not do for you to come out of the attack unscathed. Quickly now, hide the collection bag beneath that bench to your right. Trust me to keep the others occupied—and remember, you have pledged your obedience to me.

He considered resisting, considered arguing, but he wanted the chest to himself, so he did as he was told. As he started to reach for the bag, Krantz began thrashing about on the deck, and even the man who was holding the bandage against his shoulder abandoned him to help with Krantz. No one saw him stash the bag among the life vests stowed beneath the bench.

Return to me when you awaken tonight, the voice said. *Soon we will leave this ship together. I will show you where to find riches, and you will help me to find a man named Tyler Hawthorne.*

Eduardo lost consciousness.

Three days later, as the *Declan* lay in dock, the captain gave Eduardo Leblanc the pay he had earned, and a substantial bonus as well. He had tried to persuade the young man not to give up diving—he believed Eduardo had a talent for the work. But he understood completely. A shark attack was a rare occurrence, but he could hardly expect Eduardo not to fear it. In truth—and quite understandably—Eduardo hadn't been himself since the attack.

"Doc said your wound is healing remarkably well," the captain said, "and that you shouldn't have any trouble from it in the future. But— there's always more to something like this than the injury itself, of course. If there's anything more I can do for you . . ."

"Thank you, sir," Eduardo said. "I'll be fine. I appreciate all you've done for me, but I need to move on."

The captain fell silent. He had taken Eduardo under his wing, but he wasn't the kid's father, after all. Perhaps he would be fine. "What will you do now?"

"Oh, I'll keep looking for treasure—I'm just going to look for it on land."

The captain smiled. "I wish you luck. But if you fail to find it, you can always get a job with Declan Salvage."

Eduardo thanked him again.

As he watched him go, the captain sighed and shook his head. Young men could be such fools.

2

They reached a curve in the road near Tyler Hawthorne's new home. Eduardo Leblanc, who had been looking toward the wooded hillside to the left, said, "Stop the truck—pull over here."

Daniel, who was driving, immediately braked to a halt. Eduardo expected this sort of obedience from his two trainees. Lord Varre expected it.

"Is something wrong?" Evan asked.

"I saw something moving in the woods. Stay in the truck and lock its doors as soon as I get out." He paused, then added, "Lord Varre will be extremely unhappy if either of you fail to do exactly as I ask."

He could see they took this warning seriously, as they should.

"If anything should happen to me," he said, "*anything*, then you must drive away as fast as possible. Do not try to rescue me. Do you understand?"

They nodded, but he could see the dismay written on their faces.

He wondered if Daniel had paid any attention to all he had confided to him earlier in the evening. He had little hope for Evan, who reminded him too much of himself.

He looked again to the trees that stood between Hawthorne's home and the property below it and saw the bright eyes—golden in the reflected moonlight—watching.

Neither Daniel nor Evan seemed aware of the presence in the woods. He wondered if God would forgive him for bringing them into Lord Varre's service.

But what should one sin matter over all his others? Starting with taking a small chest out of the wreckage of the *Morgan Bray*.

He got out of the truck, heard the door locks snick down. He began walking.

He knew Lord Varre already sensed his rebellion. His head began to pound, but he kept walking, one step and then another, alone up the road, toward the woods where he had seen the dog. The pain increased, moving through his whole body now, intensifying with each passing second. Although he felt near to collapsing from the agony, he forced himself to stand straight and still in the road.

The dog came out of the woods, a black blur racing toward him.

Somehow, in his pain, he found the strength to ask for mercy.

Evan and Daniel watched in horror as Eduardo stood in the road, letting the huge dog race toward him. In the beam of the headlights, they saw him fling his arms open and smile as the dog reached him.

The dog made one powerful leap and fastened his fangs on Eduardo's throat.

Eduardo burst into flames. And was gone.

One moment, he had been in the road, covered in fire. In the next, he'd disappeared—with not so much as a pile of ash left where he had stood.

The dog looked toward the truck.

"Go!" Evan shouted to Daniel. Daniel wheeled the truck around and drove off.

Tyler Hawthorne stepped out of the master bedroom of his newly acquired home, onto the deck that almost entirely surrounded this level of the house.

The hillside sloped away sharply enough to allow him a view through the trees, to see the lights of Los Angeles far below, glittering through the mist that had settled over the city on this moonlit spring evening. The house was empty and quiet.

A flash of bright light appeared from somewhere near a curve in the road below, and he wondered what had caused it. A fire? An explosion or accident of some sort? But there was no smoke rising, and there had been no sound of a collision, which even at this distance he must have heard. He waited, feeling uneasy, but the night stayed quiet.

A little too quiet. The usual insect noises had ceased.

"Shade," he called softly. The big black dog had shown an unusual level of excitement about exploring beyond the fenced-in area of the property, and Tyler had let him out. Although he knew it was extremely unlikely that his closest companion would be harmed by anything in the woods, Tyler couldn't help but feel uneasy.

He waited, listening, then the crickets took up their song again. What had disturbed them?

He called again to Shade, but the dog did not return. Odd behavior indeed.

Tyler sighed and turned back into the darkened house. Although he had purchased many of the previous owner's possessions along with the property, not many of his own had yet arrived. His small staff was not due here for another two weeks. They would eventually have a guest, a man recovering from a serious illness, and Tyler realized he needed to consider all that would be required for his care. Unless he missed his guess, though, there was still a little time to make those arrangements.

He sat in an overstuffed chair near an empty fireplace and savored this opportunity to be quiet and completely alone, not even Shade at his side. No one asking anything of him.

He had youth, wealth, and excellent health. He looked at the luxury surrounding him and wished, not for the first time, that he would die.

He stood again, trying to shake off this mood. He decided that perhaps he should go out looking for the dog, then heard a floorboard creak just behind him.

He turned swiftly.

A match flared, and a voice spoke from the shadows. "Feeling sorry for yourself tonight, Tyler?"

"Colby?" he asked in disbelief.

"None other," the man said. He lit a cigarette and blew out the match.

Tyler stayed where he was.

Colby laughed. "What, no warm welcome for an old friend?"

Tyler bent to turn on the lamp next to the chair. He straightened and said, "No welcome, and no old friend."

The man standing across the room from him was fair haired and slender, slightly shorter than Tyler, dressed in an elegantly tailored suit. His blue eyes were full of amusement as he said, "I'm heartbroken."

"Impossible."

"You'll say that's because I have no heart, but really, you do me wrong."

"It's been a long time, Colby, but I doubt you've changed that much. What brings you to Los Angeles?"

"Strange occurrences. Don't you notice something in the air?"

He had, but answered, "Cigarette smoke."

Colby smiled and took a long drag, blew it out slowly. "Still self-righteous, I see. Haven't you had enough of living as you do, Tyler?"

Although he had been thinking that very thing not five minutes before, Tyler said, "If you're here to recruit me, you're wasting your time."

"Hmm. Terribly lonely, isn't it?"

Tyler didn't answer.

"Not necessary to admit it," Colby said. "I mean, really—a city of millions of souls, and Tyler Hawthorne sits alone in the dark."

"Amusement isn't happiness. Starting to realize that, Colby?"

Colby lowered his gaze and took another long drag. "Really none of your business. What have you done with your only companion, by the way?"

"He's nearby, don't worry."

Colby gave him a crooked smile. "The odd thing is, Tyler, I do feel a bit worried for you."

"Why?"

"Well, for one thing, I think those woods out there are haunted."

"As if that would bother you."

"No, of course not. But . . ." He grew serious. "But something more, Tyler, I mean it. Bad neighborhood, for all its money."

"It's where I'm supposed to be now."

Colby faked a yawn. "Yes, well, you go on being a good little scout. I'm sure that even as we speak, somewhere someone's sewing a merit badge for you. Don't bother showing me out."

He was at the door when Tyler said, "Colby—"

Colby looked back at him.

"Good to see you again."

Colby laughed derisively and disappeared from view.

Tyler was wondering if he should have done more to encourage Colby to stick around, despite the complications that would inevitably ensue, when his cell phone rang. He glanced at the number on the display. He answered and assured the caller that he would soon be on his way to the hospital.

He went to the deck again and called to Shade, waited a moment, then locked up. He tried not to worry about the dog, knowing those who had called from the critical care unit couldn't wait for him to search the woods. He told himself that when Shade heard the van start up, he'd head back.

He had just driven past the gate when a familiar dark silhouette came racing up the drive.

Shade.

Relieved, he opened the passenger door, and the dog jumped in.

"I trust I'm not keeping you from anything important?" Tyler said, closing the door.

Shade wagged his tail.

Tyler gave him a soft scratch between the ears.

He hit the remote to close the gate behind him.

"I was a little worried about you," he admitted.

Shade cocked his head to one side.

"Yes, ridiculous. But Colby visited."

Shade sighed.

"Yes, I felt the same."

By the time they reached the curve in the road, Tyler, his thoughts taken up with Colby's visit and the work before him, had forgotten about the flash of light, the silence in the woods, the dog's delay in returning.

3

Harry Williams lay dying, knew it, and although he did not fear it, fought it with every ounce of his dwindling strength. Had he not been so desperate to communicate with his wife, Catherine, just once more, he would have let go, would have given in to the tidal pull on his soul.

For days now he had lain in a dark world, unable to move, unable to speak. Comatose. Trapped in a body that would not obey him, able to hear but not to respond—not with so much as the batting of an eyelid or the lifting of a finger. He had tried. If will alone could have accomplished it, he would have come back to the family that surrounded him.

But Harry couldn't. He had fallen from the roof of his home while trying to adjust a television satellite dish, an accident he had come to accept in this sea of dark hours for what it was: stupid but unchangeable. He knew he would not recover—his injuries were too severe to allow his life to continue.

He was not destined to remain with his loved ones. He accepted this. But he wasn't ready to go. Not yet.

Catherine and the kids, his parents, his brother and sister were grieving. Already missing him. At his family's request—God bless them for following his wishes!—the respirator and the feeding tube had been removed. All this he knew. He could no longer feel physical pain. That had been true for some time now. All the same, Harry Williams was in anguish.

He had something to say. It was not, as some might have supposed, "I love you." Catherine knew he loved her, just as he knew she loved him. If he had harbored any doubts about that, her whispered pleas at his bedside would have reassured him. No—more than spoken words, their love was something down in his bones now, or deeper even than that. The children—he realized there would be no knowing who they would become one day, but against that loss he felt the peace of a man who has done his best to be a good father.

He did not need to ask forgiveness—he had forgiven, and had asked for and received it for himself. This he also knew. No, the urgent message he had for Catherine was utterly mundane, a matter of business: the location of his hidden office safe and its combination.

She might discover it somehow. She might get someone to open it for her. But all that was *maybe* and would take time. Catherine deserved to have access to the papers and the cash he had stored there. He wanted her to find the diamond bracelet he had planned to give her on Valentine's Day. The contents of the safe would help her and the kids to survive while she waited for the insurance to pay. He wanted her to have access to it now.

He had been a fool never to tell her about it. When he first realized that he would not recover, he had been angry with himself. He now thought of this failure in a dispassionate way. At this stage of the process of dying, all his passion went into hoping for one last chance to be granted the ability to speak.

Time passed in the darkness. He breathed. His heart beat. It would not last.

Only Catherine was in the room with him when the door opened.

"Oh!" she said. "You're here! I wasn't sure you'd come. Thank you!"

Harry heard the newcomer move toward the bed. A man took his hand. A doctor? No, not a doctor.

"I called you because he seems to be fighting so hard," Catherine said. "The doctors say he won't recover. But he's still alive. Were they wrong?"

"No, they weren't wrong," said the stranger, but not unkindly.

A moment later, Harry thought the stranger was mistaken. He could see again. He was standing next to Catherine at his bedside. He felt stronger than he ever had before. Then he looked down and saw himself on the bed. He looked awful.

We only have a few minutes—perhaps less than that, the stranger's voice came to him, although the man had not spoken aloud. Harry realized that he was somehow connected to the man, and hearing his thoughts.

What are you? Who are you? Harry wondered.

Never mind! Hurry! the stranger urged him. *What do you need to say?*

Suddenly Harry was certain that this was his only chance, and for reasons that he could not have explained to himself, he believed that this man was to be trusted. "Catherine, it's me—Harry," he said, and heard the stranger repeat the words aloud, felt them form and move in the stranger's throat and mouth, felt the breath that moved them. Wonderful thing, speech, he thought, but at the stranger's urging continued. "Listen carefully. There is a safe hidden in the south wall of my office. You can find it by going to the thermostat on that wall and removing its cover. There's a keypad under it. Enter this code: one-eight-five-five-eight-nine."

She was looking at him in shock.

Write it, the stranger commanded. *Otherwise she won't remember.*

With his free hand—the stranger's free hand—Harry searched quickly for the notepad next to his bed, found it, and wrote the number down. He turned back to Catherine. "Enter that and press the pound sign. A hidden panel will slide open. On the safe, enter Jerry's birthday in this order: the four numbers of the year, then the two numbers of the month, then the two numbers of the day. Everything in the safe is yours, and will help you for a while. The bracelet is your Valentine's Day present, Cath. Sorry I won't be there to give it to you." He paused, seeing Catherine looking into the stranger's eyes, but seeing that she saw him there. "I love you, Cath. Be strong. See you later."

He was back in his own shell then, and as cold as it was growing, wondrous things were happening. He heard Catherine crying and saying she loved him, too, her voice indicating that she had noticed that he was back in his body. He felt her clutch his other hand.

Are you an angel? Harry asked the stranger, knowing that only the stranger could hear him.

No, the stranger answered, in Harry's own thoughts. *Tell me—*

Oh, now I know who you are, Harry said, as a new awareness began to flow through him. *Yes. Things will be changing for you soon.*

Harry could feel the man—Tyler Hawthorne—suddenly become alert.

What do you mean?

I'm not sure, I just know I'm supposed to tell you that. Oh—also, you'll be needed in St. Louis nine days from now. The hospital room of Max Derley. Harry recited an address and a phone number, having no idea how he had learned them. He gave other details about this Missouri hospital he had never previously heard of, and the phone number of a man named Sam Gunning. He did not know how Mr. Derley and Mr. Gunning were connected, but he had a clear sense of the importance of Tyler receiving this information.

Fine, yes, but tell me—

And please stop by the hospice and check on your future guest.

I promise I will. Now, please tell me—

Harry heard the desperation in the man's thoughts and pitied him for a brief moment. *I'm sorry,* Harry answered. He had to leave—this was a matter of supreme urgency, both unavoidable and wholly desirable. Still, he managed to add, *Thank you. Tyler Hawthorne,* and bid good-bye to his last friend on earth.

The dead, thought Tyler, are damned self-centered.

He left the room before the widow could add her thanks to her husband's.

He was halfway to the van before he realized that he was not at all feverish. Then again, this hadn't been an especially strenuous assignment, so perhaps this was one of those rare occasions when he'd escape that particular side effect of his work.

Shade was peering out the open window of the van, standing on the passenger seat, tail wagging so hard his whole back end curved with it.

"Happy to see you, too," Tyler said, settling into the driver's seat. "How *do* you manage to remain so enthusiastic?"

Shade briefly nuzzled him, then sat watching him.

Tyler sighed. "I'll try to improve my attitude. I'm not sure why I find that so difficult lately." He started the van. "We have another stop, by the way."

Shade seemed undaunted.

It was just before midnight when he approached the open door of Ron Parker's hospice room, but the visiting hours here were not restricted. Although Harry Williams had passed along the message saying he should come here—his second visit today—he was uneasy about the thought of waking Ron, who to all appearances was dying from leukemia. After all, the message had been to check on Ron, not to talk to him.

So he walked quietly into Ron's room. Just past the doorway, he was brought up short by the sight of another visitor.

A slender, dark-haired woman sat in a chair pulled close to the left side of the bed. She was young, perhaps in her early twenties, probably Ron's age or very nearly. Her face was in shadow, her head bent and mostly curtained by her hair as she read a paperback by the light of a small clip-on book lamp. As he watched, she managed to turn a page using only her left hand, the hand that held the book. Her right hand gently held one of Ron's hands as he slept.

Was she Ron's girlfriend? He was certain that Ron wasn't married. Ron's late grandfather, Derek Parker, whom Tyler had befriended, had not mentioned that his grandson had a fiancée or any other attachments. When Tyler had spoken to Ron on other occasions, including today, they had discussed many things, and there was no word of a girlfriend.

And yet, what he saw here was a picture of solace and faithfulness. Ron was asleep, might well be for the night, and still she stayed with him. Kept hold of his hand so that if he should wake, he would know he was not alone.

She looked up suddenly and, startled by Tyler's presence, dropped the book and book lamp with it. The little light broke as the book went tumbling beneath the bed. She bent to retrieve it even as Tyler moved closer, ready to offer help. Ron woke up, looked around blearily, and used the control on his bed to bring the room lights up.

Even to Tyler, who had stood next to many deathbeds, Ron bore the appearance of someone in the final stages of leukemia. He was thin, his cheeks hollow. He had lost all his hair after his last round of chemo. His skin was dry and pale, except for the places, here and there, where he had dark splotches of bruising caused by the disease. His eyes, however, revealed a man still part of the world around him, however tenuous his hold on it might be.

"Amanda, are you okay?" Ron asked drowsily.

The young woman quickly straightened, rapping her head on the bottom of the rolling tray near the bed. The tray rattled, but nothing spilled. She winced and rubbed at her crown.

"Fine," she said, blushing. Tyler could see her face now—lovely brown eyes, made no less so by the small scar near one brow. Her nose was straight and her lips full. Her face was not delicate enough to be called pretty, nor beautiful by current standards, standards Tyler didn't particularly admire. An attractive woman. *And Ron's,* he reminded himself sternly.

"Tyler!" Ron said, noticing him for the first time. "Hey, man—come on in!"

Amanda's expression changed—Tyler was surprised to see her eyeing him with hostility. Did she blame him for the mishap?

"I'm sorry if I startled you," he said. "I'm Tyler Hawthorne." He extended a hand.

"Amanda Clarke," she said, going along with the handshake but ending it as quickly as possible.

"Amanda, Tyler's your new neighbor. I was telling you about him earlier."

"Yes," she said. "Umm—an odd hour for a visit, isn't it?"

"Is it? You tell me."

Ron looked between them. "Amanda—it's fine. Hell, one minute you're complaining that my so-called friends have deserted me, and the next you're driving them off. Have a seat, Tyler. What brings you out at this hour?"

Tyler gestured for Amanda to be seated before he took the empty chair on the opposite side of the bed. "I'm often awake late at night. I was in the neighborhood, and—well, I thought I'd just look in on you, give you a little company if you were awake, not disturb you if you were asleep."

"Appreciate it. I never know when I'm going to be asleep or awake lately."

Tyler turned to Amanda. "Ron said we're neighbors—"

"Yes. I own the house just below yours."

"You own . . . ?"

"Yes, I own it. I've owned it for about eight years, since my parents died in a car accident. It was in trust until a few years ago, of course."

"Sorry—I just didn't realize my neighbor was so young."

Ron laughed. "Dude, you're not so old yourself."

"You're right, I shouldn't have assumed anything."

"You aren't the only one who's surprised," Amanda said. "Ron said you bought his house—I guess I should say, his grandfather's house. I was expecting a friend of Derek's to be older."

"Oh, you know how Derek was," Ron said, giving her a quelling look. "He liked being around people who were younger than he was. He never let me call him Grandfather, Tyler. I suppose he told you that."

Tyler smiled. "Yes, he did."

"How did you meet Derek?" Amanda asked.

Tyler looked across the bed at her, saw the suspicion in her eyes. "I was interested in some antiques he was selling. We got to know each other."

"And you saw a chance to get a bargain on a house being sold by an old man in financial trouble."

"Amanda!" Ron said sharply. "You're embarrassing me, you know?"

She blushed again. "Forgive me."

Ron took her hand. "It's okay, but you've got it all wrong anyway. Tyler, don't mind Amanda, she's kind of protective of me. It's none of your business, Amanda, but Tyler not only paid a generous price for the house, he bought a lot of Derek's stuff, too. So if it weren't for him, I'd have inherited a load of debt." He paused. "I think Derek had his first heart attack because he was so worried about money."

"And losing you," she said softly.

Ron shook his head. "No, he never thought I'd live past sixteen, when I first came to live with him. So everything since has been a bonus. He thought he'd outlive me and I'd die never knowing he ended up broke. Tyler, you kept his last weeks of life from being miserable with worry, and for that, I'm grateful."

"It worked out well for everyone, although I wish Derek could have been with us longer."

"Me, too. I miss him."

They fell silent.

Tyler began to feel a familiar combination of weariness and warmth—an unpleasant warmth, the sign of the beginning of the fever. He hadn't escaped it after all. He would have to excuse himself soon, but he wished he could somehow smooth things over with Amanda, if for no other reason than the fact that they would live next door to each other for the next few years.

Ron yawned. "Sorry, I think I'm headed down for the count again. Thanks for coming by, you two. Amanda, go home and get some sleep, okay?"

She frowned. "I don't mind staying—"

"I know. But you're tired. I can tell." He turned to Tyler. "Make sure she gets to her car safely, okay?"

"Now who's being protective?" Amanda said. "But I would appreciate it."

"My pleasure," Tyler said. "Good night, Ron."

As soon as they were out of earshot of Ron's room, she turned to him and said, "I don't need an escort to my car. I just wanted a chance to tell you that I think you're the cruelest son of a bitch I've ever met in my life."

4

Really?" he said. "You've decided that after five minutes of knowing me? I'm tempted to be impressed with myself, but I have no idea how I earned the title."

"No? Did you or did you not visit Ron earlier today?"

"I did. Was that cruel?"

"Did you or did you not tell him you believed he was going to live?"

"I did. Don't you want him to live?"

"Of course I do!"

"Amanda—may I call you Amanda, or do you prefer Ms. Clarke?"

"Amanda is fine—I can put up with it for the next five minutes. What I can't put up with is having someone who doesn't know Ron at all—has no idea what he's been through or is going through—give him false hope."

"False hope?"

"Oh, and then really laying it on, Mr. Hawthorne—"

"Tyler. Even when the five minutes are up."

"Telling Ron he can come back to live in a home that should have been his."

"I agree, the house should have been Ron's—but Derek was like you, Amanda."

"What's that supposed to mean?"

"He was a little too certain that he'd outlive Ron."

"Are you threatening me?"

"No. Please keep your voice down." He sighed. "I can understand why you don't think he's going to live. I can't explain why I feel confident he will survive this round with the leukemia, other than to say I have spent a lot of time standing next to deathbeds, and—let's just say I've developed a sense of these things, and my sense is that Ron will live."

"An antiques dealer who spends a lot of time standing next to deathbeds? What, can't wait until they're cold to swindle their estates out of their belongings? I ought to report you to the administration of this hospice."

He felt his temper rising—a rare occurrence, but he knew the fever would weaken his control of it. She must have sensed she'd gone too far, because she stepped back a pace. Then, catching herself doing that, lifted her chin and moved in again.

"Let's continue this discussion in the lobby," he said, struggling to keep his voice soft and level. "I don't want to wake anyone—those who are here have enough to deal with—they don't need to listen to us bicker."

She nodded. They rode the elevator down to the lobby in silence, not looking at each other. By the time they stood near the exit, he had control of himself again.

"I collect antiques for my own pleasure," he said. "I do not sell them, so I am not a dealer. I have never—not once—purchased an antique from any of those I've counseled. I have not accepted gifts from their families after their deaths. I don't expect you to believe me, but I am well known among the staff here, so ask them."

"You work here?"

"Not as part of the staff. I volunteer my time."

She didn't look entirely convinced, but said, "I apologize. It's just that—it has been so hard for me to get to the place Ron is now, or was until earlier today. Until you came by with your predictions, he had accepted that he is dying, and was at peace with that. I didn't get there so easily, and one minute I'd seem to accept it and the next . . ."

Her voice trailed off. After a moment, she said, "Believe me, I want Ron to live. I—I can't imagine what it will be like when he's gone. But telling him that he'll get better, that he'll be able to come back to his home—a home that isn't even his now! Don't you see what you're doing to him?"

"Giving him hope."

"You're lying to him."

His skin was growing warmer, his joints beginning to ache. Tyler brought all his wandering wits to bear on the conversation and said, "Don't be so sure of that. Now, I promised him I'd see you safely to your car . . ."

"If you won't listen to reason, I'll ask the hospice to ban you from seeing him."

"Unless Ron made that request, I don't think the hospice would agree to it. Ron is ill—but he's not a child, and he is not incompetent. I doubt he would cave in. . . ." A wave of pain washed over him, and he shut his eyes.

"Are you all right?" she asked. "You look pale—"

"I'm fine," he lied. "Just tired." He opened his eyes again and forced himself to smile. "Listen, we aren't going to resolve this tonight. I really do need to get some sleep, and I am sure you've had a long day, too."

She stood looking up at him, unabashedly studying him. He fought an impulse to shift his own gaze away.

She shrugged. "I guess you're right."

As they walked across the parking lot, she asked, "Why are you so interested in what happens to Ron?"

"I made a promise to Derek. And I like Ron."

"You don't *know* Ron."

He didn't answer.

"I'm not saying your intentions are bad."

"Thank you for that," he said dryly.

They reached her car. She looked up at him and said, "You don't look well—are you sure you're going to be able to drive home? I could give you a ride."

"I'll be all right. But it's kind of you to offer."

"Well," she said, "I'm sure our paths will cross again. Good night."

"Good night," he said.

He waited until she drove off, then walked to the farthest end of the parking lot, where he had left the van. He had left the window of the passenger side open, in case Shade wanted to roam in the small park at that end of the lot. But Shade had apparently decided not to rove—he was waiting for him. Tyler crawled into the back of the van and collapsed onto the bed there.

It wasn't going to be bad. He judged, from long experience, that this one would last only an hour or two.

He regretted not being able to follow her home, to make sure she got there safely. He didn't like the idea of her driving around alone so late at night, even though she didn't seem fearful. Of anything. He certainly didn't intimidate her.

The fever spiked, and he curled up on his side, trying to ride out another wave of pain. Shade came near, breathing softly onto his cheek. The pain receded, and Tyler fell asleep.

5

Nine days later, Amanda Clarke lay in her bed in the darkness, thinking about Tyler Hawthorne and wondering if he was avoiding her. She believed she owed him another apology and being unable to deliver it irritated her. It was hard enough to admit to herself that she had been wrong to speak to him the way she had, and now it looked as if she was going to have to march up the hill to his house to say so.

Nine days since she had met him in Ron's room. Nine days since Ron had started to regain his strength.

"Let's see what happens," Ron's doctor had said today, but she was smiling. No one wanted to jump to conclusions, to be overly optimistic. At the same time, no one could deny that he was doing better. The doctor had looked at his most recent blood work and said, "Amazing. Let's hope this trend continues."

He was still very weak. He still tired out easily. But his color was better, his appetite was returning.

And he had hope. She had struggled not to hope as well. She had failed. Lying here alone, she admitted that she was nearly convinced that Ron would live, and prayed she wasn't wrong.

She heard the sound of a creaking floorboard. Not quite alone, was she?

One of her cousins, no doubt, was also still awake at—she glanced at the clock by her bed—just after midnight. Brad and Rebecca had arrived a week ago, unannounced as usual. They owned a huge house in the desert, and their trustees would have gladly approved the use of funds to buy their own place here in L.A., but when they were in town they stayed here, or on a whim, they took rooms in one of the city's luxury hotels. Amanda often told herself that she should change the locks and refuse to admit them. Telling herself what she "should" do was as far as she ever got with that plan.

Instead she avoided them as much as possible, even kept her own small bedroom on the ground floor of the house, apart from the more spacious rooms she reserved for them on the second floor. The house had a large master suite on the third floor, but so far, even her nervy cousins hadn't tried to take over that room.

She listened, but there were no further stirrings from the second floor. The only sound reaching her through the bedroom door was the mesmerizing *tick-tock-tick-tock* of the grandfather clock in the living room.

Rebecca and Brad had met Tyler. She was annoyed that they had managed to encounter him when she had not. "TDH," Rebecca had declared him. Tall, dark, and handsome. Well, she was right about that.

Rebecca already had one of her mad crushes on him. She had invited him to her upcoming party out in the desert, and said he had accepted.

Although the desert house was several hours from here, she couldn't blame Tyler for accepting. Rebecca was as beautiful as he was handsome, and together, they'd make a disgustingly good-looking couple. Or would for four weeks, which had proved to be the maximum amount of time any man in his right mind could handle putting up with Rebecca.

The thought of them being a couple even for a month made her frown. She told herself she was concerned because she didn't want problems with a neighbor. Maybe Ron would warn him about her cousin, whom Ron referred to as "Rudebecca the Train Wrecka."

Today, when Rebecca had taken a breath during her "Let me tell you in excruciating detail why Tyler is so hot" marathon, Brad spoke up and invited Amanda to the party, too.

Amanda had been sure he was just trying to spite his older sister, so she was noncommittal.

"He asked if you'd be there," Brad added. Definitely spiteful.

"You *should* come," Rebecca said, surprising her.

"You never come out to visit us, we always have to come here to visit you," Brad said.

She didn't point out that they never really came to visit her, that they never took her along to the parties they went to in L.A., that even if she just wrote about the last few years, she could put together a really thick book entitled *Signs That Rebecca and Brad Hate Me*.

"I'll think about it."

"Don't be boring," Rebecca said, and went back to boring Amanda.

She apparently bored Brad, too. "Shit, Rebecca, you talked *to* him for about twenty minutes max," he complained. "You've talked *about* him for about twenty hours now. We get the picture. If you don't want Amanda to know how desperate you are these days, shut your piehole for a minute or two."

So Rebecca fired up for an attack on Brad, which freed Amanda to escape from the house. By the time she came home from the hospice, her cousins were up in their rooms.

She dozed off and came awake with a start. She listened and heard the grandfather clock strike one.

No sound of someone prowling just outside the house.

Just a dream, she told herself. Her fears were surfacing in her dreams, not surprising on a stressful day. She had dreamed the noise.

She held her breath, not moving. Listening. Long moments passed.

No one, she tried to reassure herself, was moving stealthily just outside. No creature was stalking its prey just beyond her bedroom window. A dream.

She couldn't convince herself.

She had heard *something*.

Perhaps the house had creaked in the way old houses do, or leaves had scratched against one of the upstairs windowpanes, or the refrigerator's motor had hummed. Whatever the sound was that had awakened her, it was gone now. She exhaled softly through her mouth, drew another breath. Listened.

And heard a noise.

This time she knew it had not been her imagination. As her eyes adjusted to the dim light in the room, she saw the heavy curtains softly billow and realized she had left the window open. The afternoon had been warm, and she had wanted to air out the room. She had fallen into bed after a long day without thinking about the window—without shutting it. Now . . .

Now she was vulnerable. Now someone or something was moving around out there, just on the other side of a flimsy screen. She could hear the soft rustle of leaves disturbed by a step, the snapping of small twigs beneath the weight of a foot. Slow, stalking steps, not random movements caused by the wind.

Step. A pause. Step. A pause. More steps, slow and creeping.

She clutched the covers, tried to track the direction of the sounds. Maybe it was only a cat or a skunk. No, too heavy to be a cat, and skunks didn't move with that stalking step.

It could be a dog. She shivered, and reached up to trace the old scar on the ridge of her eyebrow.

She feared dogs. Had been terrified of dogs for years now. Not without reason.

Or—was it a person out there?

The curtains moved again. Was it her fear, or had the breeze suddenly turned chilly?

She slid out of bed and crept toward her closet. She banged one of her shins on a dresser drawer she hadn't fully closed, but managed to keep her reaction to the pain to a quiet hiss. She reached the closet, quickly put on her robe, and hurried toward her bedroom door. She opened it and stepped into the hallway, then softly pulled the door shut.

"What—?" a voice behind her said.

6

S he screamed before her cousin Brad finished saying, "—are you doing?"

"Brad! You scared me to death!"

"Apparently not," he said.

Lights came on in the upper hallway. Rebecca came out of her room and peered over the railing. Rebecca, even suddenly roused from sleep, looked perfect—as always. Rebecca and Brad were both tall, slender, blond, and blue eyed. Both favored their late mother. The look worked a little better on Rebecca than Brad, Amanda thought, but that might have been because Brad tended to sulk.

"Amanda? What is it?" Rebecca said. "Are you all right?" She saw Brad standing next to Amanda and frowned at him.

"Not my fault, I swear," Brad said, holding up his hands in mock surrender.

"That's a first," Rebecca said dryly.

"I heard someone prowling around outside," Amanda said. "It scared me. I had just come out of my room when Brad said something and I'm afraid I—I overreacted. Sorry."

"Someone prowling around outside?" Brad said, looking nervous.

"Yes. I left my window open, and just now I thought I heard someone moving around out there." She paused. "It might have been an animal, but I don't think so."

"Brad," Rebecca ordered, "go outside and look around."

"Me? Oh no. If it's her imagination, I might catch a chill, and if it's not, I don't want to think about it." He shuddered dramatically.

"Is it your imagination?" Rebecca asked, starting down the stairs.

Amanda blushed. "Don't trouble yourself."

"Come on," Rebecca said, "I'll look with you."

Amanda turned on the outside lights, grabbed a baseball bat from the hall closet, and, looking down at her bare feet, hurriedly stepped into a pair of rain boots she found in the same hall closet.

"Charming outfit, as usual," Rebecca said, and opened the front door.

The galoshes were loose on Amanda's feet, and it took a bit of effort to keep from tripping or stepping out of them, but she followed Rebecca as quickly as she could.

"I'm sure whoever it was is long gone by now," Amanda said. "My scream probably scared him off. If not, then the sounds of everyone getting up out of bed and my turning the lights on—"

"Probably. But let's look around outside your window to see what we can see."

Amanda followed, thinking that these were the moments when she could actually be fond of Rebecca. She might grow tired of Rebecca's bitchiness, her self-absorption, her moodiness—but Rebecca never sat still when action was needed. Rebecca, she had to admit, was bolder than she was.

The scent of pine trees soothed Amanda's own edgy nerves a bit. The house was situated in a canyon in the foothills above Los Angeles. The area was not wilderness, but many of the lots were large; the homes nearby were expensive. Most of the owners chose them for the seclusion the area afforded them.

Amanda's great-grandfather had been involved in the early movie industry and built the oldest part of the house as a private retreat, reputedly his love nest, where he'd sneak away to be with his mistress. No wonder, Amanda thought, he had concealed it by planting trees.

Right at this moment, Amanda wished the house was not surrounded by quite so many of them. Only one other house had even a partial view of her home. Standing on the front porch, she looked up the hill and saw that no lights were on at Derek and Ron's place—no, she had to stop thinking of it in that way. Tyler Hawthorne's house.

"So," Rebecca said, following her gaze. "He's gone."

"What?"

"Tyler. When we saw him the other day, he said he was driving to St. Louis."

"Driving? Not flying?"

"Yes." She moved fearlessly down the front steps.

Amanda followed her, Tyler forgotten. She tried not to think of all the things baseball bats wouldn't stop.

"He seemed very interested in knowing if you'd be at the party," Rebecca added, and Amanda heard the underlying message.

"I'm not interested in him." *Liar,* an inner voice said. But she knew that once Rebecca came into a man's orbit, he never thought twice about Rebecca's klutzy cousin.

"Oh, that doesn't worry me," Rebecca said, causing the last of Amanda's fear to be chased away by anger.

"I'm sure it doesn't," she bit out.

"I just wondered why he'd be interested in you *at all.*"

"He's not interested. I met him briefly at the hospice. He and Ron are friends."

"Oh." Rebecca frowned, working this out. Undoubtedly, as far as Rebecca was concerned, friendship with Ron put some kind of black mark against Tyler.

"Doesn't seem to be anyone out here now," Rebecca said as they reached the area outside Amanda's bedroom.

"It wasn't my imagination—"

"Right. Whatever. I'm going back in. I'm freezing my ass off out here—I don't carry as much weight as you do, you know, so I get cold faster."

Amanda let her go. She needed a few minutes alone to prevent herself from booting Rebecca's skinny frozen ass from here to Laguna.

Amanda decided she was going to walk back inside and tell them to leave tomorrow, and not to come back without an invitation. How would they like it if she just showed up out at their place in the desert? Not at all!

She stood in the darkness, silently composing a lecture. She envisioned delivering it, and . . . her shoulders sank.

She'd never do it. They were close to being the only family members she had left.

A light went on in one of the rooms of Derek's—no, Tyler's—house, then a moment later the house was dark again. Rebecca must have been wrong about Tyler being out of town.

She had better things to do than think about Tyler Hawthorne. She studied the ground near the window. She saw fresh tracks in the moist earth.

"A dog," she whispered to herself, swallowing hard. "A big dog."

She heard a rustling sound in the woods and whirled, bat at the ready. But the galoshes didn't easily follow the motion, and she fell flat on her face in the dirt. She scrambled up in panic, bat held ready to swing, and tried to see beyond the area illuminated by the outdoor lights of her own house.

She could hear something moving through the trees. Running.

She braced herself for an attack, then realized the sounds were retreating.

The dog—if it was a dog—was racing uphill—away from her.

Suddenly, at the edge of the darkness, four figures appeared—two men, two women. Dressed in evening clothes.

Fear and anger caused her to stiffen every muscle.

She knew exactly who they were.

And knew they were long dead.

"Go away!" she shouted.

They disappeared just as she heard the front door open. Brad and Rebecca peered cautiously around the corner of the house.

"Are you okay?"

"Yes," she answered shakily. "Just a stray dog."

They heard the roar of an engine, the squealing brakes and tires as a vehicle took the curve in the road just downhill from the house.

"Someone's in a hurry," Brad said.

Together, they walked back inside the house. She put up with their merciless teasing about her fear of dogs.

She closed the window and got back into bed. Tomorrow, she decided, she was moving up to the third floor.

She had nearly drifted off to sleep when she recalled the fright Brad had given her, and a question occurred to her. What had Brad been doing downstairs, creeping around in the dark, well after midnight?

Just before dawn, she awakened. The room was still dark, the blinds drawn, but she clearly saw four figures standing around her bed. Dressed, as they always were, the way they had been when she had last seen them alive. "Go away," she whispered to her parents and aunt and uncle. She shut her eyes tightly and pulled the covers over her head. "It wasn't my fault."

When the air grew stuffy beneath the bedding, she peered out over the edge of the comforter.

They were gone.

It took a long time to fall asleep again.

7

E van and Daniel slowly made their way down the concrete stairs. Daniel, in the lead, shielded the flame of a single candle, the only form of light they were allowed to use in there. He tried to hold his hands steady. This was difficult, given the state of his nerves. From the moment they had driven away from Hawthorne's new home, Daniel had been aware of the stench of Evan's fear, and felt sure that his own horror was equally apparent. Now, though, as they reached the bottom of the stairs, the scent of their fear was overcome by the basement's own miasma of decay.

They stood side by side, trying to peer beyond the faint pool of candlelight.

A deep voice came from a far corner.

"Put out the candle."

Daniel obeyed.

Surely one small flame had not warmed the room? But the complete darkness somehow felt colder.

"You've failed," the voice said. "Is that not so?"

"Yes, my lord."

There was a long silence. Daniel knew better than to offer information unless asked.

"Tell me what happened."

"The dog was there, my lord."

There was another silence, then the voice said, "Nonsense. He never travels without the dog."

There wasn't a chance in hell that Daniel was going to contradict him.

The next silence stretched on and on. Daniel began to shiver, not just from the cold.

"If the dog was in the house, it would have destroyed you as quickly as it destroyed Eduardo."

Daniel felt sick to his stomach, remembering.

"So, Daniel, assuming you aren't so foolish as to lie to me, how is it possible that the dog was there and yet you're alive?"

"The dog wasn't in the house, your lordship. I was searching the master bedroom when I happened to look out and see the animal running through the woods, toward the house."

"And you could see a black dog in the darkness?"

"The neighbor's lights were on. They might have had a motion sensor or something that picked up the dog's movements. I don't know, my lord."

"Perhaps someone's pet frightened you?"

"It moved—it moved very fast, my lord."

Another silence stretched before the voice said, "Fortunately for the two of you, I still need your services. You will even have a little time to compose yourselves, to try to find your courage. Let's test this idea of yours, that he travels now and again without the dog."

"You want us to go back there, my lord?" Evan asked.

"Did I indicate you should ask questions?" the voice snapped.

"No, my lord," Evan squeaked out.

"Daniel, tell me where you searched."

Daniel managed to keep his voice fairly even as he gave his report. Together they had taken the elevator installed in Hawthorne's house to the third floor, and he had started searching in the master bedroom while Evan climbed up through an access door and looked in the attic.

Daniel had systematically searched the built-in drawers and cupboards. He had smiled to himself when he discovered an antique desk at one end of a large study, rubbed his hands together, and set to work. He had quickly figured out the mechanisms that revealed its secret compartments.

"Ah yes," his lordship said, almost sounding pleased with this part of his report, even though Daniel hadn't found anything in the desk. "I believe it is this gift of yours that led Eduardo to recruit you."

"I believe so, my lord."

"And, Evan?"

Evan had learned his lesson. He was concise. Daniel already knew he hadn't found more than a few boxes in the attic and discovered nothing of value in them.

"Any other details I should know, Daniel?"

Daniel took a deep breath, and admitted damaging the bedroom door.

"When I gave express orders that nothing was to seem to be disturbed? That no sign of your presence should be left there?"

"Yes, my lord." He braced himself for the consequences, even though he knew bracing was of no use whatsoever. "I had stepped out onto the deck outside the master bedroom when I saw the dog. I turned, and realized the doors leading outside had locked behind me. In—in my panic, I jimmied one of the doors open to get back inside."

He heard no sound coming from the other side of the room, but the smell of decay grew suddenly stronger.

"Very good, Daniel," the voice hissed in his ear. "My dear, relax! You give me greater obedience by admitting your error to me. I know you were afraid to be truthful with me. Evan here is feeling rather smug about your admission of a mistake."

"My lord—," Evan began, but his next words were lost in a scream of pain.

"You will learn not to speak unless spoken to, Evan," the voice said, from somewhere across the room now. "Take him upstairs, Daniel. I don't believe he'll be able to manage it on his own. He should recover before I need you again." He paused. "You may thank me."

"Thank you, my lord," Daniel said.

"Evan?"

An incoherent murmur came from the figure slumped on the floor. Daniel and Evan hated touching the floor.

Evidently his lordship understood the murmur, because he said they were dismissed.

Evan had not been allowed the mercy of passing out, so Daniel had to carry him—no easy task in the darkness—up a narrow stairway, with the stink and stickiness of whatever was on the floor all over him. But Evan had done the same for him on occasion, so he did not resent Evan for the effort involved.

8

A week later, Ron was home. Or at least, in his former home.

He was still weak, but continued to improve. Amanda learned that Tyler Hawthorne had arranged around-the-clock private nursing care for him. After consulting with Ron, Tyler had left instructions that Amanda be allowed to visit Ron at any hour. Ron was refusing all other visitors. Amanda had not seen Tyler himself since the night she had met him at the hospice.

"He travels a lot," Ron explained. "He's home now, though. Want me to ask him to join us?"

"No thanks."

"What's bothering you about him?"

"I don't know. I'm so happy that you've recovered—"

"I know you are, but I hear a 'but' in there. But *what* . . . ?"

"But I'm worried that you'll end up in debt to him," she admitted.

"No, I've got Derek's proceeds from the house, and I can also sell some of the things Derek took with him when he moved out—paintings and rare books, although I'd rather not part with them. Besides, I've got some news." He grinned. "Maybe this will convince you that Tyler's not all bad."

"I don't think he's bad!"

"You mistrust him."

"No, not exactly." She couldn't bring herself to tell Ron that the last time she had seen Tyler, she had argued with him. About Ron. "Let's just say I don't know him well enough to trust him yet."

Ron studied her for a moment, then said, "Fair enough. Anyway, he needs help cataloging his library, and he's hiring me to do it. He's not in a rush, so I can work at my own pace, just when I feel up to it." He was grinning, and she could see the light of excitement in his eyes. "He has some wonderful rare books, Amanda. I think that's how he met Derek."

Bookish Ron. It was an ideal job for him. "Ron, I'm happy for you. I really am. But don't you wonder why he's—I don't know how to put this—"

"Showing such an interest in me?"

"Well, yes."

"I told you. He and Derek knew each other. And he likes me. And not for my hot but frail body, if that's what you're thinking."

She blushed. "I'm not."

"Oh, you were, or you wouldn't be blushing. Nope. Doesn't even think of me like a brother, the way you do. We're friends. He's not trying to get anything from me—I don't have a damned thing to offer him *but* my friendship."

She fell silent. She kept thinking of how close she had come to losing Ron, though, and how vulnerable he still was—and not just to illness. She couldn't think of a reason why Tyler would do so much for Ron, and found that between Tyler's avoidance of her and his extreme generosity to Ron, she grew more and more suspicious—even as Ron grew more and more grateful to him.

"Amanda . . ."

"Did you ever hear Derek talk about him?"

"No, but Derek rarely talked about anyone other than himself. You know that."

"True."

He waited for her to say more. When she didn't, he said, "Remember about the safe-deposit key?"

"Yes. You said Tyler thought it might have been what the burglars were looking for."

"He found the key and gave it to me. Now is that the act of a dishonest man?"

"It takes more than a key to get into a safe-deposit box. You may not be able to get into it. Do you even know which bank it's at?" She could hear the pettishness in her own voice, and hated it.

"I know where the box is, of course," he answered in a steady, quiet voice, one that she knew as a signal of his anger. It was a tone he very rarely used when speaking to her. "Derek added me to the signature card a long time ago. So as soon as I'm well enough to go out, Tyler will take me there. Tyler said that just before Derek died, he mentioned that he wanted me to have whatever is in that safe-deposit box. It was on his mind."

"Tyler was with Derek just before he died? I don't ever remember seeing him at the hospital."

"Oh, were you in charge of the guest book there?"

She sat silently for a moment, looking away from him. Clearly, he thought she was being overly protective. Was she? Maybe, she thought, we need a breather.

"Speaking of guests," she said, "for a change, I'll be one. I've been meaning to tell you that I'll be gone this weekend. I'm going out to Rebecca and Brad's house. Rebecca's throwing a party."

"Rudebecca's? You know Tyler will be there, too?"

"Yes, so you can see I'm not trying to make an enemy of him. He's my new neighbor, and he's helping you, so please don't think I have anything against him." She folded her arms across her chest. "Who knows? Maybe Rebecca will sink her claws into him and I'll have her for a neighbor, too."

"I don't think you should get your hopes up. He tells me the only reason he's going is that he has a small property of his own out there and needs to check on it. Doesn't exactly sound like he's a man in love, if you ask me. But watch out, Amanda, with all this hanging around Rudebecca—for the first time, you're starting to act like her."

She told herself that it was natural for someone who had been so very ill to be a little cranky as he recovered. She should see it as a sign of his returning strength, remember what it was like when he didn't seem to have any fight left in him, and be glad. She discovered she felt hurt anyway.

"I guess I'll be going," she said, and moved to the door.

She opened it, then heard Ron say, "Mandy—Mandy, don't."

He hadn't called her by that childhood name for years. She turned and saw the look of contrition on his face. He was holding a hand out to her. She went back to his bedside and took his hand. He drew her into a hug. "Don't be angry with me," he said. "I'm not myself these days, you know I'm not."

"Shhh. I'm not angry with you. Really I'm not. I'm not myself, either—not getting enough sleep lately."

They heard the sound of footsteps, and Tyler stepped into the room, saying, "Ron, I wondered if—"

He saw the two of them embracing and quickly said, "Forgive me, I didn't realize you had company." He withdrew, apparently not hearing Ron call after him.

Ron looked at Amanda and shrugged. "Stay a little while, okay?"

"Sure," she said, returning to her chair.

"You said you haven't had much sleep," Ron said. "Ghosts bothering you?"

She glanced at the door, making sure it was closed. Ron was the only one she ever talked to about the ghosts. "They seem to be agitated by something. Maybe because I moved into my parents' bedroom. Although—"

"Although what?"

"They don't seem unhappy when I'm in there. I mean—they never look happy, but they seem at ease. They don't linger. Actually, they're more likely to hang around when I'm outside, or in the car—they show up in the car every time I'm on the way up here."

"You've seen them here?" he asked curiously.

"No, not yet. They vanish before I'm through the front gate."

"I keep thinking they'll reveal themselves to me one of these days."

"I don't blame you for not believing in them. I'm pretty sure I'll get over the guilt at some point in my life—"

"You did *not* cause the car accident that killed your parents and your aunt and uncle!"

"No, I didn't," she agreed, not wanting to revive an old argument. "Anyway, like you, I'm not completely sure they're real. I see them more often in times of stress, after all."

"Well, you're not exactly right about my not believing in them. I keep an open mind. Besides, I know that at least in the moments you're seeing them, they're real to you. That's real enough. They don't threaten you or try to harm you, right?"

"No, never. They startle me, they make me uneasy, but other than the 'boo!' factor—you know, after eight years, they don't really scare me."

"There's some purpose to their appearances," Ron said. "Whether it's in your imagination or not."

"I wish they'd get around to telling me what it is so they could go on to wherever they're going."

They talked for a while longer, until she saw that he was tiring. So she left, telling him she'd be back to see him soon.

She didn't see Tyler Hawthorne again that day, or on any of the other occasions when she visited before leaving for the desert.

Ron's health continued to improve.

The four ghosts came to her room every night, but she was convinced she had made a good choice in relocating. She had never kept the room as a shrine to her dead parents, but until now, she hadn't made it her own. It was much larger and sunnier than her old one. She could see Tyler Hawthorne's house from the room's small balcony.

Despite their increased attention, it wasn't the ghosts who scared her or robbed her of sleep. Every night, even from upstairs, she heard a dog prowling near the house in the hours after midnight. She tried watching from the balcony, to see if she could catch a glimpse of it, but it remained hidden in the shadows below.

She didn't tell anyone about it, not even Ron, knowing he was quite worried enough about her seeing ghosts. There wouldn't be anything he could do about the dog anyway.

She began to look forward to the weekend. Her cousins would be snide, the ghosts would follow her, but she could get away from the dog.

9

Julio Alvarez saw the black Mini Cooper stop before the cemetery gates. It was just after midnight, a time when visiting hours were long over, although if you were the night watchman for a cemetery with its share of movie stars and other famous permanent residents, you never knew who might try to sneak in after dark. But Julio knew this visitor, and unlocked the gates and pulled them open. The driver of the car rolled down the window as he pulled through.

"How are you this evening, Julio?"

"Fine, Tyler. And you?"

"Fine. Thank you for admitting us."

"Tyler, I owe you so much for—"

"No, no you don't. Not a thing. I'll just park over there, all right?"

Julio gave it up. The man would never accept his thanks. "Sure, Tyler, wherever you like."

Shade didn't wait for Tyler to open the passenger door—he bounded out of the driver's side as soon as Tyler was out of the car. Once out, though, he was perfectly calm and well behaved.

"Hello, Shade," Julio said, giving him soft scratches around his ruff. "I know you want to get to work, so go on."

Tyler thanked him again and walked off with the dog.

Julio watched them for a few minutes before locking the gate again.

Most of the time, the last thing you wanted running around in a cemetery after dark—okay, second to last to a high school kid on a dare—was a dog off leash. They pooped. They peed. They dug. They rolled around in the mud on top of the new graves.

This dog never did any of that. He patrolled the place as if he had some kind of duty. Tyler had explained that he was a cemetery dog, and Julio supposed there must be darned few of them, because he had never heard of the like. Not that he mentioned these midnight visits to anyone. Would have cost him his job.

This dog wasn't like any other dog Julio had ever met. Shade had an ability to find graves that needed a little work or had been damaged. It was as if he took that as a personal affront. Well, so did Julio.

Tyler carried a flashlight, but there was nearly a full moon tonight, so he didn't use it. He walked patiently beside Shade, who was never so happy as when he was working. Tyler didn't understand all that went on with the dog, despite their long companionship, but he was aware that Shade sensed things in a cemetery that Tyler could not.

The dead were lost to Tyler, but he did not think this was true for Shade. At times, Shade would stop in a cemetery and stand very still, as if he saw something or someone Tyler could not see. Usually, whatever it was would hold the dog's interest for a time, then he would move on.

On rare occasions, he would growl. Though few things frightened Tyler these days, a growl from Shade always sent a chill down his spine.

Shade seemed to dominate whatever it was, though, for after these encounters he would step a little higher on his toes, as if exhibiting a kind of dog pride in a job well done.

Tyler found himself thinking of Colby again, of his odd visit. He wondered if he had failed to hear the real message, if Colby was growing lonely and could bring that up only by accusing Tyler of it. There were serious differences between them, ones that made Tyler unwilling to spend a lot of time with him. In truth, Shade was a better friend.

They were strolling through a particularly old part of the cemetery—always Shade's favorite place to be in any graveyard—when Tyler's cell phone rang. The dog looked back at him in annoyance.

"I agree," Tyler said, "but then, if someone is calling me now, I should take it, don't you think?"

Shade sighed and kept moving.

Tyler answered the call.

"Mr. Hawthorne? This is Samuel Gunning. I—uh, I don't know if you remember me."

"Of course I do, Mr. Gunning."

His business in St. Louis had been to help a dying man named Max Derley, who wanted desperately to convey news to Mr. Gunning—the boy being raised as Max's son was in fact wealthy Samuel Gunning's son. Gunning had been shocked, and then pleased. When Tyler left the city, Gunning was talking to the boy's mother—an old flame—about caring for the two of them.

"I'm sorry to bother you so late, Mr. Hawthorne, but here in Max's notes, it says it's best to call you at this time of night."

"Please call me Tyler. Max was correct about the time to call. How are you this evening?"

"Yes, well, you call me Sam—and I'm fine. I can't thank you enough for that, although I'm still not sure how—"

"I can't really explain it myself. What can I do for you now, Sam?"

"Well, Tyler, I just wanted to let you know that someone at the hospital where Max died has gossiped a bit, and as will happen with gossip, didn't get the story quite right. To make a long story short, I've got some relatives out there in California who never had a snowflake's chance in hell of inheriting my money, but they've taken it into their crazy heads that you cooked up some plot with Max to trick me into changing my will."

"You'll pardon me for asking this, but are you so certain they're wrong?"

"I have never been more certain of anything. He's my boy."

"You've had DNA tests done?"

"Don't need them. One look at him is enough. Besides, I know what I know."

"Then what's the problem?"

"Tyler, I've had to hire bodyguards to look after all of us here, at least until I can convince the law to do something about these folks, but I'm afraid they may also be after you. I wanted you to be on guard. I promise I'll attend to it just as soon as I can."

"I'm not afraid for my own sake, Sam, but I do have a friend living with me at the moment, and I would like to ensure his safety."

"Can I offer you help from my security service?"

"I have one of my own, thanks. I do need to know more about these relatives, though. Give me whatever information you think will be helpful."

"You have e-mail?"

Tyler gave him his e-mail address.

"Great. I'll send something to you right away. You have any questions, just give me a call."

Tyler thanked him and hung up.

Shade was watching him.

"You heard?"

The dog wagged his tail.

"Do you stay with Ron or come with me to the desert?"

Shade made a tight circle around him.

"All right, then I'd better call Danton's Security. In fact, until Danton's is able to show up, I probably shouldn't leave Ron and his medical team alone at the house—"

But Shade had anticipated his concern, and was headed toward the car at a brisk trot.

10

Late Friday night, Amanda drove down a dark desert road, asking herself why in the hell she had thought she'd ever enjoy herself for a minute at this or any other of her cousins' parties.

Well, she thought, I take that back. She had enjoyed herself for a few minutes. A really good-looking guy named Colby had spent time talking to her. It hadn't taken long for one of Rebecca's friends to butt in on the conversation, though. Colby had given Amanda a rueful look and excused himself to go have a cigarette. She saw him talking to Brad on his way out, doubtless making an excuse for leaving early. And even if he had the good sense to exit Rebecca's party before she did, besides being a smoker, she could tell he was a player, so she didn't take his momentary interest in her to mean a thing.

After that, things went downhill. She had forgotten how boring it was to be nearly the only sober person at a party full of heavy drinkers and pot smokers. She had tried not to think of the last time she had been at such a party—the holiday evening that had left her an orphan with a roomful of ghosts. She did her best to cope with Rebecca's party until the more exotic drugs came out. She knew they were probably commonplace at Rebecca's wild weekends, but she didn't think she could enjoy herself if everyone else around her was loaded. She decided to leave. Rebecca saw her leaving and intercepted her at the door.

"Thanks for inviting me, Rebecca, but—well, I think I'd better be going."

"You are the most boring thing, Amanda. But I don't think I can take another five minutes of looking at that outfit anyway. Where did you find anything with pockets that big? The length of the top is all wrong for you—it makes your butt look like the back end of a battleship—"

"Gee, why on earth wouldn't I want to stick around to hear more of this?" Amanda said, noticing that Rebecca had an audience now—an amused audience. "Good night, Rebecca."

Brad hurried up to them. "Wait! Wait! Amanda, you can't leave yet!"

"Watch me."

"No, stay a little while longer."

"Why?" she asked suspiciously.

It appeared to her that Brad didn't really have an answer, but then he smiled and said, "There's someone here who has been asking about you!" He took her elbow and steered her away from the door.

Did he mean Colby? she wondered. Maybe he hadn't left.

She allowed Brad to lead her toward a group standing near the bar. Suddenly she heard Rebecca squeal, "Tyler!"

She turned to see Tyler Hawthorne doing his best to resist Rebecca's attempt to cling to him.

Not that she could blame her cousin. He was dressed in jeans, a white long-sleeved shirt, and a leather jacket. Casual, but he made it look as elegant as a tux. He was glancing around the room, saw Amanda, and smiled.

She smiled back, raised her hand in a little wave, felt like an idiot, and turned away.

To come face-to-face with a nightmare.

She hadn't seen Todd Norenbecker in eight years. Not since the night that her parents, and Brad and Rebecca's parents, had died in a car accident. It also happened to be the night of a neighborhood Christmas party. And the night she lost her virginity to Todd.

They had been dating for a teenage eternity—three months. Todd had spent most of that time begging her to give it up to him. He had sworn undying devotion to her in the same breath with which he had said he would have to find a more "mature" girlfriend if she wouldn't have sex with him. Being incurably honest with herself, later she had owned up to the fact that she had never loved Todd any more than he had loved her. Curiosity and hormones—and for her, a long-since-abandoned, but then oh-so-strong desire to fit in—had driven her to experiment that night. An experiment that had never inspired her to try it again.

The accident that killed her parents severely injured Amanda, and she had spent several weeks in the hospital. Todd never visited her, never called, didn't do so much as send her a text message saying, "Sorry about your parents." Ron, who had always disliked Todd, had been by her side as often as possible.

"You remember Todd!" Brad was saying.

Todd smiled smugly.

"No," she said, "I don't think there's any reason I should."

Brad looked startled and uneasy, and she realized in that moment that Brad probably didn't know much of how her history with Todd had ended—Brad's parents had also died in that accident, and understandably, any thought of Amanda's love life and breakups at that time wouldn't have registered on anyone else's radar.

She started to turn away, but Todd grabbed her by the shoulder and spun her toward him.

"Hey!" Brad protested.

Todd ignored him. She could smell the booze on Todd's breath, and tried to squirm away from him. Painfully tightening his grip on her shoulder, he said in a loud voice, "Don't know me, Amanda? What a liar. I was your first and you know it! You begged me for it—"

"Take your hands off her," a commanding voice interrupted. "Apologize, and then shut the hell up."

Tyler Hawthorne. Could her humiliation be any more complete?

"Mind your own fucking business, asshole!" Todd said. He let go of her, then took a swing at Tyler.

It missed.

"Oh, thank you for that," Tyler said. His fist flew into Todd's face.

Women screamed as Todd toppled backward into the bar, then hit the floor.

"Apologize to her," Tyler said.

"It's not necessary," Amanda muttered, mortified. She ducked her head and stumbled away through the crowd surrounding them.

She heard Todd say, "Apologize to that—"

But before he could finish his sentence, there was the sound of blows, the crash of furniture, and more shouts and screams.

She hurried out the door and all but ran to her car.

Driving through the desert night helped to calm her. A motorcycle had passed her old Honda several miles ago, pulling far ahead of her on the narrow road, then settling at a steady speed that kept her car about half a mile behind it. Whoever it was had to have come from the party—although she had since passed some small side roads, there weren't any between the mansion and the point where she had first noticed the motorcycle.

Since everyone at the party had been three sheets to the wind, she was happy to let the biker pass her. Having her car rear-ended by a drunk on a bike in the middle of the desert would, she thought, be enough to send her right over the edge. When he pulled ahead, it seemed to her he was holding steadily to a straight line. Great. She had missed meeting the one other sober person there.

The motorcycle slowed a bit, and the gap between them narrowed. She was no sooner aware of this than she realized they were approaching an intersection of some kind. She saw something moving in the darkness off to the right. A truck. With its lights off.

The truck was moving, raising a plume of dust as it sped along the intersecting dirt road.

The motorcycle's brake light flared—too late.

She screamed a futile warning as she stomped on her brake pedal. The screech of tires skidding on pavement added to her wail.

She heard the bang of impact just ahead.

She caught the briefest glimpse of the rider, parted from the motorcycle like a horseman thrown from a metallic bronco, before all her attention was focused on dodging the sparking pinwheel of the bike on the asphalt of this narrow road, its gleaming mass spinning toward her car.

It struck the front end of the Honda with a second bang, coming up over the hood and shattering her windshield. Her airbag went off as the car fishtailed, then spun off the road, coming to a lopsided halt in a shallow ditch and soft sand.

Shaken by the accident, Amanda sat dazed in her car. The airbag had stung, and had given her a small nosebleed. She found a tissue and held it to her face, watching as two hulking figures dressed in white-hooded coveralls and heavy work boots emerged from the pickup truck, hurried to the still figure on the ground, and pulled the motorcycle helmet from his head.

She thought they were about to offer their victim aid, and was wondering if it had been wise of them to move him even so much, when, to her horror, they began to viciously kick his ribs, his back, his head. It was only then she saw that, in addition to the hoods, their faces were masked. She unfastened her seat belt and unlocked her car doors—then hesitated. She was no match for the brawny attackers. She locked the doors again. Lot of good it would do with the windshield smashed out, she thought.

She cowered behind the steering wheel.

They turned to stare toward her car.

She quickly dropped her head down onto the wheel, closed her eyes, and slumped, trying to assume the posture of someone who was passed out cold. She heard the approach of their footsteps and felt a sickening certainty that they would see she no longer wore her seat belt, that they had heard the door locks, that they would see the tension she could feel in every muscle of her body. *I'm unconscious. I don't hear anything. I am as lifeless as that man on the road.*

They were very near now. She kept her eyes closed. One of them rapped on the window next to her. She did not respond, nor did she open her eyes when one of them reached in through the broken windshield and touched her shoulder, undoubtedly intending to shake her—until he cut himself on a piece of broken glass.

"Son of a bitch!"

The hand withdrew. She heard the other one try the passenger-side door.

"You hear something?" the one who had cut himself said.

They stood still, listening.

"Shit," the other one said softly. She strained her own ears but heard no approaching vehicles or other signs of rescue.

"See anything?"

"See anything!" the other mocked. "By then it will be too late."

"Shhh! Listen!"

After what seemed to her to be several hours, but was really only a few seconds, she heard them move away, a few steps at a walk, then at a run.

She kept her head down. They had not spoken more than those few words, so she did not know their plans. Would they return from the truck with a crowbar or a tire jack or something else to use to ensure her silence? A gun? She hadn't seen their faces. She whimpered a prayer that they had not seen hers. She heard the doors of the pickup truck slamming shut. She heard the truck drive off, but some time passed before she could make herself sit up and peer over the dash again.

They were gone.

Hands trembling, she pulled her cell phone from her purse.

No signal.

She took a flashlight and a small first-aid kit from the glove compartment and stepped out of the car, feeling wobbly but mentally pushing herself to set her own troubles aside.

The force of the impact had thrown the man a short distance down the dirt road. She played the flashlight over the ground between the intersection and where the man lay, and was surprised to see a third path, a trail of some kind, which led away from the intersection. Could there be help within reach? A small house? The flashlight didn't illuminate much, though, and within the range of its beam she could see only a low, broken-down picket fence that bore all the signs of long abandonment. She began to run down the dirt road toward the man, glad she had decided in favor of comfortable sandals rather than high heels tonight, but wishing she was dressed in her usual jeans and T-shirt rather than the dressier pants and top she'd worn to the party. Nothing to be done about that now.

"Are you all right?" she shouted.

A stupid question, she thought angrily as she reached his unmoving form. She was half afraid of what she might see, that the damage done to him might be horrific. But although he did not stir or respond in any way, at first sight he seemed to have simply fallen asleep on the road. In a rather red-stained condition.

She knelt beside him and aimed the beam of the flashlight on his bloodied face. She received a shock. Tyler Hawthorne. Although she had known the person on the bike would be someone who had been at the large party, most of the attendees were strangers to her. She hadn't expected to recognize the rider.

"Mr. Hawthorne? Tyler?"

No response.

Beneath the already drying blood, his face was gray. She touched his cheek. It was cold. She drew her hand back quickly, then told herself not to be a fool. She moved her hand to his neck. No pulse.

She fought an urge to be sick.

Pull yourself together. He could still be alive. Help him!

She silently begged him to live.

She opened his soft leather jacket, unbuttoned the shirt beneath it, felt again for his heartbeat. There was none. She pressed her ear against his chest, heard nothing, and shouted his name again. No whisper of breath left him. She quickly looked for any sign of bleeding, found none. Not necessarily good, she knew—dead men didn't bleed. She tilted his head back and began CPR.

With each exhalation of her warm breath into his mouth, with every compression of his chest, she silently exhorted him to live.

No answering breath or heartbeat returned.

He's dead. He's dead.

But if you're wrong?

She did not stop. She began to lose all sense of time and her surroundings, the world distilled down to pressing her hands together just so, just here, counting to thirty, softly pinching his nose, covering his mouth, exhaling, watching his chest rise with the air she sent to his lungs. She was growing weary, and she felt tears of frustration and helplessness spilling down her cheeks, salting her lips and Tyler's cold face. She ordered herself to stop crying, telling herself she would not be able to breathe if her nose was stopped up with tears.

She kept working, ignoring how tired her arms felt now.

She was exhaling when she felt something very cold touch her neck. She froze. She could hear panting.

She turned slowly, and screamed.

11

The biggest, blackest dog she had ever seen stood inches from her face. Its eyes seemed to glow, its fangs glistened. Its ears were pitched forward, and it was staring at her.

She swallowed hard and held up a commanding—if shaking—hand. "No!"

It came out much weaker than she liked.

The dog ignored her, moving around her to the opposite side of Tyler. It began to lean its face toward his. It made a sound like a sigh.

"Stay away from him!" she shouted.

The dog's head lifted, then cocked to one side.

She heard a low moan.

Startled, she looked down at Tyler's face. He was still very pale, but something had changed—his skin was no longer the ashen color it had been. She leaned closer. He was breathing.

"Tyler!"

He moaned again.

This time, she let the tears fall.

She watched him carefully as she rested a moment, catching her breath, regaining her composure. The dog made her uneasy, but it had moved a little farther away from them now. Its nose was lifted, as if scenting something down the dirt road.

As she noticed this, it occurred to her again that they might not have seen the last of the men from the pickup truck.

"Tyler!"

He half-opened his eyes, then closed them again.

"Tyler, we have to get out of here. Those men might come back. Do you know who they were?"

She doubted that he had heard or understood her. But at least his eyes opened again. He stared at her a moment, frowning. He looked around him. When he saw the dog, he made a sound somewhere between a laugh and a sigh.

"Can you move?" she asked.

He didn't answer, but he rolled to his side. She stood, and felt the needles of returning circulation in her feet. She didn't know how long she had been kneeling beside him. She picked up the flashlight and turned it off. The moon had risen, a nearly full moon, bright enough to see nearby objects. She pocketed the flashlight and her cell phone. Well, big pockets were good for something, weren't they?

She watched him carefully as she stood beside him. After what seemed like a long time, Tyler raised a hand.

"Yes?" she asked.

He made another sound that was not quite a laugh. "Hell and the devil—I'm not in a schoolroom, am I? Help me to stand up . . . please."

Embarrassed, she took hold of his hand, but his grasp was weak, and she didn't think she had enough strength to help him up. The dog came back to them, circled them, and barked. It scared some last reserve of adrenaline into her, and she pulled Tyler to his feet. Tyler swayed and grabbed hold of her in a clumsy embrace.

"Wait," he said, leaning heavily on her.

She did her best to keep her balance. The dog kept circling them, its tail wagging now.

Tyler was taking in odd, shallow breaths, as if breathing was painful.

"Are your ribs broken?" she asked.

He shook his head, a no.

"How can you be sure?"

"We have to get out of here," he said, ignoring her question, but he spoke in the manner of a person who is short of breath, or who dares not take a deep breath.

"Will they be coming back?"

"Undoubtedly. Your car—?"

"Wrecked—not drivable, I'm afraid."

For another long minute he simply stood there, his arm across her shoulders. "Too heavy?" he asked, starting to straighten. "Should have asked—were you injured?"

"No, no—just relax. I'm fine. I only wonder—maybe you should lie down just a little longer?"

"I'll be all right."

"You might have a concussion," she said. "You were kicked in the head."

"Hmm . . ." He reached up and touched his lips, which she could see were swollen.

"CPR," she said.

He looked at her own swollen lips. "Amazing," he said. "Thank you."

"You're welcome," she said, and looked away.

"Let's walk to my place."

"You do have a concussion. We can't walk to Los Angeles."

"No—my home here. It's not far." He paused, caught his breath. "On the other side of the cemetery."

"Cemetery!"

She looked in the direction he pointed—she now saw that the dilapidated picket fence surrounded a few weatherworn gravestones. Near a cluster of trees, she could just make out the edge of a low building.

"My van is there," he said. "Do you think you could drive it?"

"Is it an automatic?"

"Yes." He didn't smile as he said it, but she thought she detected amusement.

"Oh. Then yes, I can drive it."

"Do you need to get . . . any belongings from your car?"

"My purse is in it," she said. "That's all I need from it now."

"I'll wait here. Get your purse . . . and anything that has your address . . . or name on it . . . set out flares if you have them."

"Maybe it would be smarter to call the police from your place. And ask them to send an ambulance and a tow truck or two."

"Don't have a phone here." At her look of surprise, he added, "It's something of a retreat . . . No computers, no phone, very low tech."

Since this speech seemed to exhaust him, she told him not to say anything more, contradicted this immediately by telling him to call out to her if he needed her, and saying that she'd hurry back, hurried off.

"So she believes she's saved my life," Tyler said to Shade.

Shade regarded him steadily.

"No, of course I won't behave as if I'm ungrateful." He drew a painful breath. His ribs hurt like hell. "It's going to cause complications, though."

Shade turned his back, staring off toward the intersection, where Amanda was lighting flares.

"Go ahead and ignore me."

The dog seemed to take full advantage of this permission.

Amanda came running back toward them, the purse banging at her side. She dropped something—the car registration? She stooped to pick it up, nearly fell over, but clambered back up and kept coming. He wondered if he had ever seen a more ungainly young woman in his life. And yet, he decided, there was some sort of grace there, wasn't there? A kind of sweet, unconscious freedom in her movements. As he kept watching, he remembered that Ron had once said she was only clumsy when she was nervous or upset. Why wouldn't she be upset, given what she must have experienced tonight? And, of course, he made her nervous. The thought made him frown.

She saw him, then came to a lurching halt, her eyes widening. Clearly frightened. He made an effort to stop frowning. He felt certain his smile looked like a grimace.

Then he realized she was staring at the dog. "I thought he would run off again," she said.

Belatedly, he remembered that Ron had told him she was afraid of dogs. "His name is Shade. He won't hurt you, I promise."

"He's yours?" She sounded horrified.

"You might say I'm his. He's a very good dog, very smart."

She rubbed at a place on her face, near her eyebrow.

Shade approached her, rolled over on his back to expose his belly, and wagged his tail.

Tyler could only stare at the dog in shock. He had never seen Shade do this for anyone but himself.

When she stood frozen in place, Tyler said, "I believe he wants to be friends."

She bent slowly, hand shaking, and quickly touched the dog's chest.

Shade waited until she straightened. He stayed low, tongue lolling from a doggy smile, tail still wagging. Looking for all the world like the most obsequious mutt on the planet.

"Does he always roam around at night?" she asked.

"Rarely. He usually stays close to me."

Shade looked back at him.

"We'd better get going," Tyler said, and tried taking a few steps.

She rushed to his side, heedless of the dog now. It was easier to walk with her help. He told himself that even when he reached the point when he knew he could manage on his own.

Except to hold the hand of someone who was dying, he had not allowed himself to be in physical contact—even such limited contact—with a woman in years. He told himself that was why he was responding to her so strongly.

A young man's body, a young man's thoughts, he told himself bitterly, but kept his arm around her until they reached his front door.

He unlocked the door, and pulled a matchbook from his pocket. He lit the candle near the door, then used this to light an oil lamp. A quick look assured him that the men who had attacked him had not vandalized his home.

"No electricity?" she asked.

"No. Entirely rustic—well, almost."

"Almost?"

"Indoor plumbing."

"No use carrying nostalgia too far," she agreed. She looked about her. He wondered what she made of the simple furnishings. A plain pine table. Four wooden chairs, the number a matter of tradition, since never more than one had been occupied at any given time. A fireplace. Unadorned thick walls. All the color in the room came from one throw rug and the bowls and cups on a simple sideboard. Amanda Clarke was undoubtedly used to far more elegant surroundings.

To his surprise, she smiled and said, "I like it. It's peaceful."

"Yes. If you'd like to wash up before we leave, there's a bathroom just through that first door. Take the candle on the sideboard with you for light."

She glanced up at him, took both the candle and a large empty bowl from the sideboard, and went into the bathroom.

The taking of the bowl puzzled him, but he had a bigger enigma before him. "Shade," he whispered, "what in hell was that all about—that business of groveling?"

Shade wagged his tail.

"She's not the queen of England, you know."

The tail wagged faster. Someone less familiar with the dog might not have seen what Tyler saw—an unmistakable gleam of amusement in the dog's eyes.

"Fine, have your joke."

The dog cocked his head to one side, then lowered it and stepped forward, softly butting up against Tyler's legs.

Tyler sighed and bent—somewhat painfully—to stroke the soft fur along the dog's neck. "Of course I'm not angry."

He heard the water shut off in the bathroom, and soon Amanda emerged, candle extinguished and apparently left behind. She held the bowl carefully with both hands. It was filled nearly to the brim with water. She carried a towel and washcloth over one arm.

He looked at her uneasily, and she said, "Now, after everything else, don't start being a baby. Sit down, please."

He obeyed, mostly out of curiosity.

She carefully washed his face, and when in response to her question he told her that he didn't have any medical supplies here, she used her little first-aid kit to put an antibiotic on his cuts and to bandage one of the deepest. He didn't have the heart to tell her how unnecessary this was, but when he saw her eyeing some of the smaller cuts, he said, "I heal quickly. No need to bandage the others."

She looked doubtful, but took him at his word, and went to work on his hands.

He looked at her long, graceful—yes, graceful—neck, the dark strands of her hair falling to either side of her nape. I must be starved for affection, he thought.

"Did I frighten you, earlier this evening?" he asked.

She blushed but kept her head bent over her work. "A little. But mostly—it was—Todd embarrassed me, that's all."

"He has two black eyes and a swollen nose. And I'm going to have to replace a few broken bottles of Rebecca's booze."

He heard her give a little snort of laughter. "Thanks. But my, um . . . honor . . . was hardly worth fighting for."

"I disagree."

The blush deepened, she ducked her head a little more, and fell silent.

Definitely too long without human affection, he decided. That must explain why having this young woman brush a warm cloth over his hands, spread his fingers, stroke them slowly and tenderly, was nearly enough to make him want to pull her to the floor with him. He began to feel grateful to the louts who had beat him to the point of not having the strength to do it. Despite his mind's wild imaginings, his body was tiring quickly, a sure sign that the fever was not far away.

"Thank you," he said.

She looked up at him. Big brown eyes. Long lashes. She wasn't hard to read—she was happy.

He shook himself. "I appreciate all you're doing, but I think we'd better get back to L.A. To be honest, I'm concerned that they may try something there."

"Ron!"

Yes, he thought, that's the way of it. Remind yourself of whose territory you're poaching.

"I've hired security," he told her. "But I'd like to get within cell phone range and check on him as soon as possible, wouldn't you?"

"Oh, yes! Let's go. Do you need anything from here?"

"No, provided my car keys are still inside my jacket. Judging from the bruises on my side—ah, yes." He gingerly extracted them from the inside pocket and handed them to her.

She was a little wary when he told her that Shade might want to ride in the passenger seat. "Won't you be in the passenger seat?"

He could feel the beginnings of the fever, knew that soon he would not be able to hide it from her. "If you don't mind, I'd like to sleep on the way home. I've got a bed in the back."

"Oh! Yes, that's a good idea. But I still think we need to stop by an emergency room. I'm so afraid—you didn't see what happened, but it was horrible, and you probably aren't fully in your senses—"

"Amanda," he said, and she fell silent. "Amanda, I have to ask for a promise from you. I know I have no right to ask it, but it is extremely important."

"What is it?"

"No doctors, no hospitals, no police. Other than warning Ron, you tell no one what's happened."

There was a long silence. "Why?"

"Are you worried about the car? I'll replace it. I'll buy—"

"No. Don't be silly. You know I can replace it myself. My concern is you, of course."

"I can't imagine why."

She blushed and looked away, but said, "I owe you an apology, for one thing. When I first met you, I was very rude to you."

"I was rude back. We don't have time for this now." He felt his skin growing hot and dry. If they could leave soon, get on the road—if she had to concentrate on driving—if he could manage to be quiet—if, if, if.

He felt his thoughts grow muddled between the fever and the injuries. "If I promise to tell you about this later, will you trust me for now?"

"You'll tell me the truth?"

"You don't know what you're asking."

"I'm asking for the truth."

When he didn't answer, she said, "Are you some sort of criminal?"

He wanted to lie to her but found he couldn't. "No."

"I don't suppose a criminal would answer that honestly," she mused aloud. "You don't look like a criminal, but I guess the really skilled ones don't."

"I'm not a criminal," he said again. He fought a wave of dizziness.

"You don't look well, Tyler. Maybe we should stay here."

"They may come back. You must get away from here, even if you leave me behind. In fact, perhaps that's the best idea."

"Forget it. Let's go."

She helped him into the van. By then he could hardly make sense of what she was saying to him. She had noticed that he felt warm. "I'll be fine," he said thickly. "Get me home."

Shade lay next to him, which further disconcerted her.

"It's all right," Tyler managed to say.

She was studying him. He could see the fear in her.

"You have nothing to fear from Shade."

"I'm only a little afraid of him. I'm very afraid for you."

"Of me, too, I suppose."

"A little," she admitted. She bit her lower lip. "God, I wish I knew what to do."

"Take me home. I promise it's the best place for me to be right now."

She moved up to the driver's seat and started the van. He stayed awake as she pulled out from beneath the carport, awake along the dirt road where she had helped him. He fought hard and managed to stay awake until they reached the nearest freeway, a distance of twenty miles. Shade lay his head on him then, and Tyler surrendered to fever and fatigue.

12

The stench, Daniel thought, was growing stronger. He tried to breathe through his mouth. It didn't help.

"Which one of you is bleeding?" the voice asked from a corner in the darkness.

"I am, my lord," Evan said meekly.

"Hmm. Minor wound, is it?"

"Yes, my lord."

"A shame." He paused. "Let me bring a few matters to your attention. What made last night different from most, Daniel?"

"Hawthorne would be separated from the dog, my lord."

"Not just separated by a few feet, Evan?"

"Yes, my lord. I mean no, my lord—I mean, you're right as always, my lord. He was to be miles away from the dog."

"So tell me, Daniel, why have you arrived here without him?"

"We were about to leave the motel, my lord, on our way to watch the house, to look for our best chance to take him, when we got a call from—"

"Yes, I know. Our friend." He sighed. "I believe the late Eduardo may have been mistaken in his choice. I often regret his lack of skill in choosing good recruits."

Daniel might have been insulted by this, since Eduardo had recruited him, and Evan as well. But whenever Eduardo's name was mentioned, he felt a sharp pang of loss. And fear. He could not forget what the dog had done to Eduardo.

"Go on," the voice said.

Daniel refocused—it was always a mistake to let your attention wander when in the presence of his lordship. "The caller said that Hawthorne rode off on his bike after some kind of fight there—said he left the party about five minutes after he arrived. Made the woman who owns the place mad as fire—in fact, while our contact was calling us, she interrupted him and hung up the phone. He didn't give us a lot of details, my lord."

"As I said, I seem to be short of good help these days. Go on."

"We figured we'd do what we could to stop Hawthorne from getting back to the dog. There was only one place to come at him by the time we heard he was leaving the party. So we waited on a side road until we saw him coming. Then we hit him, and he went flying, but it was only then we noticed that a car was driving some ways behind his motorcycle. Well, it crashed, and there was nowhere for the driver to run, so we took care of business with Hawthorne. Made sure he wasn't going to come to his feet anytime soon."

"Hmm."

Daniel didn't like the sound of that. He waited, but his master again urged him to continue.

"We decided to take care of whoever was in the car, if the driver had lived. It was a girl. Didn't look like she made it. But before we could be sure, we heard the dog."

"Are you certain?"

Daniel felt himself break out in sweat. "Yes, my lord."

"You don't really seem to be so sure. I can smell your perspiration, Daniel. Why is that?"

"I get scared thinking of that dog, my lord."

"So scared that you might run at—oh, say, the sound of a coyote?"

"I hope not, my lord," Daniel said carefully. "My lord knows best."

"And when you regained your courage, and went back to look?"

Daniel swallowed hard. "We did not regain our courage, my lord."

"You disgust me. So now there may be someone who bore witness to all of this?"

"Yes, my lord. But our faces were covered. We wore these coveralls. We took the plates off the truck."

"Plates?"

"The license plates, my lord. The ones that identify the vehicle."

"Ah yes. That is something, in any case. Bring the candle and the map to the table, both of you."

They both hated the table. A large wooden affair, it was never free of bits of hair and bone. The manacles at the corners hung empty, never yet used in their presence, but each heavy iron cuff carried its own threat. Evan and Daniel were fearful of the table, but they came forward immediately and spread the map out on its stained surface.

Daniel could feel the coldness shifting in the room even before the stench grew stronger. His lordship was within striking distance.

"Point to the place where this happened."

They searched until they found the spot. Evan pointed at it.

"Step away. Take the candle."

They did so.

There was a roaring sound. They cowered together.

"You damned idiots! Do you not see? Of course not! What do you know of such things? You struck him at a crossroads. Near a cemetery. You fools never stood a chance of taking him there!"

There was a silence. Daniel felt Evan shiver against him.

"I will say," the voice said calmly, "that the dog was undoubtedly nearby. That would be where he left it. Did you reconnoiter the area at all, Evan?"

"No, my lord. We barely had time to get in position to hit him with the truck."

After another long silence, he said, "Go back to this place. If you can discover who the witness is, do so. In any case, bring our little friend to me."

"Here?" Evan said, only remembering in the nick of time to add, "My lord?"

"Now, Evan, where else would I be?" the voice said bitterly.

13

They were still about an hour from Los Angeles when Amanda heard Tyler stirring. She glanced into the rearview mirror and saw him sitting up, rubbing his hand through his hair. Groggy, but not senseless.

The relief she felt was tempered by her continuing concern that she had been crazy to agree not to seek medical care for him. She pictured herself trying to explain to his friends, relatives, and the authorities that she had seen Tyler hit by a truck and beaten while unconscious—and when this man who had taken hard blows to the head and acted woozy told her that he would recover without help, she had just gone along with the idea, and as a result, he died. Was there a Bad Samaritan law?

At one point during the drive, not long after they had reached the highway, he had started shouting unintelligibly. She had taken the next off-ramp, pulled the van to the side of the dark, deserted road at the end of the exit. She turned the interior lights on and hurried to the back of the van, but Shade, who had been lying on the mattress not far from Tyler, came to his feet, hovering over his master. That kept Amanda from moving closer, but she could see that Tyler's skin bore the flush of fever; he was shaking and muttering in delirium.

She nearly used the cell phone to call 911, promises or no promises.

But then the shaking had suddenly stopped, and Tyler half-wakened. He seemed oblivious to her presence but aware of Shade, who snuffled at his ear, then returned to lie close to him, his head across Tyler's chest. She was trying to think of how to shoo the dog off him without being bitten when she became aware that Tyler's color was more normal, and he had calmed into a quiet sleep.

Looking at his face, she saw that the bandage she had applied had come off. The place where the cut had been had closed up, only the thinnest line showing that he had been injured there. She frowned. It must not have been as bad as it had seemed to her by the light of the oil lamp.

She watched him for a while, then dared to reach out to feel his forehead even though the dog lay so near. Shade did not stir but gazed at her with an unnerving intensity. Tyler's skin felt warm, but not fever hot. After spending some unmeasured amount of time listening to the rhythms of Tyler's breathing—with a steady counterpoint of soft snores from Shade—she returned to the driver's seat and resumed their journey. Tyler's sleep remained untroubled.

"Are you all right?" he asked now.

"I'm fine. How are you doing?"

"Better. Did you reach Ron?"

"Yes. I didn't give him many details, but he's worried about you. He said to call again when we get closer. He wants to know if you want help from any of the people who are caring for him."

"No—but I'll call him myself in a moment. First I need to make sure the wreckage gets cleared away before anyone stumbles upon it."

She heard him call someone about removing the wreckage of the car and the motorcycle. He certainly sounded clearheaded now, sounded even better than he had at his desert house, where she was sure his ribs had been bothering him.

He called Ron. He spoke softly. She tried to convince herself that she didn't really want to eavesdrop on his half of the conversation anyway.

He made a third phone call. He apparently had no shortage of people he could phone in the middle of the night, she thought, then recognized this as bitterness over thwarted nosiness and smiled to herself.

He ended the call. "Are you tired?"

"No. I'm wide awake. I like driving late at night."

"I'm just going to sleep a little longer, then," he said. "You'll pull over and sleep if you need to?"

"Yes, but I don't think it will be a problem."

"Sorry to be such poor company."

"Damned ill-mannered of you to need to recover when I want small talk."

She heard a little cough that might have been a laugh, then he asked, "Do you make small talk, Amanda Clarke?"

"I'm afraid it's not numbered among my few skills."

"Oh, not so few," he said, and lay down again.

Shade moved away from him and came up to the passenger seat. Her muscles stiffened, and she made a conscious effort not to reach up and touch the scar. She kept her eyes straight ahead.

"Is Shade bothering you?" Tyler asked.

She forced herself to glance at the dog. The huge dog. One of the biggest she'd ever seen. And just now he had a truly goofy expression on his face—eyes half closed in contentment, the tip of his pink tongue sticking out of one side of his mouth as if he'd lost track of it.

Impossible to view him as threatening.

"No," she said. "We'll be fine."

"He likes the window open a bit, if the noise won't bother you. You don't have to do it for long, but—he likes it."

She lowered the window a few inches, then, when the dog looked over to her expectantly, lowered it enough for him to stick his head out. The wind and surrounding traffic made a roar that she was sure would keep Tyler awake. When she looked back, he was lying on his side, watching the dog and smiling. Okay, she decided, worth it.

Shade looked as if he had just found the outdoor equivalent of an opium den—ears flattened, eyes closed in bliss, he was chuffing and making a kind of reverse-bobbing motion with his head, lifting it back as he caught passing scents.

Eventually he pulled his head in and gave her one of his doggy smiles.

"Enough for now?"

He didn't answer, but he kept his head inside, so she rolled up the window.

I'm talking to a dog, she thought in wonder.

A beefy security guard with a uniform marked DANTON'S SECURITY greeted her at the gates at the end of Tyler's drive, and insisted on speaking to Tyler. Tyler had apparently awakened at the sound of their voices. He stretched—a little carefully, but apparently without a great deal of pain—and began moving forward to the passenger seat, which Shade reluctantly vacated.

He greeted the guard and asked after his children, naming them. The guard said they were fine, thanked him for asking, smiled, and opened the gates.

"He doesn't have any children," Tyler said as they drove through. "But now he knows you aren't holding me hostage."

"You'd better change the code. Who knows what my intentions will be the next time I'm up here?"

"I'm afraid I'm the one who has held you hostage. Amanda, thank you."

She waved this away and they fell silent until the van was parked and the engine off.

She saw another guard in the garage, talking into a headset. He started to come toward them, but at some signal from Tyler, stood a discreet distance away.

"Amanda, I know it has been a long and trying evening for you. You must be exhausted. Do you want one of the guards to give you a ride home?"

"Nice try, but I'm not leaving until you meet your end of the bargain."

"That was concern with your comfort, not evasion."

She lifted her brows.

"All right, it was both," he admitted.

"You—you seem to be doing much better."

"Much better. Just needed some sleep. Well, let's go inside."

He got out and would have come around to open her door for her, but she was already getting out of the van. He opened the van's side door for Shade.

Ron's grandfather, Derek, had installed an elevator in the house years ago, when Ron first came to live with him. It ran from the garage to the third story, and during the times when Ron was not quite up to managing stairs, it allowed him easy access to every floor. Now its doors opened, and Ron—supported on the arm of another guard—came toward them. He was improving rapidly, she thought, then looked toward Tyler.

Speaking of rapid improvement, how the hell had he managed it? Naturally, she didn't want Tyler to be suffering, but—had she been that mistaken about his injuries?

Ron hugged her and said, "I've been so worried about the two of you . . ." His voice trailed off as he looked at Tyler. "Sorry, I thought— Amanda said—"

"We're fine, as you can see," Tyler said quickly. "Let's go inside. Amanda and I will tell you all about our adventures."

"Yes, of course," Ron said.

A small awkward silence fell. Amanda said, "Ron, you didn't tell me Tyler had a dog."

"No small talk?" Tyler murmured.

"Oh, that," Ron said with relief. "Are you and Shade friends?"

"Shade adores her," Tyler said. "I'm almost jealous."

"Isn't he wonderful?" Ron asked, petting the dog as they moved together toward the elevator.

"Quite wonderful," she said. "I'm really amazed by some of his special powers."

They came to a halt, and she was concerned to see that Tyler looked a little pale. Maybe he wasn't feeling so well after all.

"What special powers?" Ron asked.

"Invisibility, for one. How is it that I never saw him any of the times I visited you here?"

"He was with me," Tyler said.

"That's not the whole truth," Ron said. "I asked him to keep Shade out of sight whenever you were visiting. I told Tyler that you were afraid of dogs."

She glanced self-consciously at the guard, whose face remained a polite blank. Tyler caught the look, though, and said to the guard, "Thank you for your help—I think we can manage from here. Would you please tell the others that we are not to be disturbed?"

As soon as the elevator doors closed, Amanda said, "Tell the world, why don't you, Ron?"

Tyler said, "I've told no one else, Amanda."

"I doubt that guard is as deaf as he pretended to be."

"Lots of people are afraid of dogs," Ron protested.

Shade made a sighing sound.

They rode to the second floor, where Ron's rooms were. As they exited the elevator car, Ron took hold of Amanda's arm, a plea for forgiveness as much as a request for support. She laid her hand over his and said, "It's okay."

She looked up to see Tyler watching her. He looked away.

Tyler had given Ron the rooms Ron had always occupied, a suite that consisted of a spacious bedroom, a bathroom, and a large adjoining room that Ron used as both an office and a sitting room. It had a stone fireplace, bookshelves, a television, a computer, a small refrigerator, two couches, and several big comfortable chairs. Also adjoining Ron's bedroom was a smaller bedroom, now used as an office and medical-supply storage area by the nursing staff.

Ron and Amanda sat on one of the couches. Tyler lit a fire, then sat in one of the chairs. Shade moved near him, then rested at his feet.

Unprompted, Amanda told Ron about their evening. Tyler did not interrupt her, intrigued by her view of events. She finished her story with their arrival here. "And I made the whole trip sitting next to Shade," she said, not without a little pride.

There was a short silence. Ron and Amanda both looked toward Tyler expectantly.

Now or never, Tyler thought. Or—no, there were other choices, weren't there? He wouldn't lie to them, but he couldn't risk the whole truth. Not yet. To buy some time to think over his options, he asked Amanda, "Why are you afraid of dogs?"

14

Amanda gave him a look that said she was onto his ploy but said, "The reason you might expect. I was bitten by one."

"There's more to it than that," Ron said. "Tell him the whole story."

Tyler waited.

"When I was nine," Amanda said, "I was playing near our house, along the hillside. I believe I was building a fort, doing some digging. The sort of thing that always displeased my mother. Anyway, I was digging away with a toy shovel when a large stray dog came out of the trees and started growling at me. I stood up, told it to go home, to shoo, all the usual. It barked at me. I tossed the shovel at it and shimmied up a tree. It stayed and watched me. If I tried to get down, it barked and snapped at me.

"I called for help. No one came."

She paused, remembering her terror, her unheard pleas.

"I began to get cold," she went on. "I decided to snap off the biggest stick I could manage to find on the nearby branches. I got hold of a good one. I broke it off. Unfortunately, I also lost my balance and fell from the tree." She smiled. "A klutz from an early age, you see. I've always thought that fall would have been the funny part if the dog hadn't been there."

"Well, it's not funny," Ron said. "And the dog was there."

"Yes. At first, I think my falling like manna startled him, but it also knocked the wind out of me, and I broke one of my arms. He charged at me and I—well, I guess it was instinct that made me protect my neck, but he bit me hard on the face. I still had hold of the stick, and that was the arm that wasn't broken, so I hit him as hard as I could with it. He didn't let go. I hit him a second time, on his muzzle, I think, although I couldn't really see by then, and that time he released me. I remember hearing him yelp and run away.

"I managed to get to the house. I must have nearly been in shock by the time I reached the kitchen door—our cook took one look at me and started screaming at the top of her lungs. That's the last thing I remember very clearly before I got to the hospital."

She traced the scar near her brow. "I guess the plastic surgeon did a good job. This is the only scar you can see now."

"They didn't find the dog," Ron said tightly.

Tyler frowned. "Didn't find it? But then—"

"Yes, I had to have the rabies shots."

"Good God."

She sighed, then looked at Shade. "I have tried not to blame all creatures in your species, Shade, and I know you and other dogs are good dogs, but it's still very hard for me not to feel afraid."

Shade stood and moved toward Amanda.

"Shade!" Tyler called to him, unheeded. "If you'd rather I put him up in my rooms—"

But Shade had dropped to his belly, as if to make himself smaller, and moved at a crawl toward her. When he reached her feet, he laid his head on her shoes and moaned.

"I think he just apologized on behalf of all doghood," Ron said.

She hesitated, then reached down and stroked his long, soft fur. "Well, of course I see that you are nothing like that mean fellow in the woods. And yes, I'd like to be your friend. I just spook easily, all right?"

He wagged his tail.

She looked up at Tyler. "So now Shade and I have settled our business. I believe it's your turn."

A silence stretched. He walked over to the fireplace and, looking into the flames said, "You'll have to forgive me for being hesitant. In part, that's because it's not just my story to tell. But I have been given permission by the others involved to explain what I can."

"Was that the call you made in the van, the third one?" Amanda asked.

"Yes. Without boring you with the details, I helped a man in Missouri—call him Max—who was dying. He wanted to find a man who had once been his best friend, Sam. There had been a falling-out between them.

"I sometimes believe that the end of a close friendship can be as difficult or more difficult than a divorce. Think of the emotions—they are much the same. At the end, former friends feel betrayed. They act out of hurt and anger, take ill advantage of their intimate knowledge of each other, and sometimes divide whole camps of connected friendships in the wake of their separation. While couples will go to marriage counselors, there is really nothing adequate to help friends steer their way through difficulties."

"That doesn't mean there aren't good reasons to end friendships," Ron said. "If someone isn't trustworthy, it's smarter not to have anything to do with them."

"Certainly, or if the friendship was destructive. But often differences arise out of petty matters."

"Was that the case this time?" Amanda asked.

"Hmm. Not exactly. Years earlier, Sam had come to California to seek his fortune. Told his girlfriend he'd come back to Missouri to marry her one day, but he didn't ask her to give up her life there when he might well be returning to her as a failure. A month later, he received a telegram from Max. His best friend had married the girl he'd asked to wait for him."

"See what I mean?" Ron said. "Some friend!"

"So Sam thought. But unbeknownst to Sam, the woman he left behind was pregnant with his son. She knew that supporting a young family would be a financial burden for Sam, who didn't seem ready to settle down with a wife, let alone a wife and child. Max married her and raised the boy as his own. He kept her secret until he was dying."

Tyler moved back to his chair and sat down wearily.

"Are you okay? Do you need to talk to us another time?" Amanda asked.

He needed to sleep, knew his strength had not yet fully returned, but he knew Amanda and Ron were tired, too. Easier to convince them, perhaps, if they were weary. He shook his head, but laid his head back and closed his eyes. And told them of Max and Sam talking things out, without mentioning that Max was comatose at the time.

"So what does that have to do with nearly getting killed tonight?" Amanda asked.

"Ah. Sam called me from St. Louis to say he has relatives here in California who aren't pleased that he's embracing a new heir. They apparently believe I'm in on some scheme to defraud him. Sam is doing all he can to protect his son, but frankly, I'm glad they came after me and not the boy."

"Will they be arrested?"

"I don't know. Sam will pursue things with the authorities," he said. "Now, it's nearly dawn, and while I enjoy your company, I must get some rest. Amanda, may I see you home?"

"If you don't mind, I'd like to sit with Ron for a few minutes more."

Tyler hid a sudden sense of disappointment. "Of course I don't mind."

"Oh," she said, watching his face. Then she turned to Ron and said, "That is, if you aren't too tired, Ron?"

"I'm the only one who has had any sleep tonight," Ron said. "I'm fine."

"I'll give you some privacy, then," Tyler said. "Only—promise me you won't walk home, Amanda. One of the guards will drive you back whenever you're ready." He indicated the phone next to his chair. "Just use the intercom line and dial seven. That will put you through to Alex." He found a notepad near the phone and wrote a number on it. He gave it to her. "This is my cell phone number. I keep the phone with me, so if you see strangers lurking near you or you feel worried about any of this, please text or call me."

"Thank you. I hate to be such a bother—"

"Not at all."

When Tyler rose from his chair, she stood also. She came toward him and studied his face again for a moment, then said in a low voice, "Are you sure you won't see a doctor? I'm worried that if you have a concussion and fall asleep . . ."

"If it will make you feel better, ask Alex to check on me in a few hours."

"All right, I will." She surprised him with a hug and a quick kiss beneath his ear. "Good night, Tyler."

"Good night, Amanda. Thank you again."

He wished Ron a good night and called to Shade, who followed him from the room. He forced himself to give them the privacy they so clearly wanted. Let them be, he told himself sternly. You have no business pursuing her in any case.

Still, he thought of how Ron and Amanda sat near, but not too near each other. There was nothing quite loverlike in the way they interacted. Loving, yes. Devoted, yes. But were they lovers? Or friends?

None of your business, he told himself.

She had kissed him.

Just an L.A. thing. People in this city are always exchanging peu baisers. *Don't be a fool.*

He called down to Alex, requested that Amanda be given a ride home and seen safely inside. "If she'll allow it, please check the house over, too."

He undressed and made sure to plug the cell phone in the recharger on his nightstand. He crawled into bed and listened to Shade settle near him. He reached for the dog and scratched his ears and chin in a manner that earned canine sighs of pleasure. "You've saved me again, Shade, and while I'm really not especially grateful for that, I do appreciate your dedication. And, most especially, your companionship."

But the dog suddenly seemed distracted—in the next instant he came to his feet and held himself alert, his ears pitched forward. He moved to the French doors that led to the deck surrounding most of this level of the house. The deck was, Tyler thought, the dog's favorite feature of the house—he could sun himself or survey the canyon from it. "At this hour? All right."

He got up, donned a silk robe, and opened the doors. Shade immediately began patrolling the part of the deck in front of the bedroom. Tyler looked down at the place where Amanda's house stood. Only a small porch light was on.

Shade seemed disinclined to come back in. The night was warm, so Tyler left the doors open.

What did he have to fear?

Nothing. He would survive anything that might come through that door.

Which was, he thought, the pity of it all.

15

I saw what I saw."

"You had been in an accident," Ron said gently. "And for someone who survived a really horrible car wreck just eight years ago,
that must have been traumatic."

"I didn't even think about that—I swear I didn't. I was too worried
about him. Besides, you know I don't remember anything about that
other accident."

"All right. But tonight, you might have been a little dazed. The airbag
went off, right?"

"Yes, but—"

"And you had just seen something awful, and then these assholes
came over to your car and terrified you, right?"

"I admit I was scared, but—"

"And to top off everything else, a big dog comes loping up to you.
Don't you think all of that could have caused you to be a little confused?"

She paced across the room, then back. "He stopped breathing. He
had no pulse—no heartbeat. His skin was cold and gray. His wounds
weren't bleeding."

"What wounds? There's hardly a mark on him."

"I can't explain it. That's what I'm telling you!"

Ron sighed in exasperation.

"He was dead!"

"Which is how he just had a conversation with us."

"Ron!"

"Okay—which was why you began CPR. You thought he was dead. One hundred percent croaked. Total goner."

She had no answer to that.

"Look, Amanda, maybe you're right. Maybe he was dead, briefly. But you obviously revived him."

"But how did he recover so quickly?"

"How should I know? Just exactly what are you getting at, Amanda?"

"I don't know. None of it makes sense to me."

"Well, then, that's two of us."

"Sorry."

"You're tired. You've been through a lot. Maybe in the morning . . ."

"Yes."

"Don't get that look."

"What look?"

"The one that is supposed to fool me into thinking you are docile."

She brooded for a few minutes, then tried another tack. "Okay, tell me this—how old is he?"

"I don't know. He looks about our age, maybe a little older. Somewhere in his twenties anyway."

"Have you listened to him talk? He doesn't sound like anyone our age."

"Yes, I've noticed he's not like anyone we went to school with. Neither am I, so it's really nice to find someone weirder than I am."

"I've been replaced, huh?"

"Ha, ha. And if this is jealousy, no—of course no one has replaced you, Amanda."

"It's not jealousy."

"Good. But you seem to have some problem with Tyler. Other than not acting his age and rising from the dead, I mean." He suddenly grew serious. "Did he . . . hurt you in some way? Try to put a move on you?"

She blushed. "No."

"Oh, ho! So that's the problem!"

"No!"

"Hmm."

"Don't 'hmm' me."

"So you don't find him at all attractive?"

"Oh, for—yes, he's attractive. Very attractive. Satisfied? And he doesn't have the slightest interest in me, which makes him like half of the men I meet. The other half know I have money."

"That's so untrue—"

"Let's not argue about it." She smothered a yawn. "I should go home and get some rest."

He hugged her and said, "I really do think you'll feel better about all of this after you've had some sleep."

"You're probably right."

She sat in the chair Tyler had recently vacated, pressed the button on the intercom line, and dialed seven. A woman answered, and Amanda asked for Alex.

"This is Alex," the woman said.

"You're . . ." She managed to prevent herself from saying "a woman."

"Is this Ms. Clarke?"

"Yes."

"Are you ready to leave?"

When Amanda said she was, Alex said she'd be right up. Amanda hung up.

The head of Tyler's security was a woman. Named Alex. Well, why not?

She looked up to see an expression of unholy glee on Ron's face.

"You could have warned me!" she said, but laughed.

16

A few minutes later, she wished Ron had issued another warning. Maybe, Amanda thought sourly, Alex Danton had decided to get into this line of work because being a supermodel involved too much travel. She was slender, tall, blond, blue eyed, and yet her features were just exotic enough to keep her from looking like she came out of some Orange County beach girl tribe.

She smiled, introduced herself with a warm handshake, and turned to Ron. He must have grown accustomed to her, Amanda thought, because he said a quick hello and announced that he was going to bed.

"Will you be all right, sir?" Alex asked. "Anything I can do for you?"

"No, I'm fine, thank you," he said. He asked Amanda to come by after she'd had some sleep, and left the room.

Alex stared after him a moment, seemed to recall Amanda's presence, and turned to her with a smile. "Shall we go?"

As they walked to the elevator, she said, "You probably know this house better than I do, so it must seem silly to you to have an escort."

"A little," Amanda admitted.

Once the elevator doors closed, Alex said, "Neither of them warned you I was female, did they?"

"No."

"Men. Of all the stupid things . . ."

By the time they were driving past the front gates, the sky was beginning to brighten with the approaching dawn, and Amanda felt perfectly at ease in Alex's company. Alex did most of the talking, but Amanda noticed that she stayed sharply aware of their surroundings.

Amanda learned that Alex had become manager of the security business and co-owner with her mother after its founder, her father, had been in a car accident.

"He was driving a little rental car, tailing someone, when a lady in one of those fat-ass SUVs ran a red light. He was in a coma for about three weeks before he died. Mr. Hawthorne came to the hospital and helped me before Dad died. I don't know what we would have done without him."

Amanda glanced out the car window and saw something moving in the woods. She drew in a sharp breath and froze—then saw the misty forms of the four ghosts, weaving in and out among the trees. They floated effortlessly, keeping pace with the car. She turned resolutely away from them. What had Alex been saying? Oh yes—parent killed as a result of a car accident. No wonder her own mind produced the ghosts.

"I'm glad he could help you," Amanda said. "I probably could have used something like that when my folks died. But at least Ron was there for me."

"Are you two . . . ? "

"Involved? No. A brother-sister kind of thing. Not more."

"No one else comes by to see him, but I understand he doesn't want anyone else to visit just now. So . . . no girlfriend?"

"No." Amanda looked at her curiously. "Are you interested in him?"

"Ron doesn't talk to me much," Alex said, and slowed the car.

Amanda wasn't sure what to make of that answer, but decided that as long as they were exchanging information, she'd ask a few questions of her own. "Do you know Mr. Hawthorne well?"

"I don't think anyone does," Alex said distractedly. "That said, I'd do anything for him."

She stopped the car.

Amanda saw that she was staring into the woods. "What is it?" she asked nervously.

"Oh, nothing bad. Thought I saw Shade running through the trees. That doesn't make any sense, though." Alex let the car creep forward again.

"Why not?"

"He was up on the third-floor deck, last I saw him, just as we pulled away from the gates. Up there watching us—nothing gets past him." She smiled. "Probably some other dog out chasing squirrels. More I think about it, I'm sure it wasn't Shade."

Amanda wrapped her arms across her stomach, suddenly feeling it pitch.

"You okay?"

"Afraid of dogs."

"You need me to pull over or anything?"

"No, just get me home."

"Sure." She paused. "If you're afraid of them, it probably won't help to know this, but I've been around a lot of dogs and I don't think Shade would hurt you."

"I'm not afraid of Shade—not much, anyway. But if it's another dog . . ."

"Don't worry. I'm going to make sure you get in all right, and then I'll take a look around—if that's okay with you?"

"I'd appreciate it."

They each watched for any other sign of the dog as they made their way down the long drive that led to the house. "I don't see him, do you?"

"No," Amanda said.

Except for the porch light and the small lamp on a timer in the front room, the house was dark.

"You'll be here alone?" Alex asked.

"Yes. It's all right—"

"If you don't mind, I'll come in with you, just to be on the safe side."

"I don't mind." In truth, Amanda was relieved.

Asking Amanda to stay beside her, Alex did a quick but thorough search of the house.

"Okay," she said, and handed Amanda a business card. "My cell phone number's on there. Give me a call if you feel worried or see anyone hanging around here who shouldn't be. I'll take a look outside to see if that dog is around—lock up after I step outside and set your security system on, okay?"

"Thank you."

"Oh—almost forgot—Mr. Hawthorne said to tell you that until the car business gets straightened out, I'm to take you wherever you need to go." She smiled. "You will call me, won't you? I've enjoyed meeting you."

"Yes, I will. I've enjoyed meeting you, too. And please give him my thanks."

Amanda dragged herself upstairs. Whatever adrenaline had kept her going until now had drained off. She felt woolly headed, not able to keep her thoughts straight. She put on her pajamas, but she could not resist stepping out onto the balcony. Alex was finishing a circuit around the house. She waved, shrugged her shoulders, then pointed up the hill.

An outdoor light on Tyler's deck revealed Shade peering through the deck railing. He wagged his tail. She waved at him, felt like a fool for doing so, then waved good-bye to Alex.

"Set that alarm," Alex reminded her.

So she locked the door to the balcony and used the upstairs keypad to engage the security system, heard Alex drive off, and went to bed.

She lay in the darkness thinking of Tyler Hawthorne, of how horrible it had been when she thought he was dying, of those brief moments in his desert home when she felt quite sure he was drawn to her in some way—of the moments later this evening when she was quite sure he was not interested in her in the least.

She was tired, she was confused. Her muscles had started to ache from the accident.

She closed her eyes, and was nearly asleep when the room suddenly grew cold.

The ghosts were back, watching her.

"What do you want?" she asked.

As usual, they didn't answer.

17

Brad Clarke looked back at the desert mansion. No one had followed him. Good. He could have a minute of peace and quiet, which he wasn't likely to get inside the house. It was nearly dawn, but music was still blaring.

He walked along a pathway leading to one of the guesthouses. As he neared the guesthouse, he smelled cigarette smoke and swore to himself. He had been seen. The smoker waved to him—Colby.

"Thought you'd left," Brad said. "Haven't seen you around."

"Oh," Colby said in a low voice, glancing toward the bedroom window. "I've kept myself occupied out here."

Brad smiled. "Entertaining one of Rebecca's friends?"

"Oh, I wasn't so selfish that I only entertained *one*," Colby said, and Brad laughed.

"Shhh," Colby warned. "You'll wake them before I make my escape. Just wanted a moment outside before I started home again."

"Glad you could make it to the party."

"Me, too." He paused, then added, "Your cousin's cute."

"Dude—"

Colby raised his hands in mock surrender. "There's been enough fighting over her for one evening, don't you think? Anyway, I'm taking off. Thanks again for the invitation."

"You're welcome. Do it again sometime." Brad didn't remember inviting him, but then, that could be said for more than half the people here. He'd lay money on Rebecca being the one who told Colby about the party. But he said so long to Colby and turned away from the guest-houses. He wanted to avoid any other chance meetings.

He had come outside for some air, and to get away from Rebecca, who was pouting over Tyler's departure. Brad had been kind of surprised about the fight, because Tyler had seemed like such a mellow person.

"Hello, Brad."

Brad felt the color drain from his face. Evan and Daniel. "You guys can't be here!" he said in a furious whisper, looking back at the house.

"Can't we?" Evan said.

Brad struggled, but they had him in a headlock, then gagged and bound him before he had a hope of summoning help. He felt raw fear, thought he was as afraid as it was possible to be afraid—then they blind-folded him. He tried screaming into the gag, and they slapped him hard. He felt them lift him, carrying him roughly between them, and he began to cry, which made it hard to breathe.

They loaded him into the back of some vehicle—a van or a pickup truck—he didn't know which. He only knew that he was scared shitless. The metal surface he was on was ribbed and cold as ice. The vehicle bumped along and he bumped with it, jarred with every pothole, rolled with every curve.

Being kidnapped was not the experience he had seen on television. The rope chafed and the duct tape made him feel suffocated. There were no convenient opportunities for escape.

He began to realize that "kidnap" was probably the wrong word.

The right word was "murder."

They were going to kill him. He felt sure of it.

Why were they angry with him? He had called them earlier, told them right away that Tyler had left the party.

Brad missed Eduardo and wondered what had become of him. Eduardo was so much easier to deal with. Eduardo was rich and sophis-ticated, world traveled, and world weary in a way that made him seem pretty cool. Best of all, he had taken a liking to Brad and had provided an easy way to pay off a big gambling debt while Brad waited for his next payment from his trust fund.

But Eduardo hadn't been around lately. Eduardo had said that Evan and Daniel were his assistants, and that Brad should do as they asked. Now he wondered if all three of them were working for some Mafia boss.

They had always been mysterious. Brad knew it wasn't just the need for quick money that had brought him to this situation—he had enjoyed the intrigue and the chance to do something on his own without Rebecca having anything to say about it.

And until tonight, he had convinced himself that it wasn't dangerous or criminal. All he had to do was to spy a little bit on his cousin's new neighbor. Not even spy, really. Just tell them if Tyler left for a few days—they said he traveled a lot. He was to make sure Tyler was invited to the desert party, and Brad had figured out that all he had to do to make sure Tyler showed up was to invite Amanda. If Rebecca didn't get it that Tyler was interested in her, Brad wasn't so blind. He had picked up on that right away.

They had been happy with him when he told them Tyler would be at the party. And then they said Brad was to tell them when he arrived, when he left. That's all.

And that's exactly what he did! He followed his orders. He didn't harm anyone. And now look what had happened to him. It was so unfair.

The vehicle stopped.

His heart started pounding and his throat went dry.

They pulled him out and stood him on his feet. They took the blindfold off, and he blinked in the bright light of a desert morning. No buildings nearby. Nothing but mesquite and sandy hills and dirt roads. The vehicle turned out to be a big white pickup truck with a windowless shell covering the back.

Daniel took the gag out.

"Why—" Brad started to ask, but Evan punched him hard in the gut and all the air went out of him.

As the blows rained on him, he thought they would bury him out there.

They put duct tape over his mouth and eyes, made sure the knots on the rope that bound him were good and tight, and threw him back in the bed of the truck, where the landing was just one more way to inflame pain so intense it consumed every thought.

Eventually, he went into a kind of numbed state, still feeling the pain, but trying to think of how he might survive.

For a time he had hoped someone had seen them take him. Colby, maybe? That hope faded fairly quickly.

Rebecca would miss him—eventually. With the party going on, though—how long would it be before she was even sober enough to notice he was gone? Who else would look for him? No one, in all likelihood.

He had never been badly injured in his life, and any time he had sustained a minor injury, someone had cared for him immediately, done something to lessen the pain. This pain was as different from what he had felt before as a volcano was to a match.

But the pain wasn't the worst of it.

The worst was the fear.

Being so afraid—believing he was about to suffer more than he had thus far, and then be put to death—was exhausting. Over the hours, terror hollowed him out. He felt as if his skin was a shell of pain encasing nothing but more pain.

By the time they unloaded and untied him, more than his hands and feet were numb. It hurt when they pulled off the duct-tape gag and blindfold, but he hardly made a sound. He blinked at the light, and noted in a distant way that he was in the kitchen of what seemed to be an old house.

They waited only until they were sure he could stand up. They lit a candle and marched him to a doorway, then down a set of concrete stairs. They hurried back upstairs, taking the candle with them.

He had not struggled against them.

Only by using the last remaining bit of his tattered willpower did Brad prevent himself from throwing up. He hadn't noticed the smell of the basement until Evan had opened the door to the stairway. If he had felt he had any choice about it, he wouldn't have gone down the stairs at all, but whatever resistance he might have had in him had been beaten out of him hours ago.

The stench proved to be an unwelcome stimulant, reviving awareness.

There was not the slightest doubt in his mind that he was down here with at least one rotting corpse. Maybe they had killed Tyler Hawthorne, and now he was next. Whoever it was, there was no doubt in his mind that he, too, would become a rotting corpse in this basement, and he found he had just the slightest rebellion against this left in him.

It was only a thought, no more.

Because of it, he attempted to stay on his feet.

The wall behind him was cold and damp, and where it touched his skin—he tried very hard not to think about what might make it feel the way it did.

Suddenly the stench increased and the temperature dropped.

A foul breath blew against his face as a deep voice asked, "Would you like to leave here alive, Bradley?"

18

A manda's phone rang. It seemed terribly early to her, but when she glanced at the clock as she lifted the receiver, she realized it was noon.

"Amanda? It's Tyler. Did I wake you?"

"It's all right. What's up?"

"First, I wondered how you are feeling. I didn't realize how badly your car had been damaged until I got the report this morning."

"I'm a little stiff and sore, but it's not bad."

"Alex just told me that you're there alone."

"Yes." *Sort of, if you don't count ghosts.*

"Could I talk you into staying here for a few days? Just until we're sure the problem with Sam's family is cleared up? Alex will be here, and the rest of the security staff, but if you'd like to invite your cousins or someone else to stay here as a chaperone—"

She smiled to herself. "I think I can manage without a chaperone at this point in life," she said. "But thanks."

"Will you stay with us, then?"

She looked around her. Was there any reason to be here? The sad truth was, she had a completely blank to-do list. A blank calendar. A blank life.

And if she stayed at Tyler's house, perhaps she'd get over this ridiculous obsession with him.

Familiarity breeds contempt, right? Or is that, obsession breeds ratio-nalization?

"Amanda?"

"I'm here. Can you give me a little time to think about it?"

"Sure. But—say yes."

She laughed. "I'll call back in a little while."

A hot shower eased most of her aches to a tolerable level.

She dressed in jeans and a light sweater, then went downstairs and sat in the living room. She listened to a silence broken only by the ticking of the grandfather clock in the hall and the soft hum of the refrigerator in the kitchen.

I can always come back, can't I? It's not as if he's asking me to live in another country.

She went upstairs and packed a small overnight case.

She called.

"Yes," she told him.

"Thank you. I'll be there in a few moments."

Tyler hung up the phone, and took the stairs down to the garage, Shade following on his heels.

He hesitated when he saw that the dog wanted to get into the Mini Cooper with him.

"Ah—should I take you with me? Yes. I think it's best if she grows accustomed to you. But let's take the van instead, so we're not crowded—that might be too much to ask of her."

When he parked and let Shade out of the van, the dog immediately disappeared around a corner of the house. Tyler stared after him, then walked toward the front porch. He was surprised to feel anticipation. He stood for a moment on the steps, savoring it.

When had he last anticipated anything?

Vague memories came to him, from the time near his real youth.

Things will be changing for you.

That message, delivered to him at the last two deathbeds he'd attended. Was this what they meant?

He knocked on the door.

She opened it almost immediately and welcomed him inside. "How are you feeling?" she asked.

"Fine," he said. "Are you ready to go?"

"Yes, I just have to get my bag from upstairs."

"May I help you?"

"No thanks, I can get it. Make yourself at home—I'll be right back down."

As she went up the stairs, he glanced around him. The room was elegant and yet not lacking in warmth. He closed his eyes for a moment and listened to the sound of the grandfather clock, a sound he found soothing.

When he opened his eyes again, his gaze was drawn to a photograph on a side table, of two handsome young couples surrounding a teenage version of Amanda. He picked it up to study it more closely.

The setting seemed to be a party, the couples and Amanda dressed in evening wear, the adults lifting glasses of champagne. There were many other formally attired people in the background. The photograph had been taken in a large room, with a sweeping staircase in the background, a mansion, but not one he recognized. The adults were laughing, but Amanda, who was looking directly into the camera, wore a serious expression. She looked—perhaps it was his imagination, but he thought she looked hurt, and perhaps disappointed, but was putting on a brave front. He found himself wondering what had happened just before the photo was taken.

He heard Amanda come down the stairs, and turned to see her carrying a small overnight bag. She set the bag down and came to his side. "My parents, Thelia and Hudson Clarke," she said, pointing to one of the couples, "and my aunt and uncle—Cynthia and Jordan Clarke—Brad and Rebecca's parents."

"You don't look as if you were enjoying yourself."

"I wasn't," she said simply, and started to reach again for her small carry-on-size bag.

He managed to pick it up first, saying, "Allow me." He frowned, thinking of it being so light. "Is this all?"

"I can always come back here, right?"

"Alex or I will bring you back to gather anything else you might need," he said as they went out the front door.

She laughed.

"What's so funny?"

"I hear an assumption that I won't want to come back to my own home."

"I just want you to be comfortable while you're with us."

"Us?"

"Ron and me. And Shade."

"Don't forget Alex," she said, setting the alarm again and locking up.

"Yes, Alex as well. Did you get along with her?" he asked as they walked outside.

"Yes. I like straightforward people."

He fell silent, busying himself with stowing her bag in the van.

He heard a sound and looked up. "I wonder what that dog is up to now?"

She turned quickly to look in the direction of his gaze. She looked panic-stricken. "What dog?"

"Shade. Are you all right? I didn't think he still frightened you . . ."

"Oh, no. He doesn't. Not much anyway. I just wondered if you were seeing that other dog."

"What other dog?"

"Didn't Alex tell you? A strange dog has been coming around here. It was running loose in the woods between our houses last night—Alex said it looked like Shade, but we knew Shade was with you."

"You thought it was Shade?"

"But he was with you, right?"

"Yes, he came upstairs with me, but I did notice that he stayed out on the deck, watching for something last night. Perhaps . . ." His voice trailed off as he considered how little interest Shade usually took in other dogs. "Alex didn't tell me any of this, but she's been working the late shift, so perhaps over the hours I slept, it slipped her mind. Did the dog look like Shade to you?"

"I've never seen it. I've heard it, though. And I've seen tracks near the house." She shuddered. "Judging from those, it's a big dog."

He put an arm around her shoulders. "You saw tracks last night? Was that the first time?"

"No, I think the first time was the night someone broke into your house, while you were in St. Louis. But—was Shade with you then?"

"Yes. He travels with me." Seeing her curiosity about that plainly written on her face, he quickly added, "This other dog has obviously frightened you. Has it tried to get into the house?"

"Not exactly, but it isn't shy about coming close to it. That's why I moved to the upstairs bedroom—I kept hearing it at night, near my bedroom window. Maybe that makes me sound like I'm totally chicken, but—well, yes—I'm scared."

"Understandable, though. Can you show me some of the tracks?"

They found Shade intently sniffing the ground beneath her old bedroom window.

Tyler reluctantly let go of her and bent to study the ground.

"These, here in the dried mud?" he asked.

She edged closer, then nodded.

Shade came to her side, tail wagging. Tyler worried that she would be further frightened by him, but she reached out and petted him.

"You're looking for that other dog, aren't you, Shade?" she said.

Shade wagged his tail harder.

"Do you think he understands English?" she asked Tyler, who was noting that the tracks were indeed those of a large dog.

"Among other languages," he answered absently.

Her laugh caught his attention, and he smiled. "One of the gifts of dogs, you know. Our words don't matter. And even our tone of voice may not count for all that much with the brightest of them. They read our gestures and expressions, the way we hold ourselves. They probably smell our reactions as well. There's an old saying, 'You can't lie to a dog.' I believe it."

"Oh, so you have to be truthful with Shade."

He stood up. "I can be sure Shade will return the favor."

She fell silent. He realized she was studying him in a blatantly assessing way.

"I wonder . . . ," she said.

"Yes?"

She took a deep breath. "I understand you're involved with grief counseling."

"Not . . . professionally," he said cautiously. "I just try to be of help to people whose deaths are imminent. And of help to their families."

"Are you planning to go back to the hospice?"

"Yes, I'm going over there again this afternoon."

"I'd like to come with you."

"I'm not sure—"

"Please!"

He raised a brow. "It's not a place most people are anxious to visit."

"I don't know if you can understand this, but—there's one thing I want more than anything else." She drew a deep breath, as if screwing up her courage. "I want to be *useful*."

He started to make a glib reply, saw how earnest she was, and instead said, "Tell me what you mean."

"I mean—having some purpose, doing some good. Not just being a locust."

He smiled. "A locust, is it? I haven't seen a lot of signs of you being an überconsumer."

She laughed and shook her head.

"Right," he said. "Let's see—how much of your spare time is spent shopping?"

"Not much," she admitted.

"Your car—solid and dependable, but not new?"

"True."

"I don't mean to stick my nose into your finances, but I have the impression you could be chauffeured in a Rolls if you wanted to be."

"I could be, yes. I'm a trust funder. I've never had to work a day in my life and never will. The idea of taking a job from someone who needs one bothers me. I say I'm a locust because I'm living off the harvest someone else brought in—the money my great-grandfather and grandfather worked to earn."

"Not your father?"

She glanced around, making him wonder if she had heard someone approach. He glanced around as well, but no one else was nearby.

"My father wasn't a very serious person," she said. "You've seen the photo. He was handsome, my mother was beautiful, and they were the life of any party they were invited to—and they were invited everywhere. They flew on private jets to go to parties on other continents." She paused. "They usually teamed up with Brad and Rebecca's parents. Two gorgeous couples, full of life and fun. When they ended up with me, they must have thought someone swapped babies on them in the hospital." She looked up at him. "Are your parents living?"

"No. You, Ron, and I have that in common."

"Tell me about them."

"My parents?"

She nodded.

He thought of giving her the story he usually told, a set of half-truths that kept others from asking further questions. Instead he said, "I never knew my mother—she died giving birth to me."

"Oh!"

"My father and I didn't see much of each other before I moved away from home. I didn't understand then—well, I suppose I expected to be able to spend time with him in a future we weren't destined to have together."

"I'm sorry—"

He shook his head. "No, no need to be. I've found that grief eases over time, but regret has real staying power. All those things you wish you had said to the ones you loved." He paused, then asked, "Do you miss your parents?"

He tried to read the look that came into her eyes when he asked that—almost one of amusement, he thought, and he wondered why.

"To be completely honest," she said, "they've always been—I mean, they always *were* difficult people to live with. The adults who knew them thought they were a lot of fun. For me, as their kid, they weren't so fun. They drank a lot. They were so crazy about each other, I think they just didn't have much room left over for me. They were away from home more than they were here, so, for the most part, I was raised by a succession of nannies—none of the nannies could put up with the carnival atmosphere here for more than two years at a time. It probably sounds crazy, but for all of that, I loved them, knew they loved me in their own weird way, and I wish to God I could talk to them."

"They died in a car accident?"

She nodded. "We were all at a party. The one in the photo, as it happens." She blushed again, and he couldn't figure out why. She went on quickly, "When we were leaving, I was the only one who was sober, and I tried to convince the adults to let me drive. They insisted that my learner's permit only allowed me to drive before eleven at night. I pointed out that I could drive at any hour when one of my parents was in the car, but Aunt Cynthia—Brad and Rebecca's mom—said I was wrong. She insisted on driving."

She swallowed hard and looked off into the distance.

"We didn't have far to go, just a few miles. But the few miles were through the canyon. I don't really remember the accident itself, or much of anything that happened after we left the party, but I'm told the car went over an embankment. I was the only one wearing a seat belt. I was told the others were killed instantly."

"You had a head injury?"

"Yes. They say that's why I don't remember the accident."

"It's common, you know, that type of memory loss."

"That's what they say, but—it's hard to walk around with that piece missing. Brad and Rebecca have a theory that I caused the accident and I'm repressing it out of guilt."

"That's ridiculous."

She shrugged. "Who knows? I never will. I woke up in the hospital. A concussion, three broken ribs, and a broken ankle. My father's aunt told me what happened. Ron visited me every day."

Ron. He swore to himself that he would not interfere in their relationship. He stepped away from her.

"Anyway," she said resolutely, "that's all in the past. I want to move on with my life. I can't just sit around being useless. I've been thinking about what you do, and it seems so important. I'd like to see if it's something I could do one day, if I got training, and some experience. I'm not afraid of being around people who are sick or dying. Maybe—maybe I could even be of help to you."

He had a dozen excuses to offer her, a dozen more ways to put her off doing this at all. But he had made the mistake of watching her face, and he had seen the longing there. He tried glancing away, only to find that Shade was staring at him, too.

He had spent too many years with the dog not to be able to read that particular look—he was being compelled. He sighed. *Apparently I'm the one trained to be obedient.*

"Tyler?"

"I suppose so," he began.

"Thank you! Oh, thank you!" She launched herself at him and held him in a fierce hug. He managed to keep his balance, at least physically, by awkwardly returning the embrace.

"You don't know what this means to me," she said, "but I promise—I promise!—I won't get in your way. And if—if someone doesn't want me to be in the room with you, then I won't argue or say a word. I'll—I'll just wait in the hallway until you're done talking with them. And—"

"All right, all right," he said, laughing.

She leaned back in his arms, smiling up at him. Suddenly she frowned and let go of him. "Your ribs! Oh my God! Oh, did I hurt you?"

"No, not at all. I'm fine." *Confused as hell, but fine.* He let her step back from him.

She held her head to one side. "You are, aren't you? I mean, I don't feel as bad today as I thought I would after that accident, I'm just a little sore. But you—I'm kind of amazed."

He looked away. "I'm sure it looked worse than it was. I—"

"Don't lie to me," she interrupted. "Please don't." Her smile was a little wistful as she added, "Don't say anything to me you wouldn't say to Shade."

He looked down at the dog, whose tail was wagging. *What are you so all-fired happy about, Shade?*

"All right," he said aloud. "But I was going to tell you the truth. I was going to say that I heal quickly."

"Hmm. And that's not all there is to it, right?"

A silence stretched, then he said, "Right." If she started asking him questions now, he would tell her the truth, the whole truth, and then— then he would have to disappear from her life. He would have to leave her, let her go on to whatever life and lovers she was destined to have without him.

He found himself especially unhappy to think about her having lovers. Even Ron. It was something like learning your girlfriend had a crush on your little brother.

His whole life was spent uprooting and reestablishing himself as need be. He knew that come what may, he would survive the loss of her.

He was so very tired of surviving losses.

Tired of surviving, period.

"Are you all right?" she asked. She was looking up at him, brows drawn together in concern. Those lovely brown eyes . . .

Well, maybe not so tired of surviving after all.

If he told her who he was, what he was, he was fairly sure she'd either disbelieve him or hold him in disgust. He would lose any chance of growing closer to her.

If he didn't, well—the outcome was the same, wasn't it?

"I'm okay," he said. "But I have a question for you."

She looked at him expectantly.

He screwed up his nerve and said, "You and Ron—are you—well, it's none of my business really, but—are you—?"

She grinned. "Lovers? No. I suppose a lot of people assume we are, but no. We're close friends. I don't think I could love a brother more than I love Ron, but long ago we figured out that we never wanted to date. As I told Alex, it's always been more like a brother-sister thing."

"Oh," he said, and found himself grinning, too. "Well, thank you. Shall we go?"

"All right, but don't think I'm giving up."

"Giving up?"

"On getting answers to *my* questions."

She turned and walked toward the van.

She stumbled over something along the way, caught her balance, and moved on.

Ron had told him that everyone knew she was a klutz, but maybe people watched the wrong set of movements when they watched Amanda.

It was in that moment after she stumbled, he thought, that you could see her at her best. An elegance in the way she recovered her balance, her style of moving on. It required something more than mere grace.

He smiled to himself and followed her.

19

T wo conditions," Tyler said, just before they entered Benecia Wright's room at the hospice. "First, if they object, no argument, you wait for me in the hallway."

"Of course," Amanda said.

"Second, you respect both the Wrights and me, and keep whatever you see or hear completely confidential."

"I promise I will."

Tyler sighed. "I hope this isn't the second stupidest thing I've ever done."

"What took first prize?"

"I'll tell you another day, perhaps. Right now, we're in something of a hurry." He went inside the room.

Benecia's husband, Larry, was distracted with grief, and seemed not to notice that Tyler had brought Amanda with him. Still, Tyler asked if he objected to her presence, and was quickly assured that he didn't mind.

"I've been so worried that you wouldn't make it in time." Larry drew a shaky breath. "She's fading."

Tyler saw this was true. A former bartender and chain-smoker, she had been losing her battle with cancer for several months now.

"I just want to tell her," Larry said, choking on his tears, "that she's the only one I love. Ever loved. And—to ask her forgiveness."

Tyler sat at the other side of the bed and lifted one of Benecia's dry, frail hands. *I like her,* he heard Benecia say, from somewhere in her mind.

Who?

Your young woman. She's the answer to your prayers.

He shifted uneasily. *Not my young woman. Now. Benecia—*

Well, you should do something about that, you fool. And you're old enough to know better. Tyler was the only one in the room who heard her raucous laugh.

I was under the impression that you might have something to say to Larry?

He heard her laugh again. *All right, here we go.*

"Larry, you dumb son of a bitch," he said aloud.

Far from being offended by this form of address, Larry sat up straight and said, "Benny?"

"Yes, honey. Don't you know I forgave you all that long ago? I know I'm the only one who's ever really held your heart, no matter who else got hold of that big—well, there's a young lady present, so I'll just say, no matter who got hold of anything else of yours."

"It's true, Benny. You're the only one I've loved. But—I just wish we had more time together!"

"You make the most of whatever time you've got, Larry. Nobody has forever, not even this couple who are helping us out now. You find another woman, that's okay by me, Larry. You're not a man who should be alone. You'll be a good husband to the next one, I know."

"I want you, Benny! Nobody else."

"I'm touched by that, honest to God, I am. You're the only one I wanted, honey. But it's nearly time for me to go, and that's that. Now, listen up. You called Sarah home from college, right?"

"She'll be here any minute now."

"I'll wait for her—that's about all I'll be able to do. But you bury me, then send her right back to school—you got that? She'll want to stay around and take care of you, and don't you let her. You tell her it was my dying wish that she get that degree, okay? Promise me."

He promised.

"Well, good. I love you, Lar-Bear."

"Benny! Don't leave me!"

"Don't be silly. I can't stick around and you know it. But I'll be waiting for you. Now, you let Tyler and his friend leave us, so we can have a few minutes together before Sarah gets here, okay?"

Tyler said a silent good-bye to Benecia, who told him he would be busy with other matters for a week or two, and would know when and where he would next be needed. She then urged him not to waste time. *You may not have as much of it as you think you have, Tyler Hawthorne.*

He tried to ask her what she meant by that, but she told him he wasn't so stupid he couldn't figure it out, and that while she was much obliged to him for his help, she wanted to spend what little time *she* had left with the people she loved.

He let go of her hand.

20

Amanda was sitting silently in a corner of the room, not moving. No telling what she was thinking, but his guess was that she was in something like a state of shock. He walked over to her and whispered, "Are you all right?"

She nodded, but looked back and forth between him and the woman in the bed.

He held out his hand in mute invitation, and she took it in hers, seeming relieved by his touch. She allowed him to lead her from the room.

He didn't let go, not as they walked down the hallway, down the stairs, out of the building, across the parking lot—toward the far corner of the lot, where he had left the van in a shady spot. Every step along the way, he waited for her to say something or to pull away from him. She did neither. She seemed content to be holding his hand, but her brows were drawn together in thought.

He was afraid to speak first, afraid whatever half-cast spell they were under would be broken.

There had been a time, he knew, when two unmarried persons of the opposite sex, walking hand in hand without chaperonage, might have been—to say the least—frowned upon. Things were not so now.

There had also been a time, not too long ago, when couples "went steady" and often walked hand in hand. That, too, had changed. In some ways, holding hands was more serious now than it had been a generation or so ago.

In this time, in this place, with this woman—what did it mean to her? What did it mean to him?

A desire to be connected to her. To trust and be trusted. To . . . see where this would lead.

She might not feel any of that. Still, he held on, acknowledging to himself that he was so absorbed in savoring the contact, he was having trouble thinking straight . . .

When they reached the van, she let go. He tried not to let his disappointment show. He said, "There's an open lot just beyond these trees. Do you mind if I let Shade stretch his legs a bit before we leave?"

"No, that's fine." Shade was let out and the van locked. They stood together beneath the trees and watched the dog romp through the grass.

Amanda said, "Just tell me it's not a trick."

"A trick? Oh—you mean, what happened with Benecia?"

"Yes. I can't imagine that you're the kind of person who would intentionally try to fool her husband, even in the name of giving him comfort. But—"

"I see. You're worried that I only pretended to have some ability to communicate with her."

"I don't mean to hurt you or offend you," she said quickly. "I—I just can't exactly figure out what happened in there."

He smiled. "You haven't hurt me. I'm glad you're skeptical. Let's see. I could have picked up the information about her daughter from the nursing staff or Larry, or even another patient. And, as you mentioned, I could have been saying what I thought he wanted to hear."

"I don't think you would do that," she repeated.

"Con artists specialize in finding the weakness in another person, and having that other person practically exploit himself or herself. Who could be more vulnerable than the guilt-ridden husband of a dying woman, eh?"

"How on earth would you have known he had fooled around with other women?"

"Oh, if I simply guessed at it, the odds would be in my favor where adult males are concerned."

She digested that thought in silence. Shade came back to them, lying down in the grass near their feet.

"About those adult males," she asked. "Would you be in the minority?"

He smiled. "I've never married."

"Okay. But you're good looking and rich and—so, are you a player?"

"If I said I once was, but I haven't been for a long, long time, you'd take my word for it?"

She laughed. "I see your point." She paused, then said, "But I would take your word for it."

"Why?"

"Well, I guess Rebecca taught me a few things."

That didn't sound good. He said carefully, "She's experienced, I suppose."

"Very. In some ways. Not so much in others."

" 'Not so much' how?"

She frowned, as if puzzling out how to explain it. "Take trust, for example. She has almost none. She's really cynical. You can be taken in with cynicism, you know." She looked up at him. "It can make you fail to trust the people you should. You never get anywhere in life that way."

"No," he said in a tone of wonder, "I don't suppose you do."

"It's kind of the irony about being a trust funder—most of the people who live off trusts stop trusting."

"For understandable reasons."

"Maybe. In the end, I suppose that's the worst thing a con artist does to people—makes them afraid to trust other people, and their own judgment. Rebecca has known a lot of con artists of . . . a certain type."

He thought over what she had said. He wouldn't have guessed her to have made such a study of her cousin, nor to have been so sympathetic to her.

"So," she said, "if you think you can trust me, tell me what went on with Benecia."

"It's not easy to explain. The truth is, I've never really talked about it much."

He was silent for a long time. She waited.

"It's a gift, you might say." *Although I did pay for it,* he thought bitterly. "You talked earlier about usefulness? This is my one bit of usefulness in this world. It's a little complicated, but basically, if I'm near someone who is dying, who is close to breathing his or her last breaths, sometimes I can help that person communicate with loved ones."

"Wow." She took a deep breath. "Wow," she said again. "But, is it sad for you? I mean, being with someone so—so intimately, and then letting them go?"

"Sometimes, yes, brief though our acquaintance may be. I have met some remarkable people over the years. And I'm fortunate in that I seem to be called to help those who are ready for death—I'm just there to settle some matter for them before they let go."

"So, are you a mind reader?" she asked uneasily.

He smiled. "No. I have only that one connection, for that brief time. Your thoughts are safe from me, Amanda."

"I'm not so sure that's true," she muttered.

"Believe me, in the short time I've known you, there have been many times when I would have loved to know what you were thinking."

She blushed.

"Take now, for instance," he said, and her blush deepened.

"So, if you aren't a mind reader, what do you call this? Are you a psychic?"

"No. I don't think of myself as a mind reader or a psychic. It's not ESP."

"What do other people who do what you do call themselves?"

"I've only met two other people who did this. One gave it up completely. The other has been dead for many years. The one who died—he never gave me a name for it. I've read some old folktales that indicate there are others . . . in my situation, let's say. They've been known by various names. The rare English texts on the subject refer to us as the Messengers. If there is an 'us,' that is. I suspect I am the last of them. I've searched for others, to no avail."

They heard a car park nearby.

"If you don't mind," Tyler said, "could we talk more about this at home? I'd rather not be overheard."

"Sure," she said, and they walked back to the van.

He put Shade in the back and was just moving to open Amanda's door for her when the dog began growling.

Amanda's face went pale.

"Don't worry," Tyler said quickly. "He's not growling at you. But I wonder what's bothering him?"

He stood still, listening. Shade continued to growl.

"Wait in the van for me," he said.

"I don't think so," Amanda said, and stepped behind him.

She followed him as he moved cautiously around the van. A silver Lexus was parked in the next stall. He had seen it before, he was sure.

Behind him, Tyler heard Amanda draw in a sharp breath. "That's Brad's—"

Tyler turned to see that her speech had been cut off by an arm wrapped around her throat.

Brad held a knife in the other hand and was aiming its tip at her heart. He pulled her back a few paces. Despite his weapon and hostage, his eyes were wide and fearful. His face was bruised and scraped, as were his hands. He looked as if someone had beaten the hell out of him.

Tyler tried to slow his own breathing, held his hands open and out at his sides. He looked at Amanda's terrified face and did his best to communicate to her that he would not let harm come to her. How he was to ensure that, he had no idea, but he knew they had to try to be calm, to get Brad to calm down.

"You don't want to hurt Amanda, Brad," he said in a low, steady voice.

"We're going to go for a ride in my car, Tyler," Brad said, pulling Amanda harder against him.

"All right. But Amanda can stay here."

"No. Amanda, reach into my left pocket and get my keys."

She did as he said.

"Now press the button to open the trunk."

She did.

"Hawthorne," he said, "get in the trunk."

Before Tyler could respond, Amanda hit a second button on the keys, setting off the car alarm.

"No!" Brad screamed, and grabbed the keys from her. He shoved her to the ground as he hit the button to cancel the alarm.

Tyler launched himself toward Brad. Brad slashed with the knife, and Tyler felt a sharp sting along his ribs as he knocked Brad over. Brad struck his head against the van as he fell, and dropped both knife and keys as he landed in a stunned heap.

Tyler picked up the weapon and keys and stood up quickly. He moved toward Amanda. "Are you all right?"

"Yes."

As he reached toward her, to help her to her feet, her eyes widened. "You're bleeding!"

He looked down at his side, pulled his torn shirt away. "Caught the tip of the knife. Just a scratch."

"It looks deeper than a scratch to me."

"Hmm. The bleeding has nearly stopped, see?" As she stood, he looked her over more carefully. "You're hurt."

"Just scraped up a little." She was staring uneasily at Brad, who moaned. "Is he going to try that again?"

"I doubt it, but let's get him into the van and take him to the house."

"You're willing to take him to your house after that?"

"Take a look at him," he said, stooping back down next to Brad.

Brad's gaze was unfocused. All the fight seemed to have gone out of him.

"Who hurt you, Brad?" Tyler asked gently.

Brad closed his eyes and moaned. He curled into a ball.

Amanda, still wary, came closer.

"He's in need of a doctor," Tyler said, "but I don't think your family would like the police involvement and publicity we'd get if we took him into the hospice to ask for help."

"Brad, what got into you?" Amanda said. She turned to Tyler. "Why was he trying to do that to us? I mean—he's Bradley! He never even got into fistfights as a kid. And—look at him!"

"Yes. We'll have to try to ask him about all of that later. I don't think he's himself right now."

Tyler coaxed Brad to his feet and helped him to the van's side door. Brad opened his eyes but seemed disoriented.

"Is he drugged?" Amanda asked.

"It seems so. Are you still feeling afraid of Shade?"

"No. Sorry. He was obviously trying to warn us."

"He does have a fierce growl. But I promise he won't harm you. If you'll open the door, I'll settle Brad in back."

She did so, and although Shade sniffed all three of them, he did not growl or attempt to bite Brad.

Brad, becoming aware of Shade, made a whimpering sound and cowered away from him.

"It's all right," Tyler said. "You'll be all right."

"He'll kill me!" Brad said.

"No, he won't harm you. He's really a gentle dog—provided you aren't trying to harm me."

Brad looked between Tyler and the dog and Amanda. He suddenly burst into tears. "Amanda! I didn't mean it."

"I know, Brad."

He began to weep harder. "I'm so scared!"

"Everything will be all right, Brad," Tyler said. "I promise you. I'll keep you safe."

"Can you? Can anyone?"

"Yes."

"I'm so tired. Scared and tired."

"It's all right. You don't need to talk now, just rest, okay?"

"He'll kill me," Brad murmured again and lay down and closed his eyes.

21

After the doctor left, Amanda went looking for Tyler and found him in the library. He was sitting at a large desk, bent over some paperwork. He had changed clothes, and she suddenly felt grubby still wearing the clothes she had put on this morning. He wasn't dressed up, but the jeans and long-sleeved shirt he wore looked good on him.

Shade had been sleeping on a rug before the fireplace, but he came awake when she entered, and wagged his tail. At the thumping sound, Tyler looked up, saw her, and smiled. She felt her breath catch.

"Hello, Amanda. Have you had dinner?"

"No, not yet," she said. "I'm not very hungry."

He apparently didn't believe her, because he picked up the phone and called the kitchen, asking that some sandwiches be brought up to the library. After hanging up, he moved from behind the desk and led her to one of the sofas in front of the fireplace. He paused to gently take her hands in his, and turned them palm up.

"Do the scrapes hurt?"

"It's really nothing. I'll be fine. Brad's the one I'm worried about."

He let her hands go and motioned for her to be seated. To her disappointment, he sat at the other end of the sofa. Yet there was something in the way he looked at her that made her decide she needed that distance if she was going to concentrate on the conversation. Did he need it, too?

"How is your cousin doing?" he asked, bringing her thoughts back to Brad.

"He's asleep now, I'm glad to say. I'm supposed to wake him in a few hours because he may have a concussion, but I wish he could just rest. You talked to the doctor?"

"Yes. He was worried, as I think we all are, about how Brad obtained some of his injuries."

"Did Brad tell you who hurt him?"

"No, although from what I could gather, it has something to do with our friends from the desert."

"The men in the truck?" she asked, bewildered.

"Yes. He kept apologizing to me, saying he never would have told them I left the party if he had known what they had in mind."

"But then—how would Brad know Sam's relatives?"

"I don't think he does. Although that's not certain—I couldn't get very clear information from him. Did you have any luck?"

"No. He isn't making a lot of sense. I'm really worried about him. Whatever drug was in his system seems to have worn off, but he's still confused. The doctor said it might be because he hit his head." She paused. "I called Rebecca, but I couldn't make her understand that he's been hurt. She's—not too sober at this point."

"Eventually she'll come looking for him, I suspect."

"Not right away, I hope." Seeing his look of surprise, she said, "They're brother and sister. When they get together, it doesn't take long before they bicker. He's in such bad shape, he needs to rest. I don't think her company would do him a lot of good right now."

"Hmm. Maybe we won't press her to come here, then. Instead I'll ask Alex to try to discover where he has been."

"Do you think she can do that? I'd really appreciate it."

"She's very good at her work. What else did the doctor say? I should ask first—do you feel comfortable with this doctor, or would you rather have someone else in to see Brad? Are you all right with Brad staying here, or do you want to move him to a hospital?"

"Oh, the doctor is wonderful. I like him a lot. If you don't mind keeping Brad here, I think it would be best. It's quiet, and the doctor thinks the best thing is for him to be kept as calm as possible, to let him rest. And Brad knows Ron, so he won't have a lot of strangers around him like he would in a hospital."

"Yes, I think you're right. Right now Ron is sleeping. I've asked Alex to send him to us when he wakes up, so that you can tell him about your cousin."

"Thanks, although I don't know if I'll be able to explain much to him. Brad seems so scared."

"Yes, I noticed that, too," he said. "Someone has terrorized him. But I couldn't make sense of what he tried to tell me about who it was."

"Did he say something about a dark cellar, and a voice, and something rotting?"

"Yes. But he couldn't say where the cellar was, or whose voice it was. He said he had been beaten by 'Daniel and Evan.' Are those names familiar to you?"

"No. I have no idea who they are."

"Hmm. We'll have to wait and hope he can tell us more after he's rested."

"Yes, I guess so. And please—I've asked the doctor to send his bill to me, but he said I'd have to work that out with you. So let me know how much it is, and I hope you'll let me know of any other expenses so that I can pay for anything this costs you—"

"Don't worry about it. Since I injured Brad, I'm happy to help pay for his care."

"You injured Brad! Oh no—he hurt you! Did the doctor look at it? Did you need stitches?"

She heard the slightest hesitation before he said, "No. I'm fine, really."

"Tyler—"

"Seriously, I'm fine."

There was a light tap at the door, and Tyler moved to open it for a middle-aged man bearing a tray laden with sandwiches, fresh fruit, and two glasses of milk. He set it on a table at one end of the library. Tyler introduced the man as Ben, a member of his staff.

"We have soft drinks or wine or beer, if you'd prefer to drink something other than milk, miss," Ben said.

"Milk is fine," she said. "Thank you."

Ben, assured that nothing else was needed, left the room.

She sat down and began to eat one of the sandwiches. "These are really good," she said. "I guess I'm hungry after all."

"Good." Tyler cut an apple into neat pieces and placed them on her plate. "Ben's an excellent cook."

"Did you meet him through your work?"

"Yes, a little indirectly."

"I have a feeling there's a story here. Were you at the deathbed of one of Ben's family members?"

"No. I was at the deathbed of his former employer." He fell silent for a moment, then said, "I suppose most of this is public knowledge, so I won't be breaking confidences. What the public doesn't know is the background I'll give you. When he lay dying, Ben's former employer was anxious for my help because he wanted to confess to poisoning his first wife. He committed the murder in order to be free to marry the woman who became his second wife. Ben had been convicted of the crime."

"That's horrible!"

"Yes. Fortunately, the man's second wife—to whom he made this confession—did the right thing. Her soon-to-be-late husband told her where he had hidden a written statement and evidence that would clear Ben's name. The widow could have refused to be helpful—destroyed the statement and evidence, and avoided the scandal that followed. But even though it was difficult for her emotionally and in every other way, she led the fight to free Ben."

"Did you testify about it?"

"No. That would have been a little awkward."

"Oh—yes, I can see that."

"Once she made up her mind, she was unstoppable."

"Is Ben bitter about what happened to him?"

"If he is, he hides it from me. He has every reason to be, of course. Even though eventually he was released and there were public statements about his innocence, he found it difficult to find work." He paused and smiled. "That was my gain. I hired an excellent personal chef."

He took a bite of one of the sandwiches. Amanda breathed an audible sigh of relief.

"What?" he asked.

"I was starting to wonder if I was going to be the only one eating."

He smiled. "No, I can't resist Ben's cooking."

"Oh." She took a deep breath and straightened her spine. "Well. There's a reason I'm relieved to see you eating."

He raised a brow in inquiry.

"I—no, you'll think I'm crazy."

"I don't think that's likely. What's on your mind?"

"I've been wondering if you're, like, um—a vampire," she said in a rush.

He tried to suppress a laugh and failed. "Really? Just wondering? You'd have dinner with a vampire?"

"Well, not that I was *convinced* you were, but—"

"My teeth seem a little pointed and sharp?"

"No! And I've seen you walk around in the sunlight, but—"

"I think there may even be a little garlic in the chicken sandwiches."

"Yeah, well—"

"And I'm sure there's a mirror around here somewhere that would show I have a reflection."

"Okay, okay. No need to rub it in."

"Sorry."

She narrowed her eyes at him. "That grin isn't exactly repentant."

"No, sorry." He suddenly grew serious. "There are questions you have about me, I know. I stand a much better chance of having you decide *I'm* crazy—or worse—when I answer them. But ask away."

She had dozens, but where to begin? "After dinner," she said firmly.

"Then I'll ask." He didn't rush her. She let him finish his sandwich, and they moved to the sofa again, sitting at opposite ends. Shade looked between them, as if sensing their tension. But he didn't move from the rug.

"Okay," she said. "Twice now, I've seen you injured, but you seem to recover faster than is humanly possible."

He stayed silent.

"Well?"

"What's the question? Am I human?"

"No—yes—oh, start with telling me if I'm right. Is that true—do you heal fast?"

"Yes. I don't recover instantly from every injury, but what would require months of convalescence in another person generally takes only a few hours of rest for me."

She swallowed hard. "Oh."

He frowned, and his gaze left hers. He watched Shade, who had lowered his head to his forepaws. After a moment he said, without looking at her, "Go on."

"What about disease?" she asked.

"I haven't suffered an illness in years. Many years." She thought he sounded unhappy, but she couldn't understand why. Since she didn't know if she'd ever work up the courage to ask him these questions again, she persisted.

"Can you heal other people? Did you heal Ron?"

"I have no power to heal anyone. Ron's recovery was his own."

"But you gave him hope."

He shrugged. "If so, it had nothing to do with any extraordinary power of mine."

She thought for a moment, then said, "Last night, in the desert, I thought you were dead. Were you?"

"For a time, yes, I believe I was."

He still hadn't looked at her, and now she thought that was just as well. It was one thing, she realized, to insist to yourself that you had seen someone revive from death. It was another thing to hear the previously dead man say it was true.

"How is that possible?" she asked.

"If I told you I don't know," he said, "would you believe me? For the most part, that is the truth. There is a history I can give you, but that history doesn't really explain the—let's call it the process. So, in fact, I don't know how it works. If I could get it to stop working, I would."

"What do you mean?" she asked.

At last he looked toward her. "Amanda, there is nothing—absolutely nothing—I long for more than death."

22

Of all the shocks she had received in the last twenty-four hours, Amanda found that this one hit her the hardest. "You don't want to live?"

"No."

"You mean all the time I was giving you CPR—no, wait—that was useless, wasn't it? I mean, I'm not the reason you revived."

"No, but—"

"Was that amusing to you? Or were you just disappointed?"

"Amanda, no, please don't mistake what I'm saying."

She looked away from him.

He moved closer to her and gently took her face in his hands. "Do you think I'm so heartless, so cold?"

Actually, she thought, when he touched her, cold was the last word she'd use. She found herself unable to resist raising her eyes.

"Amanda, out there in the desert, you forgot all your own troubles and fears and came to my aid—"

"Not really, as it turns out—"

"You didn't know that at the time. Despite having witnessed a horrible collision and being terrified, I'm sure, by what followed, you didn't just sit there, weeping over your own misfortune. Do you know how many people would have been paralyzed by their fears in such a situation? But not you. You came to my side—to the side of someone who had done nothing but irritate you and make you angry—"

"That's not exactly—"

"Someone you mistrusted, who had just embarrassed you by making a scene at a party."

"You were sticking up for me. I know that now. At the time . . ."

"At the time I was calling attention to something you were handling in a much quieter way, while I was failing to control my temper. I frightened you."

"Do you have a temper? You don't strike me as a hothead."

"I will admit it rarely surfaces, but it's there. I won't lie to you—which would be pointless, given what you witnessed at the party. But I found it took everything I had in the way of self-restraint to keep myself from killing that little son of a bitch." He paused. "I'm not proud of hitting him."

"He did take a swing at you."

"Oh, he had it coming, I suppose, and I did shut him up, but—it wasn't really a fair fight. It never is with me, you see."

"I don't see."

He dropped his hands from her face and stared into the fire.

"Todd still has his black eyes, I'm sure. His nose must hurt like the devil. Me, I'm fine. He didn't know what he was up against. It's really not right for me, invulnerable as I am, to strike blows at those who are weaker, who will suffer consequences that are never at stake for me. There's nothing courageous in my going into a fight—I know I won't suffer what my opponent will suffer. There's no risk involved for me."

He fell silent, then said, "Do you know what quality I've come to envy in those around me? Frailty."

"Frailty?"

"Yes. Ask yourself—is there any courage where there is nothing to be overcome? Where there is no vulnerability? I would say I might as well be a machine or a stone, but even machines rust and stones wear down, while I go on and on, unchanged. I look at other humans and wonder if I have the right to call myself one of their number. I look at someone like

Ron, who has struggled almost all his life with illness, with death hovering over his shoulder. I look at people like Larry, Benecia's husband, who stayed at her side and saw a woman he loved, no matter what disease had done to her. They have courage." He turned to her. "You have courage."

"Me? Oh, no."

"Yes, and not just because of your love for Ron—"

"Sisterly, you understand—"

He smiled. "Yes, sisterly." He grew serious again. "You've known Ron a long time, and the bond you have kept you at his side. But we shared no such bond last night. I was all but a stranger. You probably didn't even know I was the person on the motorcycle, did you?"

"Not until I got closer," she admitted.

"You did everything you could for me, and kept at it even when it appeared there was no hope of saving me. Stayed with me, even when Shade approached—this, when he must have represented all your worst fears."

"I had nothing to be afraid of and I was—"

"Again, you didn't know that at the time. He frightens people who aren't afraid of dogs. And despite that, you stayed with me. You were generous, even at risk to yourself. That means a great deal to me, even if you don't see the value of it. You thought I was amused by your kindness? You can't imagine how very far I am from feeling anything like amusement over what you did for me. Please don't think for a moment that I would ever ridicule you for helping me. And if I've failed to say it before, thank you."

"Well, you're welcome," she said, feeling embarrassed. Then she remembered what he had said just a few moments ago. "Tyler, when you say you want to die—"

"Don't worry. I'm not suicidal—"

"That's not what I meant." Her eyes widened. "Could you commit suicide? I mean, is it possible?"

"No, I don't think so."

"*Don't think*—so you haven't tried it?"

"Are you making a request?"

"Of course not! Of all the dumb things to ask me! And you didn't answer my question."

He shifted uncomfortably beneath her gaze. "You'll have to forgive me if I—say dumb things. If I don't explain this well. I've never talked about this directly with anyone who wasn't on his or her own deathbed." He paused. "I've never tried to kill myself outright, but I'll confess that there were years, early on, when I did live recklessly. I suppose I was testing my limits. Or rebelling after I realized what a bad bargain I'd made . . ."

"Bargain?"

"It's a long story, and I will tell it to you if you care to hear it, but for now, I'll put it in the simplest terms I can. I was dying, and in exchange for my life, I agreed to become—oh, the messenger boy of the nearly dead, let's say. I wasn't merely spared from death, however. I gained Shade as a companion and protector. I gained the ability to survive any illness or injury. Beyond that, I remain in the prime of my life, in prime condition."

"You don't age?"

He hesitated. "An interesting question. Physically, no."

She could hear the shakiness in her voice as she said, "I've thought you were about my age, twenty-four. In your early twenties anyway. Although—most of the time, you don't act much like you are my age. You act older."

"I am older. Much older. But physically, yes, I'm twenty-four."

She stared at him, not saying anything. She couldn't resist studying him, looking for lines, or gray hairs, or weathered skin.

"I know I look as if I'm your age," he said. "In fact, with the exception of changes in hairstyle and clothing, I look exactly as I did when I was twenty-four. The only scars I bear are ones I acquired before then. I'm extremely fond of those scars now."

It was a lot to take in. Some part of her brain kept saying, "This is impossible." But it fit with what she had already seen, what she already knew to be true on some deeper level. If he had said, "You imagined everything, nothing that happened out in the desert was real," she would have known he was lying. Still, the truth was not so easy to take in either.

He was regarding her steadily and, she realized, a little nervously. The man who had nothing to fear was afraid. Afraid of her?

No. It suddenly became clear to her that he *needed* her to believe him. He had carried this secret for God knew how long and now—

Shade suddenly came to his feet, just as the ghosts appeared, at the far end of the room. It made her jump, and Tyler asked, "What's wrong?"

"Long story of my own," she said, forcing her gaze back to him, ignoring the dog and the crowd at the other end of the room.

"Shade startled you, didn't he?" he said. "Shade, where are your manners?"

Shade lay down, but he kept looking toward the ghosts. Could he see them? She remembered reading once, long ago, that if you thought there was a ghost in the room and looked between a dog's ears, you'd be able to see it. She had always wondered who would want to do either.

So here she was, watched by ghosts, ghosts who were seen by a dog that seemed to understand every word spoken to him. She didn't understand how Tyler's "bargain" worked, but she knew—deep down *knew*—he was telling her the truth. She took a resolute breath and said, "I'm sure it was really hard to tell me your secrets."

"I don't blame you if you don't believe me. I really don't. All I ask is that you not repeat what I've told you to anyone else."

"And if I do believe you?"

He looked at her in surprise. "You believe me?" he said, and seemed unable to say more.

"Yes, I believe you, Tyler Hawthorne."

He reached out and squeezed her hand, and said, barely above a whisper, "Thank you."

The ghosts started to move closer, and Shade growled.

"Shade!" Tyler said, letting go of her hand. "What's gotten into you?"

The ghosts retreated. She found herself feeling angry with them— not for the first time. She was determined not to let them interfere in what was happening here, whatever it was, between her and Tyler.

"How long have you been alone?" she asked.

He smiled. "As for being alone, I'm not, really. Shade has been with me from the start, and he's an excellent companion. And the dying are invariably willing to befriend me."

"I can understand why. Let me make sure I understand. For a short time, a few minutes, really, the dying are completely open to you, and tell you their secrets."

"Yes."

"And then you have to say good-bye to them."

"They are always happiest right at that moment. It's as if they gladly surrender to whatever draws them away. At that point, I don't think they really notice my being there—or anyone else's presence—as they leave."

"But you don't ever get to leave."

"No."

"Hmm. And while I am sure Shade is a great comfort to you—"

"More than you can imagine."

"I'm sure that's true. But—does he talk to you?"

"Not in words, no. But he's excellent at conveying meaning."

Shade wagged his tail, but he kept his eyes on the ghosts.

"And you befriend a few people, like Ron. Like me."

"That doesn't happen very often," he said.

"I can understand why. You've got all these secrets, both your own and those of the dying, and you can't afford to have someone discover what I learned out in the desert."

"That's part of it."

"So if you befriend someone who isn't dying, you have someone to talk to for a period of time—without really being able to tell them your own story, of course. And then what?"

"After a few years, I move."

"Because otherwise people start to wonder why you aren't aging the way they are."

"You begin to understand why Los Angeles appeals to me."

"I'm sure it won't take long for people to be begging you for the number of your plastic surgeon."

He smiled.

"So, when were you born?"

"In 1791."

"Seventeen ninety-one!"

He shrugged.

"Oh. Really?"

"Really."

"Seventeen ninety-one—A.D.?"

That surprised laughter from him. "Not, I will admit, the question I expected at this point. Yes, 1791 A.D."

She waved this off. "I can't help how my mind works. So what happened to you? When you were twenty-four, I mean. That would have been—1815?"

"Yes."

"Were you here then, in Los Angeles?"

"No, I was in Europe. I was born in England, but at seventeen I joined the army and spent several years fighting on the Continent. I made a brief trip home, but in 1815 I was back and fighting in Belgium."

"With the British army?"

"Yes." One corner of his mouth quirked up. "What can I say? Having spent roughly two centuries in the U.S., I've lost my accent."

She didn't let that sidetrack her. "The British army in 1815—you were fighting Napoleon?"

"Yes. Boney, we called him. Have you studied history?"

"I like it, but I haven't taken more than basic classes," she admitted. "Sorry. Does that bother you?"

"No, not really."

There was a soft knocking at one of the doors leading from the hallway. Amanda saw the ghosts vanish as he called, "Yes?"

Ron came in. "Hi! Alex told me you were in here. Mind if I join you?"

"Not at all," Tyler said. "How are you this evening?"

"Better, although I wish I had more energy. My sleeping schedule is so crazy. I haven't been awake much today, and now I'll probably be up all night. What time is it? Almost eleven-thirty? What did you two do today?"

"We went to the hospice," Amanda said, then looked to Tyler.

"I'll let you tell Ron whatever you want to about today. As for me, I need to take Shade out for a bit."

"Whatever I—"

"Yes, anything," Tyler said, standing. He turned to Ron and added, "We have another houseguest—Amanda's cousin Brad."

"Brad! No wonder you looked so shaken up when I came in here, Amanda. Brad! Of all the—"

"He's been badly injured," Tyler said quickly.

"Oh! Oh . . . I'm sorry." Ron looked at Amanda in confusion. "I thought he was with Rudebecca."

"One of these days," Amanda said, "you are going to call one of the other Rebeccas we know by that name."

"Not a chance. I like Rebecca Davis," he said, naming a friend who now lived on the East Coast. "I like Rebecca Johnson. Those are wonderful Rebeccas. Nice people. The Trainwrecka, though—"

"I hate to interrupt this fascinating recital," Tyler said, "but I need to get going."

"Maybe we could talk more, when you get back?" she said. "If you aren't too tired."

"Of course. And don't hesitate to call if you need me. You still have the cell phone number?"

"Yes—but—you aren't just walking him here, around the grounds?"

"Sorry, no. He has a few favorite places to roam, so I'll be taking the car. But I'll be only a few minutes away. And Alex and her crew will be here to protect you while I'm gone."

23

Tyler went to his room, found the slender packet of handwritten sheets, and ran his fingers over the paper, so unlike the paper of these times. The words were inscribed in his best copperplate, written with neatness and care—once she became accustomed to the style of the hand, she should be able to decipher it. He wondered if the day was coming when no one would be able to write without the aid of a keyboard.

If so, he'd be around to see it, wouldn't he?

He shuddered.

He took the sheaf into her room, a guest room. She had not had time to make any personal impression here, hardly time to do more than unpack.

He began to set the papers on the desk, then halted and turned to the bed. Ignoring all the warnings in his mind that this was trespass, and his fear that she would see this as an insult, he pulled the light comforter aside and set the papers on the soft sheets below, near but not quite on her pillow, then left the room.

"I don't know what she'll make of it, Shade," he said later, as they walked together through the cemetery. He paused and stared out over the tombstones. "I hardly know what to make of all of this either. Courtship, at my age? A little ridiculous, isn't it?"

The dog stopped and stared back at him, then butted his head against him. From long experience, Tyler knew this to be a gesture of comfort. He reached to stroke the dog's soft, tufted ears. "Thank you. I've often wondered if you long for the company of another dog, but you've never seemed more than mildly interested in other canines." He paused. "And I don't know where to find another cemetery dog for you. Should I try again to find someone else who does what I do? The closest I've come is Colby."

Shade walked on. He always seemed disapproving or indifferent to any mention of Colby. Tyler could hardly blame him.

"Colby once told me there are no others, but he's never felt compelled to be truthful. I feel strongly that there must be others, and yet whenever we've traveled—not the smallest bit of success, was there? Perhaps I've kidded myself, hoping we'd at least be able to meet an animal who could provide better companionship for you than I do."

Shade looked up at him again, this time with an intensity that made him wish he could read the dog's mind.

They walked on for a while. He confessed to Shade, "I can't stop thinking of her."

Shade turned to him and wagged his tail.

"Yes, that's all very well until I imagine what sort of future I would be offering her." He sighed. "It would be better, don't you think, if I could find someone else who is in my situation?"

Shade looked away from him, then moved off, back toward the car.

Tyler tried to shake off the sensation of having disappointed the dog.

24

D aniel awoke to the sound of something tapping against his bedroom window, a soft, relentless, irregular beat. He turned on his bedside lamp and pulled back the curtain. He stifled a cry of revulsion—the screen was crawling with small brown beetles. Even as he watched, more flew to join the ones now clinging to the mesh, making the tapping sound as they landed against it.

He dropped the curtain into place and scrambled off the bed. He dressed hurriedly and headed out down the hall toward Evan's room. Evan's door flew open before he reached it.

"Goddamn!" Evan said. "You should see what's happening!"

"Bunch of bugs on your window screen?"

Evan nodded. "Yours, too?"

"Yes, we better tell the boss."

Evan paled. He whispered, "You think so? He's already unhappy about that fucking wimp."

"It was *his* plan. Did you think for one minute that plan was going to work?" Daniel whispered back.

"No, I did not. Not for one minute."

They fell silent and made their way toward the kitchen. Daniel heard the sound of running water as they came closer to the kitchen door.

He put a hand on Evan's forearm, halting his progress. "Did you leave the water running in the kitchen sink?"

Evan, listening to the rushing sound coming from the other side of the kitchen door, shook his head.

Daniel steeled himself and pulled the door open. He flipped on the light and jumped back against Evan. "What the hell!"

The floor was moving. From beneath the door on the opposite wall, which led to the back porch, a steady stream of brown beetles squeezed through an opening and joined the others that filled the kitchen floor. In the next moment Daniel saw that they seemed uninterested in coming through the door he had just opened—in fact, they did not come near Daniel or Evan. Instead, they all moved in one direction, clambered over one another in their eagerness to reach one destination: the door to the basement. There a great pile of them scrabbled against that barrier in a futile frenzy to overcome it.

"Open the door!" the voice from the basement called.

"My lord?" Daniel answered.

"Open the door to the basement, you fool! Let them come to me!"

Daniel tried not to think about the crunching beneath his shoes as he walked over to the door and unlocked it. He opened it, and the beetle river plunged past him and down the stairs. He felt the rush of them against the sides of his shoes, and stood paralyzed. Even when he squeezed his eyes shut, he could hear the click of their bodies knocking together, a sound that became louder, as if someone were pouring gravel down the stairs. After another moment, though, it began to taper off.

"Not enough! Not enough!" the voice from the basement said angrily.

Daniel opened his eyes.

"Evan!" his lordship commanded from below. "Open the door to the porch!"

"Yes, my lord!"

Daniel looked back to see Evan cross the kitchen floor. There were not so many beetles now, and though the stream continued to come in from beneath the porch door, Evan was able to cross the floor without stepping on any of the insects.

But when he opened the door, what seemed to be thousands of the beetles came rushing in, scrabbling over Evan's shoes toward Daniel, who quickly moved back from the doorway to the cellar. They charged past him, and again the flow down the stairs became noisy, their shiny, hard wing cases battering together in their eagerness to go below.

Eventually the river of beetles became nothing more than a trickle, although a steady procession of them still made its way from the open door.

His lordship spoke again, and it seemed to Daniel that his voice was stronger than ever before.

"You shall leave that door open, Evan, until I tell you otherwise."

"Yes, my lord."

A silence fell, and then Daniel realized that this was not quite silence. There was a continuous crunching sound coming from the basement.

At last there was a pause. "Daniel, you need not bring me any more remains. As you have probably guessed, I'm able to feed myself now."

"Yes, my lord," Daniel answered, a little shakily.

His lordship laughed, but his voice was sharp when he said, "Do not interfere with anything that comes through that door, do you both understand me?"

"Yes, my lord," they answered in unison.

"Good. Now, soon I shall finally be able to emerge from this hovel and find us a decent place to live. But when we leave this house, you must never use my title when addressing me before others. Do you understand?"

"Yes, my lord," they answered again.

Daniel wanted to ask him what they should call him, but didn't dare. He saw Evan open his mouth and shot him a look of warning, which Evan had no trouble reading. They waited in silence for dismissal.

"Henceforth," said the voice, "refer to me as Mr. Adrian. You might as well start practicing that here at home. I don't want any slipups in public."

"Yes, sir," they said.

"Very good. Daniel, take off your shoes and toss them down the stairs. Leave the door to the basement open."

"Yes, Mr. Adrian."

When this task was accomplished, the voice said, "You may go. I bid you both a good evening."

They wished him a good evening in return, as they had been trained to do. They exchanged a look of shared fear and confusion, but did not speak to each other as they made their way to their rooms, except to say good night when they reached their doors.

Daniel took off his shoes and climbed back into bed. He lifted the curtain over his window. The screen was empty. He let the curtain fall back into place.

He did not fall asleep again for several hours, but over that wakeful time no answer to his most worrisome question occurred to him. Even his dreams did not tell him how he might escape from someone or something he must now call Mr. Adrian.

25

Amanda decided she would let Tyler be the one to tell his own secrets to Ron. She wanted time to think over all Tyler had told her, to sort through her feelings. So she told Ron about Brad's misbegotten attack, leaving out the part about Tyler's quick recovery from injury. Instead, she talked about Brad's wounds, her worries that he had been drugged. She hardly needed to say more after that—Ron's earlier derision of Brad was forgotten, replaced by his ready sympathy. They discussed and quickly dismissed a list of possible enemies.

"I can think of one or two people who might have wanted to punch him out," Ron admitted. "He doesn't always know when to shut up, you know what I mean?"

"Yes. But this wasn't just a punch thrown in anger."

"No. I don't know anyone who'd be that mad at him. That mad at Rudebecca, maybe. Do you think someone would try to get to her through him?"

"Then why set him loose and tell him to attack Tyler and me?"

They could think of no answer to this.

"Whatever makes sense as a reason for taking him—getting back at Rebecca, ransoming him for money, whatever I can think of—doesn't make sense as a reason to let him go or to tell him to go after you," Ron complained.

"I don't think we're going to have any answers until he's feeling better," Amanda said. "If then. The doctor said that whatever drug Brad was
given might have affected his memory—it will be some time before the
lab tests come back to tell us what he was given. In the meantime, Tyler
is going to ask Alex to look into who might have kidnapped Brad."

"Hmm."

"What?"

"You think she's really a serious detective?"

She stared at him in surprise. "Ron, has anyone working here been
less than the best?"

"I guess not."

"What's going on? Did she do something to upset you?"

He lowered his gaze. "No. Not at all."

He was hiding something from her, and she felt a little dismayed by
that, then realized that when it came to Tyler, she was hiding much more
from Ron.

"So," Ron said, as if reading her thoughts, "you and Tyler seem to be
getting along better."

"I don't know what I would have done without him." She paused,
then added, "But it's not just gratitude."

Ron said nothing, but when he looked up at her again, he was grinning.

"What?" she asked.

"I can't answer that without irritating you." He stood up. "I'll see
what's going on with Brad. You look as if you could use some sleep."

"I was hoping to talk to Tyler when he gets back."

"So at least take a nap. He doesn't seem to sleep much, so I'm sure
he'll still be up if you conk out for an hour or so."

"You're right, I could use some sleep—but I hate to abandon you."

He shrugged. "There's always someone awake around here. Maybe
Alex has learned something more from your cousin."

The room she had been given was spacious, with access to the deck that
ran all along this level of the house. Moonlight filtered in through the

French doors that led to the deck, and she used that soft light to navigate her way to the maplewood desk, where she turned on a small lamp.

She had unpacked her bag earlier, before going to the hospice with Tyler. That seemed so long ago now.

She washed up in the large bathroom and changed into her night-gown. Turning off the desk lamp, she thought of closing the draperies against the moonlight but decided against it. Instead, she opened the doors and stepped out on the deck. The view from here was lovely, far better than the one from the secluded home her great-grandfather had built below. She could just see a corner of her house, and realized that from a little farther down the deck, one would have a fairly clear view of it. A breeze came up, bringing the scent of the nearby pine trees to her. She thought she heard the sound of an animal—the strange dog?—moving in the woods and hurried back inside. She nearly closed the French doors but told herself not to be ridiculous, there was no stairway from the deck to the ground level, nothing a dog could climb to reach these rooms. She discovered a mechanism to pull a hidden screen door across the doorway to the deck, and set the screen in place. The warm breeze came up again, and she moved toward the bed.

She turned the bedside lamp on and immediately saw what the moonlight had failed to reveal—a small sheaf of heavy paper had been laid against her sheets.

Heart hammering, she carefully lifted the pages. The paper did not seem fragile, despite its apparent age, but she handled it gently. It was thick and not quite smooth. She liked the heavy feel of it. The writing was in an old style, what seemed to her to be a sort of calligraphy, neat lettering flowing evenly across the page, in lines as precisely spaced down its length.

She lay down on the bed on her side, set the pages back against the sheets, and began to read. She soon became accustomed to the writer's hand and made out the first line:

Think of this tale as an imagined story, if you must . . .

26

Think of this tale as an imagined story, if you must . . . I do not claim to understand all of the events that occur in it, and have little hope that any other will hold this story to be a truthful account. I have done nothing more than lived it, and if my living it could be changed by your disbelief. I would urge you with all my heart to be a skeptic. But if by any chance I can spare another from my fate by recording these events, perhaps it is best I do so, and in such case I would urge you not to doubt a word of it. . . .

Three days after the Battle of Waterloo, I awoke in the absolute darkness of the blind, as I had every other day since the fighting had ceased. I did not—and could not—open my eyes as I awoke from what I knew to be a dying man's dreams.

I did not need my sight to know that I was no longer listening to Miss Merriweather's laughter. Nor was I on horseback, racing my father and my brother through the meadow just beyond the home wood. I was not watching soldiers take up hiding places in rain-soaked fields of maize.

Without being able to see my surroundings, I knew I was lying flat on my back, unable to move, pinned beneath the body of my own horse. Poor old Reliant. I assumed I must be hidden beneath the big trooper, because although both friend and foe had passed near me, I had not been noticed.

The dreams had formed from a patchwork of memories. Even before I had left England, Miss Merriweather had married and died in child-birth. Three years earlier, in 1812, my father had died, and my brother had inherited the title and estate. The memory of the field of maize was more recent—I had seen the soldiers taking this position just three days ago, in anticipation of the approach of Napoleon's army.

Had my comrades or enemies seen me awaken, the watchers would have found it difficult to note any difference between my sleeping and waking states. Most would have assumed Captain Hawthorne was dead.

I could not see, could not move, could make no sound. My tongue was dry and swollen. I had, from the time I had fallen in the midst of fierce fighting, been cursed by my remaining senses.

I could feel my uniform, skin, and hair, all stiff with my own blood. I felt the mud drying beneath me, the weight of my dead horse crushing me. I felt relentless pain in my skull and chest and arms and legs. I felt hunger but, most of all, thirst.

The stench of the smoke and gunpowder of the battle had been re-placed by the sharp-edged rot of the corpses strewn across the ground—the tens of thousands of men who had died at Waterloo.

I wasn't sure how long I had lain there. I did not know the battle's outcome. I was grateful to have been spared some of the sounds of battle, sounds I had often heard in previous engagements, but never at such a pitch, never so fierce in all my experience. Now I longed to hear an English voice. I prayed that Reliant had been killed almost instantly. The horse was cold and silent now.

For a time, after I first awakened, I had heard sounds that let me know the battle was not long over—the cries of injured horses, the moans and screams of the wounded and dying men who had fallen not far from me. I could then still smell the acrid smoke of rifle and cannon.

As the hours and days passed, the sounds changed, becoming softer and more piteous as men too wounded to walk or crawl cried out for water or food. Their cries weakened, those nearest me apparently succumbing, while from a little distance a murmur of prayers and pleas continued.

Now there were smaller sounds—flies buzzing, rodents scurrying. Birds, at some business I did not want to imagine. In the far distance, the sounds of carts and horses and men. But no artillery fire. It was the time of collecting the wounded and the dead.

I would most probably be numbered among the latter soon, expiring of thirst or starvation if not of my wounds.

Perhaps because of the wound to my head, I had no clear recollection of what had happened to me. I could remember very little beyond seeing my batman killed—a man who had been my groom at home and who had followed me when I left for the Peninsula. But he had been lost early on in the fighting.

Despite the horrors of what I later determined to be the last three days, I did not wish for death. What little strength I had went into one prayer: *Let me live.*

I was repeating it endlessly to myself when I heard the sound of panting, then snuffling.

Here. I'm here! I silently cried to what I was sure was a dog.

As if in confirmation, I heard a soft whine. The dog began digging. A large dog, I guessed, from the sound of earth being frantically clawed away. He uncovered my hand, tugged at the sleeve of my uniform.

Oh, good dog! Good dog! But you'll never move poor Reliant. Have you a master nearby?

I knew the dog was most probably a stray, but I found myself picturing an owner who might be sympathetic to me.

Help me.

I heard footsteps. They stopped nearby. The dog kept digging.

"This beanstalk?" an Englishman's deep voice said in a puzzled tone. "Good heavens. Are you certain you want to be looking up at such a tall master, Shade?" I felt the man take my hand as he added, "It's not too late?"

The dog dug all the more furiously.

I'm alive! I'm not dead yet.

"No, nor shall you be," the man's voice answered, as if he had heard my thoughts. "If you'd rather live."

Oh yes, I'd rather!

"Good. But you must understand what I offer you."

Anything!

"Come, take a look."

Suddenly I felt whole and free of pain, and yet not in my own body. I stood as if within the man, looking down through his eyes.

I gave a cry of horror as I saw my own condition. Little wonder he had thought me dead. I was covered in mud and all but invisible beneath the horse, only saved from being completely crushed because I had landed in a shallow ditch. My eyes were closed. My face was blackened with dried blood, my hair matted down near a severe wound on my head.

My attention was drawn to the dog, one of the largest I had ever seen. He had long, black fur and large dark eyes. He looked up at me—or perhaps I should say at his master—pausing briefly in his efforts to dig my body free, and wagged his tail.

"Back to work, Shade," the man's voice said harshly. The dog's demeanor changed and he bristled, but he obeyed. Perhaps he had seen me, after all.

The man looked about him, forcing me to do the same.

Before me was carnage beyond my worst imaginings. I had seen battle, and its aftermath, but nothing to equal this. Bodies—and parts of bodies—lay everywhere around me. In the distance, I saw soldiers working to find the wounded and take them from the field. Here and there, human scavengers sought to rob the dead of their belongings. The ground had been churned by hoof and boot and wheel, and among the bodies one saw crushed caps and belts, the bright blue or red of a torn uniform, a feather bent and buried in the mud.

And as far as the eye could see, covering this grim landscape, a strange snow—thousands of scraps of paper. Letters, diaries, undelivered messages to families, friends, and sweethearts. Lost thoughts of tens of thousands of poor souls, whose last words drifted in fragments across the battlefield.

Would that I could deliver them, I thought.

My host—as I began to think of him—laughed. I felt it as if it were physically my own laughter, and I despised him for forcing me to participate in what seemed to me no joke at all.

"Don't be so quick to fire up at me," he said, amused. "It is merely that you will find your wish granted, if not quite in the manner you expect."

I continued to look about me and was going to ask, "Whose victory?" But viewing that carnage, the question seemed unanswerable to me in that moment.

"Wellington and his allies," my host said, again hearing my thoughts—and again I felt the words form on his tongue, the movement of his teeth, the vibration of his throat, the very breath it took to speak. It seemed to me there was some bitterness there.

For my part, despite the cost so clearly shown before me, I felt a rush of pride in our forces and relief that Napoleon had suffered such a defeat. In the next instant, I found myself returned to my own body and darkness.

This, I decided, has all been a fantasy, the delusions of a dying man.

"Are you certain, Shade?" I heard him ask again, almost as if in disgust.

The dog had made great progress, having loosened most of the soil around and beneath me. I felt the warmth of the dog's breath as his teeth took hold of my uniform collar. He began to pull. I marveled at his strength—I felt myself begin to move from beneath the horse. The pain was excruciating. I again lost consciousness.

I awoke on the battlefield sometime later. I was still in pain, still too weak to move so much as a finger, but these conditions were nothing to me—for my sight had been restored. The first thing I saw was Shade. He lay next to me. His head was up, his ears pitched forward. He watched me and seemed happy to have my attention in return. He wagged his long tail.

Above me, a bored young man stood looking down into my face. He was of slight stature but muscular build. I would have guessed him to be a youth, not more than sixteen, but something in his eyes said he was far older. His clothing was exquisite, his pale face handsome—if somewhat marred by a frown. His long white fingers were bejeweled, and in one of his hands he held a silver flask engraved with an elaborate letter *V*. He seemed entirely out of place in this wretched valley.

He stifled a yawn, then bent to give me water from the flask, gently lifting my head, helping me to drink. No wine from a crystal goblet was ever more appreciated than that drink of lukewarm water.

"Thank you," I rasped, able at last to speak, but he said nothing in response. He waited a moment, then again helped me to drink.

He consulted his watch, returned it to his vest, and said, "We haven't much time. Are you well enough to talk?"

"Yes—please, allow me to thank you—"

His eyes became hooded. "There is no need, I promise you."

"Who are you?"

He hesitated, then said, "I am Varre." Seeing my confusion, he added, "Lucien Adrian deVille, Lord Varre. I have a bargain to offer you, Captain Tyler Hawthorne—listen well. You may yet die on this field, slowly and painfully, every opportunity taken from you. Or you may leave here, and within the next fortnight be restored to wholeness, unable to sustain injury, free from all illness—other than occasional, brief fevers. I warn you these may be painful and troubling, but you will never suffer them for more than a few hours. You will not age, but remain in the prime of life."

"Not age!"

"Please do not interrupt me again." Despite saying this, he did not immediately continue. Just as I thought I had offended him so deeply he would abandon his offer, he went on. "Some of your older scars may not be taken from you, but any injury you received here at Waterloo will heal within hours. Any disease you now carry within you will be cured, no trace of it will ever be found in your body. You will be given work to do—nothing beneath a gentleman's station—and enough funds to make a new start in life."

He smiled, perhaps reading my thoughts. "I'm not the devil. You may serve whatever master you choose. That is not up to me. Do you think it is the devil's work to comfort the dying?"

"Am I to become a priest, then?"

He laughed. "No. Only that you must visit those who are dying. They will draw you to themselves, in fact, and tell you what you must do. You must keep the dog by you. It won't be difficult—he will always find his way to you."

I closed my eyes, thinking again that I was so lost in fever, I was imagining the whole.

"Look at me, Tyler Hawthorne, and give me your answer. Do you accept this bargain?"

My skin felt as if it were on fire, I was injured and weak. But I do not deceive myself that any of this prevented me from sensing that Lord Varre might not be telling me all I needed to know.

"Will you be guiding me in this new occupation?"

"No. As soon as we have completed this . . . transaction . . . you will not see me again. Do not attempt to find me."

On this point, he was adamant, but in truth, I was relieved to know that I would soon be shot of him.

"Do you accept this bargain I offer you?" he asked again.

"Why do you offer it?" I asked. "Why do you abandon your . . . 'occupation,' as you call it, and leave youth and health and wealth behind?"

"Oh, let us say I am giving myself a promotion." Again he laughed, and I realized how much I disliked it. He had the sort of laugh that never invited another to join in the joke. "You need not concern yourself with my welfare, Hawthorne. Not that I imagine you do."

I remained silent. He started to walk away.

"Wait!" I said, horrified by the prospect of being abandoned once again to this sea of the dead and dying.

He turned back to me and smiled. "Do you accept the bargain, Tyler Hawthorne?"

I would live. I would heal. That much I believed. That much I longed for.

"Yes," I said—fool that I am.

27

Varre reached for my right hand again, and placed a ring on my index finger. He tucked a card into one of my pockets and said, "This man will see that you have all you need when you are ready to return to England."

The look on his face was one of triumph. He's utterly mad, I thought. And I'm going to die here a madman, too. Yet I felt relief from the worst of my wounds, a lessening of pain.

"Thank you!" I said again, for that much alone, although I was still half convinced that all I was experiencing was a product of delirium.

I heard his laughter as he walked away from me.

The dog stayed by my side.

I managed, with the greatest of efforts, to move my hand enough to see the ring Varre had placed there. It was a silver mourning ring, a memento mori, and appeared to be quite old. Looking at its death's-head, I felt an urge to work it from my finger and leave it for the scavengers to find. But even this small feat was beyond my strength. I left it on my hand.

Shade began barking. I had never heard the like, and I worried that he might frighten any help away. Apparently someone wise in the way of dogs realized the nature of his call, though, for he quickly drew the attention of others. Before long I was lifted by strong hands, and added to a blood-soaked, rough cart, already more than half loaded with other wounded.

Those who read this story so many years later may find it strange that days after the battle we were still being gathered, but the number of dead and wounded at Waterloo was more than forty-seven thousand, creating a city of casualties on a strip of land roughly two miles wide and six miles long. That I was not left among the dead seemed to me a miracle.

The dog followed the cart as it gathered as many other wounded as it could hold, and trotted alongside as it made its jolting progress toward a nearby village. To the creaking of the cart were added the quiet prayers, soft moans, and occasional fevered cries of those of its passengers still able to speak, many whose suffering far outstripped my own.

When the cart had traveled what seemed to me to be as far as Spain, but was probably no more than a few miles, I received a shock. As I lay pressed against the others, feverish but marveling at the continued lessening of my pain and the wonder of my rescue, I suddenly heard a man speaking to me, and just as quickly realized that he was not speaking aloud.

Captain Hawthorne, sir—if you please, sir—will you give the letter tucked in my boot to my wife? And tell my Sarah that I died telling you of my love for her?

"What is your name, and how do you know mine?" I said, frightened.

A soldier walking beside the cart had been praising Shade, but he broke off at this and said with a pitying look, "Baker, sir. Sergeant Thomas Baker. And you told us your name when we found you—or should I say, this fine fellow—Shade, is it?—found you. Just rest, Captain Hawthorne. We'll have you on the mend in a trice."

But no sooner had he finished speaking than I heard within my mind, *Sorry, sir. I didn't realize you was new at this. Private William Makins. You need say nothing more aloud, sir. I can hear you just as plain as you hear me.*

And Makins, who seemed utterly calm and at ease, went on to tell me that he came from a certain village, the name of which I immediately recognized, as it was not far from my home. He told me how to find his own home. He told me of his gratitude to me for taking the Messenger's job.

Messenger? I silently asked.

Yes, sir. You'll be the one who comes to us as is dying, and allows us to say what might otherwise have been unsaid to them we love. As time goes on, you'll be able to do more to help us. And you'll bring us such a peace, sir. You'll be called to us, and give us what we've no right to hope for, but is thankful for all the same. It's a good thing you're doing, sir—never forget that when the job seems hard to bear, as I'm sure it will be. God bless you, sir, he said, and died.

"Sergeant Baker," I said weakly, "I believe Private Makins . . ."

He looked over and sighed. "Makins, you say? Was that his name? Probably shouldn't have picked him up, but I thought he might pull through. Not in your unit, though. Did you know him before the war, sir?"

"His home is not far from my own."

"We're almost to the hospital station now, Captain. If you can bear it—"

"I have lain among the dead for three days now, Sergeant. I shan't be troubled by poor Makins."

I spent several weeks in the place where they took me, although only a few days recovering from the fever and what those who found me assumed to be relatively minor wounds. By the time I left that village, Makins was only one of nearly a hundred men I had listened to. I began to keep notes, taking down their names, the names of their loved ones, the words they spoke to me. I became a great favorite among those who were tending to the wounded for the care I gave the dying, the ease I might bring to a restless patient at his last, my willingness to write to the families of the deceased.

I wrote to the Brussels address on the card Lord Varre had left with me, telling the agent named on it where I stayed, and saying I would be remaining there for the foreseeable future, but would come to him as soon as I was able. He replied by sending a courier who brought a large sum of money to me in mixed currencies, and a note assuring me that he would be happy to be of service should I need any additional funds or assistance.

I used some of that first sum of money—what those around me considered to be an inordinate amount of it—to have a special coffin built along the lines of one I had once seen made for a wealthy merchant. It was fashioned from iron. The remains of Private William Makins, who was among the many dead not yet buried, were transferred to it, and it was filled with alcohol and sealed. This, I had been told, would preserve those remains for the longest time possible. I planned to take Private Makins's body back to England. Although nothing could leave me out of favor with the staff of the hospital, who saw this as a noble gesture, I have no doubt that others thought me a lunatic, even if they did not directly express this opinion to me.

If they had, they would have found me in complete agreement. At that time I did not believe Lord Varre's promises of long life and eternal good health and youth, even though I knew my wounds had healed unnaturally quickly. I was soon rid of the initial fever—although now and then it would return with a vengeance and incapacitate me for a few hours—and gradually I regained my strength. I told myself that perhaps the fever had induced hallucinations, that I had never been as severely wounded as I had thought I was. Still, something far out of the ordinary had happened to me, and I could not deny all of its effects. In truth, I spent most of those days in terror, and if it had not been for Shade, whose presence had a calming effect on me, and the counsel of the dying, I am certain I would have lost my sanity.

In those first weeks, contrary to what the staff of the hospital believed, it was the dying who comforted me. In my moments with them, their candor and tranquility soothed me. It was their care of me, their uncomplicated concern, that allowed me to grow accustomed to my new responsibilities. It was little enough to thank them by penning a letter to a family member or sending a memento to a friend. In whatever time I had free, I did what I could to help those not so close to death, bringing them water, reading to them, writing missives home for those who were too wounded or ill to do so, or who were unlettered.

I had written to my brother, who had thought me dead, reports having reached him from those who saw me fall in battle. His letter in return I found quite moving, and he urged me to come home. I put it off. I sold out of the army, but given my sincere belief that I could communicate with the unconscious, I did not want to return only to be placed in an asylum.

Through my visits to the hospital, I gained a valet. Even before the war, Merritt had taken care of his young lieutenant, who now lay dying of a wound from a saber. He had been his batman on the Peninsula, and returned to the Continent with him after Napoleon escaped from Elba. Merritt was a quiet man, and did not flinch from any task the care of his wounded master required.

One evening I told him I would sit with the lieutenant, so that he might sleep for a few hours. He refused, saying he did not think the lieutenant would last the night.

He was right, and as the final moments of the lieutenant's life drew near, I felt the nearly gravitational pull the dying had on my attention. I took the lieutenant's hand.

You can trust Merritt, he said. *Let him know you can hear me.*

No, thank you. I'll either be thought mad or frighten him.

Frighten Merritt! I'd like to see you try. Tell him I said there's a creaking third step on the second landing at Wyvern's Lair. Go on, man, do it. Haven't got much time.

So with great trepidation, I repeated the message aloud.

Merritt's eyes widened, and he stared hard at me, then said slowly, "So there is."

"Yes, you old fox, and a boy's treasures hidden in a wooden box in a hollowed-out oak in the home wood." I blushed and added, "Or so he says."

"Yes, Captain," Merritt added, tears coming to his eyes. "So there is."

As you can see, Captain Hawthorne, the lieutenant said to me alone, *he can keep secrets. He's a good man—has a gift with animals, as well—and I understand that your own batman was killed. Will you take him on?*

I looked across at Merritt. *I will ask him, but I do not want him to feel pressured into becoming my servant out of love for you.*

I knew you were the right man for him! You won't regret it. And now, if you would be so good as to tell him . . .

What followed was a mixture of reminiscence and requests. The reminiscence showed the lieutenant to be a man of good humor and kindness, if not completely able to keep himself out of scrapes. He told Merritt not to blame himself for this injury, and to seek my help in sending certain items home to a beloved aunt.

"For you know I liked her above all the rest, Merritt," I repeated on the lieutenant's behalf.

Merritt spoke to me as if I were the lieutenant's ears, which I realized I was, as the lieutenant answered him. The lieutenant mentioned that I might need help back to my rooms, as this visit had put a strain on me.

A short time later, the lieutenant died. The fever set in on me not long after, and I was grateful for Merritt's assistance in returning to my lodgings. Although I recovered quickly, he did everything possible to provide for my comfort in the hours when the fever laid me low, not seeking his own rest until dawn.

When, after the lieutenant's burial, I asked Merritt if he would work for me, he readily agreed to do so.

"I must ask," I said, "that you do not tell others of . . ."

"Your gift, Captain? I would not think of doing so, sir."

"There is a dog . . ."

"Yes, I've made his acquaintance. Shade, I believe you call him. He's a fine gentleman, isn't he?"

"Yes," I said, somewhat at a loss.

"It will be my pleasure and honor to serve you, sir."

In the coming weeks, I saw that the lieutenant was right. Merritt was a discreet and capable man, and his assistance freed me to spend more time at the makeshift hospital.

Eventually the dying made clear to me that I was to return to England.

Your gift will go with you to England, Captain, one of them told me, *so never fear. Be sure to give the dog a walk in a cemetery now and again.*

A cemetery?

Sure, he's a cemetery dog—didn't you know? And they need their time among the graves. No shortage of graves here, of course, but it won't be the same when you go back.

I thought about this, and felt a rising tide of uneasiness over my return to England.

There's a bit of business for you to attend to there, Captain, but if England doesn't suit you, sir, you'll find another home. God bless you, Tyler Hawthorne, and many thanks for your kindness to me.

Before I could ask him what "bit of business" he meant, he died, and his thoughts were lost to me.

28

Our passage back to England was largely uneventful. The most unsettling moment came before we set sail, when I visited Lord Varre's agent in Brussels, who gave me to understand that I was now an enormously wealthy man. Since I had assumed that the amount sent to me a few weeks earlier was the largest portion of what Lord Varre had intended me to have, I was shocked. When I ventured a question regarding the source of this wealth, he said that Lord Varre had left a letter for me. The letter informed me that this was merely a small portion of his own wealth, which he was willing to share with me. These funds came from his alliance with an Italian merchant's family and investments made on the 'Change over many years. I must keep in mind that these funds must be made to *last quite a long time*.

The meaning of those five underlined words was not lost on me.

The agent happily arranged our passage. He did not question my need to add Merritt, Shade, and the casket of Private Makins to those arrangements. He took care of every detail, including the purchase of a team of horses and a carriage for my use in England.

Merritt helped me to deliver Private Makins's remains to his widow, a beautiful young woman who seemed overwhelmed by my attention to her late husband's burial.

"Your husband was a great help to me at Waterloo," I told her. She accepted this without question. I gave her his last letter, as he had asked. I left a sum of money with her that would ensure she would not be forced within the next few years to seek a new home or spouse out of desperation, telling her that these were the earnings of her late husband, from a venture we had entered into together. This was not entirely untrue.

I saw that Merritt seemed quite taken with her, and she seemed to feel very much at ease in his presence. But she was still in mourning, and he quite rightly honored that. We took our leave after the funeral.

The thought that Merritt might return to marry her one day made me consider my own affairs. I was of good family, and upon my father's death had inherited a comfortable property, a part of the estate not entailed to my brother. This, combined with my wealth, and the fact that so many men had been lost in the late war, would be enough to ensure that a great many families would be glad of any courtship I pursued with an unmarried daughter. But I hesitated to look for a wife.

I did not yet accept that all Lord Varre had told me was true, but niggling doubts would not be banished. What if I were to marry and not only outlive my wife—and children and grandchildren—but appear to be younger than they once they had passed the age of twenty-four? It seemed impossible, and yet envisioning such a situation was enough to cause me to remain reticent.

My brother's happiness at my return from war was evident—he had thought me lost at Waterloo. His welcome was warm and deeply gratifying. His wife was expecting their third child, and his two boys, then aged seven and five, made quite a to-do about their uncle the soldier and his large dog.

Although my brother and I reminisced late into the night, I awoke just before dawn and, unable to fall asleep again, got up and lit the fire that had been laid in the fireplace in my room. I had already learned that I could forgo sleep without ill effect, although sleeping felt good, and I took pleasure in it when I could manage it. I was wide awake now, though, so I grasped the handle of the water pitcher next to the basin, preparing to wash my face. I felt a small, sharp pain—the handle of the pitcher was chipped, and I had cut my hand. I was fortunate that Merritt was not yet up and attending me, because no sooner had I pressed a clean cloth to the wound than it healed. If I had not seen the bloodstains on the cloth and the handle of the pitcher, I would not have been sure I had been cut. I quickly wiped off the handle and burned the cloth in the fire. Shade watched me with interest but did not move from the hearth rug.

I stood staring at my hand. What if all that Lord Varre had told me was true? What if I had been given more than the ability to speak to the dying?

Impossible! Every man died. Some part of my brain whispered that everything else Varre had said was true, so perhaps I was, after all, immortal. My next rash temptation was to take out my pistols and test this premise in the gravest way possible. I was not quite desperate enough (or foolish enough) to try it, especially not in my brother's home, but I took my penknife and stood by the basin again. I deliberately cut myself. It stung. It bled. It healed almost instantly.

I cut it again. Deeply. It hurt more, bled more, but healed nearly as quickly as the previous two wounds.

I opened the window of my room and, making sure no one was watching, emptied the bloody water from the basin into the flower beds below.

I sat on the bed, shaking.

Another man might have rejoiced in the prospect of being unable to remain wounded. Perhaps it was the cumulative effect of weeks of unsettling experiences, but my own reaction was one of dread.

What had I become?

I moved to my knees and prayed, as hard as I had prayed when I lay dying at Waterloo. "Am I still human?" I whispered wretchedly. I tried to take the memento mori ring off my finger. It would not budge. I considered removing the finger.

I began to wonder if on that battlefield, when I lay reaching so desperately for life, I had instead taken hold of the unforgivable. I begged God for answers, for guidance.

I waited and waited, but heard no divine reply.

I knelt there for some time longer, feeling utterly forsaken. Shade approached me and laid his head on my hands. Eventually I moved to sit on the bed, and he placed his head on my knee. I stroked his soft fur and, as so often happened, found myself calmed by his companionship.

In the days since my rescue, had I done evil? I could not believe that comforting those men was wrong, or that their words or reactions to me signified a partnership with the devil. If I had known in advance that I would be able to help them in this way, would I have refused to do so by refusing the gift? I couldn't bring myself to say that I would.

Something within me spurned the idea that I would be immortal here on earth. There would be a way out of this bargain. I would accept my lot and do my work, and hope for release. Despair seemed unlikely to lead me to anything good.

I was calmer, but not without concerns. What if I were to be in a carriage accident or injured under some other public circumstance, and this instantaneous healing were witnessed by others? What if someone were to see me recover almost spontaneously from even a minor wound, as I had just now?

Perhaps I could become the ideal soldier. But again my wounds might be seen to heal rapidly, or I might be the only one to survive a deadly engagement. If I were to walk into the War Department and so much as start to suggest that I was unable to die, I'd be sent to Bedlam to do my battles.

If Lord Varre had been telling the truth, and in appearance and strength I remained twenty-four and unharmed forever, what place could I occupy in the world?

I had many questions, and I believed only one person was likely to have answers for me: Lord Varre. I began to feel certain that I should seek him out, and learn as much as I could from him.

I rang for Merritt, dressed, and hurried to the library. There I took my brother's copy of Debrett's from the shelf and looked up Lord Varre. His estates were situated in the north of England, a journey of three days from my brother's home.

So it was that I expressed regrets to my hosts, saying that urgent business called me to the north, but that I expected to return soon. I left with their protests in my ears, wondering if I was embarking on a fool's errand.

29

We reached Lord Varre's estate in the early evening of the third day of our journey. It was a secluded manor at the end of a long lane. Its appearance surprised me—given the "portion" of his wealth passed on to me, as well as his ostentatious dress and haughty manner, I had expected a palatial estate on extensive grounds. Instead, I found a well-cared-for but relatively modest manor, surrounded by trees that hid it from the main road.

This lack of opulence didn't matter to me. I had spent most of the journey rehearsing speeches and listing questions for Lord Varre. At last I would have my answers. I cared not if I received those answers in a palace or a hovel.

I was admitted by a frowning young footman, who took my card but not my hat or cloak. He spoke in low, almost whispered tones, and said that he regretted to inform me that Lord Varre was not receiving visitors. His lordship had taken ill, and was not, in fact, expected to live.

I was shocked, and stood considering what my reply to this should be, when an elderly butler, who looked rather starched up, descended the stairs and asked in a solemn voice if I was the gentleman who owned the dog sitting on the front steps.

I said that I was, expecting to be told that I should remove the animal—and myself—forthwith, but the butler merely nodded and ordered the footman to admit the dog into the house, to help my valet to take my luggage to the green bedroom, and to offer any other assistance required to make his lordship's guest comfortable. He ordered another footman to take my hat and cloak.

"Thank you," I said, "but while I hope to speak to his lordship, I wouldn't wish to further burden the household at such a time—"

"You are no burden at all, sir. Indeed, you are most welcome. Do I have the honor of addressing Captain Tyler Hawthorne?"

I felt relieved. His master had mentioned me. "Yes—although I've left the army now, so it's no longer 'Captain'—"

"I understand. I am Wentworth, his lordship's butler. I will take you up to see him shortly, but perhaps I may offer you some refreshment first?"

"I'm in no need, thank you, but if I might wash up a bit before seeing his lordship—?"

Before I could say more, Shade was let in, and he greeted Wentworth—who seemed equally delighted to see him—as an old friend. The greeting further relieved my mind. I was by then beginning to appreciate Shade's ability to judge character.

The footman reappeared to say my room was prepared. Wentworth said that I should ring whenever I was ready, and he would personally escort me to his lordship's rooms.

The room I was given was clean and comfortable, if not in the style I expected of Lord Varre. Merritt was waiting for me, and began to help me to make myself more presentable.

As I dressed, I noticed that the figure of a large dog was carved in black marble and set into the mantelpiece.

"Our Shade to the life, isn't it, sir?" Merritt said. He then informed me that he believed the stables were in good order, as was the household, then paused and added, "Although I will say, sir, that none of them is very old, Mr. Wentworth being the exception, and no one else in service here for long. They're none of them from nearby, the locals apparently having a fear of the place."

"A fear of it?"

"Something to do with illness in the place, sir. Strikes it regular, they tell me."

"Are you uneasy, Merritt?"

He gave me a look of disbelief. "What, me, sir? After facing Boney and his friends for half my life? I should think not, sir."

I smiled. "I'm glad to hear it."

Wentworth escorted me down a hallway, Shade following. The butler seemed to think nothing of the dog accompanying me. My anticipation grew. Now, untroubled by fever or fear of dying, I would be able to express myself more clearly. I would have answers to my questions.

He took me to a small antechamber, then opened a second door and ushered me into a large bedroom, heavily draped and darkly paneled, lit only by a single candelabra. Still, the light was enough for me to see the face of the man on the bed. I came to a sudden halt, shocked.

The man was not Lord Varre.

He was a man of perhaps sixty years of age, although illness might have added years to his appearance. He was propped up by pillows, pale and thin.

I was on the verge of offering profound apologies when I remembered that the butler had known my name. If I was mistaken, then how had he come to expect my arrival?

"Come in, come in, Captain Hawthorne," the man on the bed said, his voice soft but clear.

I moved closer. I studied his face and saw a definite resemblance to the man who had rescued me at Waterloo. Lord Varre was surveying me with as much interest as I had him.

"Wentworth," he said, "please see that we are not disturbed."

"Certainly, sir. I shall be just outside your door should you need me."

The butler gently closed the door behind him.

"I am doubtless not whom you expected to see," the man on the bed said, then sighed. "I suppose you were looking for a much younger man?"

"Your son, I presume?" I said.

"No, sir. I am Marcus deVille, Lord Varre. The man you met was Lucien Adrian deVille, known by his family as Adrian—my great-great-great—oh, who knows how many generations he encompassed? A grandfather of mine, you might say."

"I don't understand . . ."

"Aye, who could blame you? Come here and sit by me, and I will tell you what little I know."

I obeyed. Shade came with me, and was recognized. Again he was greeted as a member of the household.

"Excuse me, but did this dog once belong to you?" I asked.

"Shade? Oh no, no. He was owned—if he can be owned—by Adrian, the man who introduced himself to you as Lord Varre. As I understand it, Shade has now attached himself to you. In this house, he will be treated as royalty. I owe him a great deal."

He suffered a coughing fit. I helped him to a glass of water.

"Thank you . . . I will speak plainly," he said. "I am in ill health, and haven't time to tell you all you should know, let alone fill your head with a lot of rubbish that will do you no earthly good. I take it you can sense that I am not long for this world?"

This was true. "You are gravely ill, sir, but I believe you will see at least another dawn."

"More than I hoped for," he said, unperturbed, "but still not so very long. So let me begin by saying that I know you are nearly immortal, will not age, are able to recover from any wound or illness, and have another gift besides—which Adrian thought a rather stupid request, when most men would have asked for lovers or wealth. He asked for wealth when the gift was given to him. But you, you weren't so selfish, were you?"

"Perhaps, as he said, I was merely stupid."

"Do you regret it, being able to help the dying?"

"No," I answered at once.

He smiled, and fell silent for a moment.

"You are more than he bargained for, Captain," he said at last. "And

I'm glad of it. Let me tell you a strange tale. Centuries ago—I know not how many—a young man became enamored of potions and magic and the dark arts. He was a brilliant scholar and gathered every manuscript he could, and sought out alchemists and necromancers and objects reputed to have magical powers. He learned of an old man who lived in a small village and was rumored to be a sorcerer. This young man had already made a habit of pursuing every rumor he ever heard of those with supernatural powers, although he was already quite cynical about these matters. He found a great deal of fakery among those who claimed to be magical. This particular old man did not try to baffle him with incense or drugs. Indeed, he simply said he had been waiting for him.

"He gave the young man a ring, a mourning ring, and near midnight, took him to visit a cemetery. The young man was not frightened, as some might have been, and spent his time admiring the ornate crypts of the aristocrats who were interred there.

" 'I wish I were wealthy,' the young man said, and looking slyly at the crypts added, 'and alive to enjoy it.'

"The old man said he had expected no less—nor more—of him. Soon a great black dog appeared, and although he never admitted it to another, I have read the young man's journals, and know that at last he was frightened."

Lord Varre began coughing again. "Perhaps," I said, giving him another sip of water, "we should continue this after you've had a little sleep?"

"No, no," he said. He lay back and closed his eyes, but went on with his story.

"I imagine you know the bargain the old man offered him. That dog was Shade. A cemetery dog. They are rare. Some are harbingers of death, I'm told. But that is not Shade's role, as nearly as I can tell. He protects you. He has some special connection to those in your line, who have the power to talk to those too injured or ill to speak.

"Adrian had little patience for such work, though. He was surprised to learn that the sorcerer had died not long after they had met, and had left his fortune to Adrian. In this way, Adrian did indeed become vastly wealthy.

"There were problems, though. He soon realized that his lack of aging was noticed by those around him. He would need to travel. He was always a restless person, so he did not mind this. As he roamed the world, braving places others feared, he saw endless opportunities and began to make money in shipping and trade.

"As he traveled he continued his studies of black magic and potions. I have never been certain where he was born. At times, I have believed he was Spanish, as some of his oldest documents are in that language, and he seems to have called himself Hidalgo de Seville for a time, but that may easily have been yet another name he created for himself.

"Wherever he was from, wherever it was he went, at some point he decided to come back to England. He made himself useful as a warrior. Unable to be much disabled by his wounds, he became a valued and feared knight, and earned the title of Baron Lucien Adrian deVille, Lord Varre. He was given these lands. The original house is long gone, but the attic and cellars are full of his papers and other belongings.

"He didn't much like it here, I'm happy to say. He loved having the title, but there was that old difficulty, you see. He married and remained here for eleven years, at the end of which time his wife died bearing him his third son, who did not survive infancy. He took his remaining sons with him on a voyage to Italy, and left the care of the manor to a trusted steward, with whom he corresponded frequently.

"By this time he had become an expert poisoner. If his diaries are to be believed, he enjoyed a dalliance with Lucrezia Borgia."

The old man opened his eyes and stared at me. "Supposedly, after a decade abroad, Lord Varre and his youngest son died in Italy, where they were buried. Indeed, there is an elaborate crypt bearing our family name near the villa he owned there. His eldest son inherited titles and land, and returned to England."

"He died? But—"

"Supposedly. The young man who returned to England was said by one and all to greatly resemble his father. So much so, he was mistaken by some to be his father, until they realized that his father would have been a middle-aged man. He was a generous landlord and master, so these questions did not trouble others for long. And if he did not seem to age, well, his father was the same, wasn't he?"

"You're saying it was indeed Adrian. But if so, what of his sons?"

"There were indeed two bodies buried in that crypt in Italy."

"His own sons!"

"Adrian's love of himself always surpassed his love of his family. The only shows of sorrow I have ever read in his diaries were oblique references to his losses. Losses he had caused, of course."

I was speechless with dismay. Lord Varre lay quietly, allowing me time to consider all he had said.

"The Borgias!" I finally choked out. "Good God—if this occurred at the beginning of the sixteenth century, do you mean to say it has gone on for three hundred years?"

"At times, he left us in peace. And he learned other tricks, of course. Stagecraft became one of his accomplishments. A trusted servant would be well paid to help him to present himself as a much older man. There were rumors from time to time, but the servants learned, of course, that there was a high penalty for indiscretion. Mostly, he traveled, seeking thrills that were harder and harder to find.

"When he wasn't at home, he took on other identities. He was a master forger and created himself as a German *Freiherr,* a French *comte,* an Italian *visconte.* His wealth and address made him believable, as did hundreds of years of acquiring fluency in a wide range of languages. He sometimes remained in these guises even when he returned here. He would be the cousin who was a German baron, a French count, or an Italian viscount. A bright young man, he seemed, so self-possessed. He charmed everyone, and those who had lived in the area for a long time noted the family resemblance. He began to take his sons and grandsons to the now well-populated crypt in Italy. Eventually his offspring became aware of the pattern, so that when he found the need to spend time in England as Lord Varre, his sons easily became convinced that it was better to live one's life as a wealthy gentleman in France or Italy than to die young and join one's ancestors in that crypt."

He again suffered a coughing fit, and I begged him to rest his voice for a while. He did, and Shade laid his head on the bed beside him. He gently stroked the dog's fur and smiled. "Ah, Shade. What a comfort you are, old friend."

Shade made a low sound of pleasure.

"You doubtless wonder," Lord Varre said after a time, "why Adrian was willing to give up such power to you. You received the care of Shade, and a ring, and some other—gifts, I take it?"

"Yes, at Waterloo." I showed him the ring.

"Adrian arrived here again not long after he met you. I had never seen him without Shade. He told me of his plans for you. You were meant, Captain Hawthorne, to be an unsuspecting temporary vessel, one might say."

"Temporary?"

"Yes. This past winter, Adrian began to receive messages from the dying—he avoided them for the most part, but in the recent war-filled years, this was not easy. He had become an admirer of Bonaparte, from all I can gather. He was rather disturbed, for once in his life, by boredom and complacency, because the dying told him there would be another. At long last, he would be allowed to die. Shade would choose a new master on a certain date in June, at a certain place. So Adrian hurried back here. This was the second time in my life I had seen him, this time posing—of all things—as a young cousin of mine returned from America."

He brooded for a few moments, and it seemed to me that some strong emotion was acting upon him. Indeed, he wiped brusquely at his eyes before he went on.

"His manner was a remarkable thing for me to observe—Adrian, whom I had every reason to hate—was in a panic. He produced a key and ordered Wentworth, the only one of my servants who is aware of the true state of matters, to unlock a set of rooms in the cellars that have been forbidden to the rest of the family. He began scouring his books and at last seemed to believe that he had found a solution to his troubles.

"He did not tell me the whole—but he mentioned that it had something to do with a mourning ring, some power he invested in it."

"This one?" I said, holding up my hand. "The mourning ring he gave me at Waterloo?"

"Perhaps. I cannot be certain. He collected them. I have asked Wentworth to give you that collection. You are also to have his remaining books and papers." He frowned. "Do not fail to take them, Captain Hawthorne."

I assured him I would do as he wished.

"Good . . . good. In any case, Adrian told me that he must go to Belgium but would return shortly. Now he was quite pleased with himself. He believed he had retained his power of regeneration—that is, of recovering from wounds. It would take him a bit longer without the dog, he said, but he would recover. There were other cemetery dogs and he would find one and draw it to him.

"I had already seen that he had developed the power to bring others under his influence. I, myself, found him difficult to resist, and he seemed to find my resistance more amusing than troublesome. His influence was not merely over humans, most of whom were glad to do his bidding. He could bring birds to his hand. If there was an ill-tempered horse in the stables, he could ride it as if it were a child's pony. I have seen him coax a fox from its lair and pet it as if it were a cat.

"He felt confident that he had a method of reclaiming his full power, but he also saw an opportunity. His plan was to grow a bit older here, with me playing his grandfather. He would wait a little more than twenty years, and when his body reached forty-four in natural appearance, he would reclaim his gift from you."

"Why did he want to reach that age?"

"When he had first stopped aging, he noted that although some men lived to be seventy or more, a great many men did not live past forty. As time went on, more men lived longer, and he foresaw this trend would continue. In this day, a twenty-four-year-old man is considered to be a young man. He felt at forty-four he would be taken more seriously in business dealings and the like, and yet still be young enough to travel and partake of sports, take mistresses, and father children."

"So," I said, feeling a mixture of relief for my own part and disgust with Adrian, "I will be free of this in twenty years?"

He gave me a sorrowful look. "I'm sorry, Captain Hawthorne. I must most sincerely beg your forgiveness."

"I'm sure you have it, for I can think of no wrong you've done me."

"Oh, but I have, you see." He placed a trembling hand over mine. "Forgive me, Captain Hawthorne, but in this very house, I murdered Lucien Adrian deVille, first Baron Varre."

30

M urdered him?" I repeated blankly.

"Yes, I daresay you don't believe such a thing is possible."

"Of you? No, indeed—"

He laughed, which induced another choking fit. "Bless you, my boy," he said, when he was able to speak again. "Bless you for that. But I'm afraid I'm as damned as Adrian. Perhaps twice as damned, for I have caused you take his place for . . . well, the future is not foreseeable." He glanced at Shade. "This old fellow may know how long you must remain as you are, but I do not." He looked back at me. "Adrian told you that you cannot be killed?"

"I hardly believed him."

"It is true. Indeed, Adrian bragged to me of exacting revenge on anyone who had tried to murder him—many of those men were my ancestors. In the sixteenth century, a group of them had overpowered him and stabbed him in the heart. They sought the dog, too, but this was wrong of them. As it happened, he proved more fierce than Adrian himself, and eluded them. Still, they were happy—Adrian did not stir. He did not breathe, nor did his heart beat. So, certain he was dead, they covered him in chains and threw him into the sea."

Despite everything I now knew about Adrian deVille, a horrifying vision arose in my mind, of being in his place. I thought of being brought back to life again and again, only to drown moments later—and to repeat that fate forever.

Lord Varre seemed to understand why I paled. "No need to waste your sympathy," he said. "Adrian told me he awakened the next morning in a small cottage, one of his many homes here in England, places where he keeps papers and possessions hidden. He placed various protections on these places so that none would disturb them. Thus, while my ancestors were dancing for joy, thinking themselves free of him at last, he was in a comfortable bed, Shade at his side. He was taken with one of his fevers, but while he waited for this to pass, he plotted his revenge."

He fell silent. Many minutes passed before he spoke again.

"Should you decide to take Shade on a walk through the family cemetery, you will see a great many weatherworn markers for a single year late in the sixteenth century. Anyone will tell you that the plague struck the area, and hardly a man was left standing as a result of it."

"He caused it?"

"Adrian boasted of bringing it to the place."

"But that means—he took his revenge on the innocent as well?"

"Children, women, men who had nothing to do with the plot— diaries from the time recount terrible suffering. Early on, when the head of this house and all his family died, Adrian reestablished himself here as the heir to the barony, and turned a deaf ear when any of his remaining persecutors begged for mercy for their families.

"Although little survives in the family records from the time before the plague, there are a few letters and diaries from the times that followed. Stories have been handed down for generations—family tales of 'Our Monster,' as he became known. What I tell you next, I've learned in part from those stories and writings, and in part from Adrian himself.

"When he returned some thirty years later, his own anger toward the place had not abated. He did not bother with charm now. He was more debauched than ever, behaving insultingly to the women here, and cruelly to the children. He had spent this time, it seemed, learning to inflict pain on others. The family sent their servants away, in order to protect them, and would have sent their own women and children from the place had not Adrian forbidden it. Among the servants, a few stout-hearted men stayed to be of whatever help they could. One of them bore the name of Wentworth."

"An ancestor of your butler?"

He smiled. "Yes. Adrian felt invulnerable, but he was only one man, and the family awaited their chance. One night when he was, as usual, drinking heavily—perhaps you have noticed a change in the way drinking affects you?"

I shook my head. "I enjoy wine as much as the next man, but I'm afraid too much of it makes me so ill, I—" I broke off.

"Assuming you respond to alcohol as Adrian did," he said calmly, "you will find that you now have what is commonly called a 'hard head.' It will take a great deal of drinking before you begin to feel the effects of alcohol, but you may then go on to become remarkably inebriated, to the point of passing out. A moment or two after you reach unconsciousness, you will awaken clearheaded, but suffer nothing more than a brief, slight fever. No headache, no queasiness. In short, you may become stewed to the eyebrows without being punished."

"I find the prospect less attractive than you may believe."

He smiled. "You are not much like your predecessor."

"You were telling me about the second attack on him?"

"Ah, yes. That time, his downfall was at the hands of a raven-haired girl of fifteen, one of the fairest daughters of the house. She was his own granddaughter, but this made no difference to him. He flirted with her as if she were no relation to him. She decided to turn this to good use and enlisted the help of the rest of the household. She was a brave girl, but she professed a great fear of the dog, and on a night when Adrian was drinking and making amorous overtures, she asked Adrian to shut Shade away. For reasons we do not understand, Shade meekly allowed this."

He paused and scratched the dog fondly on the ears.

"The girl gave a signal as soon as Adrian was well separated from the place where he had locked Shade away. Adrian was set upon again. This time they burned his body and scattered his ashes in the wind.

"They went back to the manor and were of a mind to harm the dog, but the girl stopped them. I do not know that they would have been able to do any of the things they intended to do to Shade, for he is capable of defending himself. She came close to Shade and said, 'You will protect us, won't you?' and set him free.

"The men argued with her, but she paid them no heed.

"Again the dog sought Adrian, and had no difficulty finding him. Again Adrian awoke alive and whole in a place of his own. But for reasons he would not disclose to me, he did not return until long after that young woman had married and died in childbirth. With one notable exception, whenever he came back to visit this place, he reverted to his most charming manner. He usually came here, as I've mentioned, in another guise, most often posing as a European cousin who outranked a mere baron. He might be demanding, insist on special treatment and the best rooms, but he brought his own servants, paid for his luxuries, and threatened no one."

"The notable exception?"

"This last visit. He returned here two weeks after Waterloo. He was demanding, as usual, but also unhappy—he could no longer drink to excess. He needed sleep. He grew hungry several times a day, and it was no longer the kind of mild sensation he had previously thought of as hunger.

"His arm was in a sling—he had been slightly injured on his journey north and the wound had become infected, a matter of some carelessness on his part in treating it, developed over several hundred years of never needing to concern himself over minor wounds. While here, he bumped his head, which raised a lump. Listening to his howls over it, one would have thought the world was coming to an end.

"The realization that he was now humanly vulnerable was emphasized by the fact that he arrived without his dog. Never before had I seen him without Shade. It was immediately clear to me that Shade had in some way restrained Adrian's worst behaviors on visits to this household.

"I also learned that whatever supernatural gifts Adrian had lost, he was not entirely without power. His temper led to unhappiness with the staff. The staff who upset him began to suffer painful maladies and serious injuries. Two died. Other servants began to talk of the house being accursed, and despite the shortage of work in this area, they quit. That was when I went to him and begged him to have a care. I needed the staff to see to his comfort. What's more, my two sons and their families would be closing up their London houses and returning here for the summer. I expected them at any moment.

"He laughed in my face and told me he'd do as he damn well pleased."

He again fell silent. I waited for his story to continue, but then I saw that his eyes were filled with tears. Shade came closer and sighed softly. Lord Varre gradually regained his composure. "Late that same evening," he said, "I learned that my sons and their wives and their four young children were numbered among those who perished in a fire at an inn, a place where they had stopped along the way during their journey north. The youngest was a boy of four."

His face grew set. "After the funerals, I went to London, telling Adrian I needed to settle my sons' affairs. I did, but I had another purpose as well: to discover whether anyone matching Adrian's description had been seen in either of my sons' homes. He had indeed visited, posing as a young émigré cousin. A maid he had trifled with recalled that he had asked one of my sons for recommendations for places to stay along the road north.

"I knew Adrian had been responsible for their deaths," Lord Varre said. "He would doubtless arrange for mine as well, and 'prove' that he was next to inherit the title. I knew that I had little time to act.

"I remembered the stories I had heard of his previous 'deaths,' but I prayed to God that without Shade, he might be denied his restoration to life. I returned home determined to neither eat nor drink anything Wentworth had not prepared himself, and to keep a sturdy footman by me at all times. I had developed a plan, and I asked for Wentworth's help, something I had no right to do, but he readily agreed to give it.

"The evening after my return, Wentworth brought a bottle of the best brandy in our cellars to the table, and I feigned readiness to refuse it, but of course Adrian insisted we drink to ease our sorrows, although he showed no more concern for their loss than a cat feels for the loss of a canary. As usual, he drank to excess, calling for additional bottles when the first was emptied. I convinced him to remove to the library, where we could be more at ease. He agreed and took the most comfortable chair for himself. I had expected this.

"He continued to drink, saying his arm was troubling him, and this might help him sleep. Fortunately, he did not worry that my own glass was nearly untouched—this meant I would not be taking brandy he wanted for himself. He remained unconvinced that he had lost his former immunity, and like many a drunkard before him, believed he held the reins of a horse that had instead fully harnessed him. He dozed off in his chair.

"When I was sure he was deeply asleep, I rose from my own chair and quietly dismissed the footman who had been standing just outside the door, ready to intervene should I fall under attack from Adrian. Wentworth arrived just then, carrying a new bottle. We entered the library together. I moved toward the desk, where I had earlier placed a dagger. I had just opened the drawer when I heard a rather sickening thud. I looked up to see Wentworth wiping off the bottle he had used to strike a very nasty blow to Adrian's head.

" 'You'll forgive the liberty, my lord,' Wentworth said, 'but I believe I owe something to all the generations of Wentworths who have suffered this man's presence.'

"I asked if Adrian still lived, and Wentworth announced almost regretfully that he did. 'I have prepared a place in the cellars, my lord. Upon reflection, it seemed better not to carry out our work on this Aubusson.'

"I gradually realized that Wentworth, so devoted to me and my sons and grandchildren, was furious with Adrian, and had only just restrained himself from murdering Adrian outright. He was also thinking more clearly than I was—he was right that we should not leave stains upon the carpet. I took the dagger and its sheath from the desk and hurried to help Wentworth carry Adrian to the cellar.

"This was not difficult. He was not a large man, and I had not yet fallen ill."

He paused.

"I will not make you suffer every detail of Adrian's murder. Despite my hatred of him, I found it distasteful. Still, I will tell you that it was a long night's work. I left nothing to chance, and in the end, nothing was left but an iron chest filled with ashes and ground bones. This chest I surrounded with iron bands and heavy locks.

"We took it to a seaport. There I entrusted it to a dear friend of mine who was on his way to his family plantation in Jamaica. He solemnly swore to me that he would not attempt to open it, and would drop it into the deepest part of the Caribbean. I watched him set sail on the *Morgan Bray*." He fell silent, then said, "I may have sealed his fate."

He pointed to a newspaper. I picked it up and saw the article that had caused his dismay. The *Morgan Bray* had been caught in a storm off Jamaica and gone down with all hands aboard.

"The chest was at the bottom of the sea, just as I had asked, but Adrian took my friend and all the crew with him."

"Such storms are common in that part of the world, I am told," I said.

"I suppose you are right," he said, but sounded thoroughly unconvinced.

"If this news has made you fall ill, my lord—"

"No, no. Whether these matters and the loss of all my beloved children took its toll on me, or whether Adrian had already planned that I would sicken, I do not know, but by the time I returned home from seeing the *Morgan Bray* set sail, I had already fallen ill, and became as you see me now, a dying man. I am now the last of my name. I have arranged for the care of my servants and the disposal of my wealth.

"But until today, I worried that I might have damned myself for naught. I feared that Shade would leave your side and seek Adrian, that Adrian would reappear in some cottage or hunting box not far from here, and come forward with his false documents to claim the title. I had inquired of you from the army, and was first told you were dead, and then that you were alive but injured, and finally that you were no longer with the army and were traveling to Brussels. I hardly knew what to believe until Wentworth told me of your arrival."

He looked at Shade again and smiled. "I can see his loyalty is to you now, Captain. I cannot tell you how greatly I am relieved."

He died two days later, a day after a visit from his solicitor, and not long after a visit from the local vicar, who appeared quite shaken when he left. With Wentworth, I was at Lord Varre's bedside when he died, and we received the last of his confidences. I will not betray his trust. I will only add this note to this part of my narrative—I do not believe for a moment that he was damned.

Of Lord Varre's wealth, the largest part went to his servants and to aid the poor of his parish, most especially to those returning soldiers who had served in the recent wars. I was surprised to learn that I was a beneficiary of his will, but this made it easier for me to take away those objects that he had entrusted to me, most of them possessions of Adrian deVille. Added to these were family papers, his own collection of books, and a small collection of miniatures of his family members.

This last bequest, the solicitor said, reading from the will, "is given to you to remind you of the importance of having accepted a gift." The solicitor seemed hopeful that I would interpret this for him, but I am afraid I disappointed him.

31

Amanda finished the last of the parchment pages and set them carefully on the desk. All her first thoughts were of Tyler, and what he had been through. She thought of him spending so many years keeping secrets, going to one deathbed after another.

A little earlier, she had heard him return, heard him speaking softly to Shade as he walked down the hallway past her room. She thought of going to him, to talk to him about the pages he had left for her.

She hesitated.

She asked herself if she believed what she had just read.

Yes, she thought, *I do.*

And yet, none of this fit into her experience. She told herself sternly to consider the possibility that he was crazy, convinced of his delusions, but right out of his head—or that this was a hoax. She knew she had to be on guard against con men—that had been drilled into her own head from childhood on.

Okay, if this was a hoax, the pages she had just read could have been written yesterday, faked to look aged. But that phrase, "written yesterday," took her thoughts to the previous day.

No, they couldn't have been written yesterday. Not while he was lying on a dirt road in the desert, dying. Not with all that had occurred yesterday and today.

She took a deep breath and let it out slowly.

She had seen him revive after the accident. She had seen him heal—twice, now—from serious wounds. She had watched him use his gift with the dying.

He wasn't crazy. It wasn't a hoax. Strange, but not a hoax.

She admitted to herself that given the degree of attraction she felt to him, she might not be able to think about him objectively.

She got up again and put on a light robe. She would check on Brad, she decided.

She was crossing the room, headed toward the door to the hallway, when the ghosts appeared. She drew in a sharp breath and put a hand to her throat, but managed not to yelp.

Tyler's story made her think of them a little differently now, she realized. He didn't see ghosts, so why did she? She studied each of their faces, trying to read their expressions.

Not disapproving this time, she noticed. Her aunt and uncle looked worried, her parents—serene.

She could not recall a time, during the years her mother lived, when she had ever seen her look like this. Even the childhood photos she had seen of her mother, years before marriage, had not captured this quality. "You're beautiful, Mom," Amanda said.

Nothing in her mother's expression changed—or did it? Something in her eyes. Didn't they lighten just a little?

Then it occurred to her that they were standing between her and the door.

"Is this a message of some sort?" she asked.

They said nothing. Made no gesture.

She waited.

They drifted toward her.

They had been near her many times over the years, but she had never seen them close distance in this way. She felt frightened, and realized that although they often startled her, they had never before scared her.

"Why are you doing this?" she asked, hearing the tremor in her voice. "I'm just going to see Brad!"

Her mother seemed to shake her head, just slightly. They came closer still, and she began to feel cold.

Closer yet, and now the air was icy. She shivered. "Don't!" she whispered.

She turned in blind panic, knocking over a vase that crashed to the floor behind her. She ran to the French doors leading to the deck and wrenched them open. Crossing the deck in quick strides, she gripped the railing and took great gulps of air. The night was cooler now, but still warmer than she had felt in her room.

"Amanda?"

She turned to see Tyler, who must have been standing there all along. Shade was next to him, looking at her with his head cocked to one side.

"Are you all right?" Tyler asked, moving toward her. "I heard something crash—are you all right?" Somewhere inside the house, an intercom tone rang. He ignored it.

"I broke something," she said, trembling. "A big vase."

"It doesn't matter," he said, coming closer still, almost touching her now.

His cell phone rang.

"Answer it," she said, thinking that if someone was dying, she was not going to be the one who kept that person from speaking his last thoughts.

"It's Alex," he said, puzzled. He answered. "Hello, Alex, what is it?"

He looked at Amanda with a slight smile as he said, "Everything's fine. I'm afraid I knocked over a vase. . . . Yes, I appreciate your vigilance. Everything all right otherwise? . . . Good, I'm glad the two of you are watching over Brad. . . . Yes. . . . Good night, then."

He put the phone away.

"Thanks for covering for me," she said, "but if she's with Ron, he'll know who's breaking things."

"It's none of Ron's business, is it? Besides, I don't think he'll tell on you. It doesn't matter."

"You keep saying that, but you don't even know which vase I broke. I think it was an antique."

"Were you hurt?"

"No."

"Then everything that was of value to me in that room remains unscathed."

She smiled.

"What happened?" he said quietly. "What frightened you? Was it what I gave you to read? If so—"

"No, no! I'm glad you gave that to me. Thank you for trusting me."

"I believe I'm the one who should thank you."

He was looking down at her, and she could not mistake what she saw in his eyes. She held her breath, certain that in another moment he would touch her, perhaps even kiss her.

He did reach for her, then dropped his hand. She allowed herself to breathe again, and wondered if she should make the first move. She was distracted as Shade came rushing toward them. Amanda froze, but the dog continued past them.

"Becoming more like me after all, are you, Tyler?" a voice said, startling them both.

Tyler turned, keeping her sheltered behind him.

"I believe that's the worst insult you've given me, Colby," Tyler said.

Colby laughed.

"Colby?" Amanda said, stepping out from behind Tyler. What was he doing here?

"We meet again," Colby said, eyeing her up and down. "Although if I'd known how delightful you look in a nightgown . . ."

Tyler took a step forward. "It's been a long while, Colby, but if you think the outcome might be different this time—"

Colby raised a hand to his jaw in rueful reminiscence, shook his head, and laughed again. "Temper, temper, Captain Hawthorne. Just for that, I don't think I'll tell you what I've learned."

"Get out," Tyler said. "You're a damned liar, so I don't care to hear your stories."

"Damned, certainly," he agreed. "But aren't you, as well?"

"Shade," Tyler said.

"Now, now," Colby said. "You know Shade will protect you if I truly try to harm you, but he has no interest in me otherwise. Really, Tyler, I hesitate to question your manners, but I do wonder if living in America has been good for you."

"Get out," Tyler said. "Must I say it a third time?"

Colby looked at Amanda, then back at Tyler. He smiled. "Miss Clarke doesn't seem to feel so strongly. In fact, she looks curious about me."

She was indeed, but she wasn't going to do anything to help Colby upset Tyler. She stayed quiet.

Colby gave a little bow. "You know, as curious as I am about her in return, I think I will leave—but you might want to keep Miss Clarke with you, Tyler. Otherwise I may come back to renew my acquaintance with her."

He walked around the corner of the deck.

"Is he gone?" she whispered to Tyler.

"Yes," he said, still staring after him, as was Shade.

"How did he get in here, past your security?"

"A knack of his," he said absently. Then in a tight voice, "How did you meet him?"

"At Rebecca's party."

"Rebecca's party?" He frowned. "I didn't see him there."

"I think he left before . . . before we did."

He turned back to her and seemed to come out of whatever dark thoughts were on his mind. "I apologize for the fright that must have given you. Are you all right?"

"Yes," she said, but shivered.

He put an arm around her and said, "Let's go inside." He started to steer her toward her room, then stopped. "I have a question to ask of you, Amanda, and I hope you know you can answer honestly. I have no doubt that if I take you back to your room tonight, Colby will . . . will get past my security again, and . . . visit you." His face showed a kind of grim determination as he said, "If you would prefer to wait for him . . ."

"No."

He visibly relaxed. "Then I have a suggestion to make, and I hope you will understand that my reason for making it is your protection. You know that I don't need sleep?"

"Yes—except with the fevers, right?"

"Yes, but this has nothing to do with the fevers. If you would allow it, I would watch over you tonight."

"Watch over me?"

"What I'm asking is—would you please sleep in my room tonight? I'll be near you, but I promise I won't—I won't impose on you."

Telling him that it would hardly be an imposition didn't seem like such a great idea. Obviously, he didn't exactly have the hots for her, since he was able to suggest that she sleep in his bed—alone. And when she thought about it, why should someone with a couple hundred years of experience want anything to do with her? He probably thought of her as a child. This offer of watching over her was one indication of how likely it was that that was indeed how he viewed her.

Her pride nearly made her refuse the offer. Then she thought of returning to her room, and the ghosts, and Colby's threat.

She'd be near Tyler. He wouldn't let her come to harm. And maybe, if they were able to talk a little, she'd understand him better.

"All right," she said.

"Thank you," he said, and she could hear his relief.

If there was a little awkwardness in the moments when she got into the bed, that became secondary to a moment of sweet pleasure when he sat next to her and combed his fingers through her hair.

"Good night, Amanda," he said, and lightly kissed her temple before turning off the bedside lamp.

"Good night, Tyler," she said as he stood. She inhaled the scent of him from the pillow and smiled ruefully to herself in the darkness. *You are pathetic,* she told herself, but inhaled again.

By the moonlight, she could see him standing near the doors leading to the deck. She could just make out his features.

"How long do you think you will live here?"

"I don't usually stay anywhere more than half a dozen years. Ten years at most."

"This is L.A., Tyler. No one ages."

"I will admit that it is a little easier to have my . . . differences . . . go unnoticed in a big city, or any place where people live out their lives without paying much attention to their neighbors, but eventually I'll have to pull up stakes."

"People in Southern California move often, too," she said. "Ron's grandfather was the only one of our neighbors who lived here for more than five or six years."

"That may be so, but over time—well, the bureaucracy catches on. I can't, for example, look as if I'm twenty-four on all my DMV records or passports."

"Oh. What do you do?"

"Let's just say I've become as good a forger as Adrian ever was, and if you'd like to visit some of the cemeteries where I'm supposedly buried as my own ancestor, it will be quite a tour. I differ from Adrian in that I did not murder anyone to fill a coffin." He paused. "I will admit that this age of computer records has made it a little more difficult, but I have managed."

"You do know that Ron's an excellent hacker, don't you?"

He smiled. "Yes. We've found it an area of mutual interest. And—I am fortunate because some of the people I've helped have been willing to help me without asking a lot of questions."

"Or come to work for you, like Alex and Ben?"

"Although I pay them, I do regard them more as loyal friends than employees." He paused. "I say that knowing that in another five or ten years, I'll have to abandon them. Keep this in mind, Amanda—sooner rather than later, I'll have to pull up roots."

He couldn't deliver the message any plainer than that, could he?

She felt a kind of despair, then told herself to grow a spine. He had already told her more about himself than he had told anyone else. If he didn't care about her, he wouldn't have brought her into his bed—even if he wasn't in it with her. Yet.

32

Tyler asked himself if he had lost his mind.

He wanted nothing more than to crawl in next to her and make love to her all night.

He could think of nothing that would be more disastrous.

He was—to understate the case—an old man. She might see him as young, might even feel as drawn to him as he was to her. But he was constantly aware that his youthfulness was a charade.

And if he ignored that, what could he suppose would happen in the very near future? She would age, and he would not. That might not bother her at first, but eventually it could not help but affect her—and would most likely subject her to ridicule.

She would die, and he would not—thinking of it was nearly unbearable.

Suppose they decided to seize whatever moments they could find? She had lived all her life here. Being with him would require her to live with constant upheaval.

He thought of all of these objections, and more, and still wanted her, was tempted to be with her, consequences be damned.

Suddenly, Shade came racing into the room, and Amanda gave a little scream. Shade halted near the bed and started barking—while staring at the far wall.

"Shade!"

He stopped barking but continued to growl ferociously at the wall.

Tyler turned the light on but couldn't see what was bothering the dog.

Tyler turned back to Amanda, who had leaped from the bed and was cringing in the far corner of the room, her face paper white.

"It's not you," he said quickly, and took her into his arms. He held her and tried again to get Shade's attention. Had the dog lost his mind?

"Let him growl," she said, peering over Tyler's shoulder.

"I know you're trying to get used to him," Tyler said, "but really, this is too much to ask—I don't know what's gotten into him. He usually only does this in cemeteries, and then only rarely. He growled a couple of times during our walk tonight."

"Ghosts," she said.

"Well, I've never seen them myself, but that's my theory, yes."

"It's not a theory," she said, her voice a little stronger. In fact, she seemed to be over her initial shock. "Good dog, Shade! Keep them away!"

Shade gave a quick wag of his tail but kept growling.

"Them?" Tyler asked in dismay.

"My parents and my aunt and uncle," she said angrily. "Who have no business being here right now!"

One part of his brain recognized that he was experiencing a rare emotion: fear. The rest was employing every ounce of his willpower to keep him standing there.

"Your parents?" he said faintly.

She looked at him. "You will not convince me you are scared of ghosts! You just went walking in a cemetery after midnight!"

"Shade protects me from them on those walks," he said as Shade's growl grew louder. *And will protect me now.* The thought calmed him. Shade was with him, no ghost would be able to harm him.

"Protects you? You can't be killed, right?"

"There are worse things," he said. "Ghosts present a particular hazard to my kind."

"What hazard?"

"They see my kind as caught between their world and the world of the living. They would have me live an existence closer to theirs instead of this one."

Amanda stared toward the wall, then said to those she saw there, "I would never forgive you for that! Never!"

The room grew colder, and he felt her shiver. He held on to Amanda, determined that just as Shade protected him, he would protect her.

Shade stopped growling.

"They're still here," Amanda whispered. "But they seem to be staying put."

Shade settled near the foot of the bed. Amanda had grown pensive, and Tyler watched her face as his heartbeat returned to normal. He should let go now, he told himself. He held on to her as he led her back to the bed, then reluctantly released her. She got back under the covers, scooted to the middle of the mattress, and patted the top of the comforter.

He resisted for half a second before sitting down next to her.

"If a ghost attacked you—you'd become a ghost, too?" she asked. "You would die?"

"Not exactly. As I understand it, ghosts aren't all alike. If I allow a certain type of ghost to approach me, it can have a kind of persuasive power over me. It would try to change my nature to one closer to its own. And since I can't die—well, I'd become like Colby."

"Like Colby?" She swallowed hard. "He's not human?"

"That's hard to answer. Colby isn't a ghost, but he's also not fully one of my kind either—and he's certainly not merely human. He has some of the powers of each—he got past my security because he can appear and disappear at will, show up at one place, then another. Yet he doesn't have the invisibility of a ghost—he can't hide his presence from the living in that way. Like me, he is in his own body. His skin, were you to touch it, would feel like that of anyone—solid, warm-blooded. He has my powers of agelessness, of recovery, but he can't hear the thoughts of the dying."

"So what is he?"

"A creature completely devoted to pleasure and mischief, as nearly as I can tell." He fell silent, thinking of Colby's visit. "I really handled things the wrong way tonight. Colby loves to provoke, and I allowed him to provoke me. He's older than I am, and far more experienced in finding another person's weaknesses. Lately I've worried that he's in trouble or needs to tell me something, but I haven't controlled my temper long enough to allow us to reach a point where he could confide in me. I should know by now that in any encounter, first he has to try to push my buttons, just to have his fun. It's his nature."

"What makes you think he's in trouble?"

"The number of times he's been in contact." He paused, then said, "Perhaps he's happy in some way I don't comprehend. But lately, I think he's regretted giving up his usefulness. He's a man without a purpose, in essence. Agelessness is not an existence I could bear without a purpose. And I do not envy ghosts, who may be devoted to some purpose, but are unable to do much about it."

"I can understand why you wouldn't want their existence. I have to admit, I haven't really thought about what it's like for the four who haunt me. I've always been fairly sure they weren't real."

"How long have you seen them?"

"When I woke up in the hospital, after the accident, they were in the room. Ron and I have been trying to come up with an explanation for them for years. At first, I thought it was just my head injury, and then I thought it was guilt, you know, especially because they wear evening clothes, dressed like they were on that last night. But they weren't even buried in those clothes." She glanced at the dog. "It's kind of a relief to know Shade sees them. I've thought I was crazy."

"You've had to cope with seeing ghosts for eight years?"

"Yes. Only those four ghosts. They don't harm me. They don't speak. Just startle me now and then. I'm the only one they bother. For whatever reason." She frowned. "What is the reason? I mean, why do they hang around me?"

He thought for a while, then said, "They may be protecting you."

Something else was troubling him, though. "All these years, Ron is the only other person who has known about them?"

"Yes. I once tried telling Rebecca and Brad about them. Years ago. They really didn't let up about that for a long time."

"You told me they blame you for the accident. Do you blame yourself?"

"Most days, no. Some days, I think I should have stood up to them. Rebecca says, 'You knew they were drunk, why didn't you insist they call a cab?' And I don't really have a good answer for that one."

Tyler looked toward the wall, at which Shade was still staring. "Have you asked them if they blame you?"

"I don't think there's much I haven't asked them. But they don't respond."

"Do you blame her for your deaths?" Tyler asked, hoping he was looking somewhere near them.

Her eyes seemed to follow some movement, and she started crying.

"Amanda—what's wrong?"

"They shook their heads."

He took her hand. "I'm sure they never blamed you."

"They're agreeing with you." She wiped her tears away with her free hand, then said, "They've never made so much as a gesture in my presence until now. Just stared at me. Ask them why the hell they're answering you when they've never answered me!"

He did so.

"Now they're shrugging. I guess they don't know."

"Is Amanda's guess right?" Tyler asked, speaking to the ghosts. "You don't understand?"

"Um, I don't think they know how to reply. My aunt and my mom are nodding and my dad and my uncle are shaking their heads."

"Oh, I see," Tyler said. "Shrug if you don't understand why it is you can't speak to her."

"They're shrugging."

"But I'm acting as some sort of bridge between you and Amanda?"

"They're nodding."

"Why are you here this evening?" he asked.

"They're pointing between us," she said. "Because we're together?" she asked indignantly.

Tyler repeated the question.

She turned to Tyler. "It's a little phony of them to act as if they care about me now."

But they did care about her. Of that, Tyler felt sure. They didn't blame her for their deaths, so they weren't haunting her out of vengeance. They lingered to protect her. And here he was, sitting on a bed next to their daughter, and he could not deny that he desired her. No wonder they had chosen this moment to appear.

He looked down into her tear-stained face. "Are you all right?" he asked. "Is there a way to get rid of them?"

"Believe me, if I knew of one, I would have used it a long time ago."

"I wonder if there is some way I can help you with this."

She studied his face. He had already become used to this, he realized, this straightforward, unabashed examination of him. Hours ago, he had decided to let her take her time to see whatever she could see in his eyes, the set of his mouth, whatever else it was she chose to stare at, and had not taken offense. Of course, it gave him a chance to study her in return.

"You aren't making me a project, are you? I mean, I'm not just some poor soul in need of assistance?"

He smiled. "No. Far from it."

Her attention was diverted. "They're gone."

He breathed a sigh of relief.

"Sorry about that."

"You have nothing to apologize for. Are you going to be okay?"

"Yes, thanks."

He stood up. He wondered if he was imagining the disappointment he saw on her face. He turned out the light and settled on the floor next to her.

"Maybe I shouldn't stay in here," she said. "I'm afraid of what the ghosts might do to you."

"Shade won't let them do anything to me. But we need to figure out what they want, I think."

She brooded in silence over that. After a few minutes, she said, "I feel guilty, taking your bed from you."

"Don't. I'm fine. Truly."

Eventually, she fell asleep.

He listened to the rhythm of her breathing, watched her face in repose.

He did not doubt that something had drawn them together—his ability to free up her communication with her ghosts was just one more sign of that. He was equally sure that despite the strong attraction he felt for her, he had a choice in the matter. He simply had no desire to look elsewhere. Something about Amanda just felt . . . right.

He thought of her acceptance of him, and felt a kind of contentment unlike any he had ever experienced. Something more than gratitude—although he was indeed grateful.

He desired her, but he wasn't going to hurt her, or fail to proceed with caution. He would not spend the next two hundred years regretting carelessness with her.

Shade got up and stood next to him long enough to accept a few soft scratches on the ears and chin, then left to stand on the deck again. There, he intently watched something out in the woods. The ghosts must have relocated. Or perhaps Colby was enjoying himself by teasing the dog. If so, he wouldn't get away with that for long.

It was nearly dawn when Shade came in to settle beside him.

Tyler watched the sky lighten—just before, contrary to all his intentions, he fell asleep.

33

He awoke before she did, showered and dressed, and took a phone call from a doctor he had worked with in the past. He returned to the bedroom in time to see her stirring into wakefulness. She smiled up at him and stretched in a feline way—uncurling to extend her arms, back arched, toes pointed. He felt his mouth go dry.

"Good morning," she said.

"Good morning."

Her eyebrows drew together. "You're dressed. Do you have to leave?"

"Not right away, but yes."

"Can I go with you?"

"Sorry," he said. "For my own part, I wish you could. But for this gentleman—"

"It's okay," she said, a little too quickly. "I don't want to suffocate you."

"It's not that at all," he said, trying to rid himself of images of certain wonderful ways to find himself "suffocated."

"Do you have time to have breakfast together?"

"Yes, that would be great." He called Ben on the intercom and asked that they be served in the private parlor off his bedroom.

When he took her into it, he said, "Having sitting rooms off bedrooms is something from another era, I suppose, but it's a feature of the past that I find comfortable."

If Ben was surprised to be serving a young woman who was dressed only in a nightgown and a robe, he did not betray it by so much as a smile. But when Tyler passed the kitchens with Shade on his way out of the house, he heard Ben whistling—as much a first as the breakfast arrangements.

He drove to a hospital near downtown Los Angeles. As arranged by the doctor who had called, he was taken to a ward where a homeless man lay dying.

The dying man's breathing was irregular. His gray hair lay in long, thin strands on his pillow. His frame was thin and covered by wrinkled, leathery skin. His cheeks were hollow and his open mouth revealed that his few remaining teeth were badly decaying.

Tyler had never seen him before in his life.

"Dr. Riley said you might know who he is?" the nurse asked hopefully.

"Yes," Tyler said, taking the dying man's rough hand in his own.

Horace Dillon, and I've got family in Orange County. He gave Tyler the name and phone number of a niece who lived in Newport Beach. *She doesn't know I've been living like this—haven't seen her in about three years—but tell her I got enough saved to pay for my own burial.*

"His name is Horace Dillon," Tyler said, and repeated the contact information for the niece, along with a warning that she would have no idea that her uncle was homeless or had been ill. The nurse hurried away to make the call.

Kind of you to be here with me. My niece won't get here in time, but that's all right. We weren't all that close, but she'll see I get a headstone and she's welcome to anything left after that. She's married to a wealthy man, but a burden is a burden, and I never wanted to be one to them.

There was, Tyler noticed, no rancor in this. Horace gave Tyler the banking and burial plan information his niece would need.

Before you go, though, Mr. Hawthorne, I got a little information to give to you.

Thank you—please feel free to call me Tyler.

Always hard for me to address my seniors by their first names, but all right. First, I must say I pity you.

He was not the first of the dying to say this to Tyler, but today it rankled.

There's no need, Mr. Dillon. Right now, I'm the happiest I've been in centuries.

Because of the young woman, you mean. But that's why I pity you. I wouldn't want to have to make the decision you'll be making.

Tyler nearly let go of the man's hand.

Don't blame the messenger! Shouldn't have to say that to you, of all people. Now, I only have a few seconds here, so listen. It's up to you. You've longed for a way to be where I am, but you know you have to pass this work on. She's the one, if you're ready. Give her the ring. Then let Shade find the other dog.

Other dog?

You already know what I mean. The question is, will it be her or you?

What?

She's the one, Tyler. The next one to do your work. If you want to give her the job—up to you. Oh, and beware of an old enemy. That's all I can say, except, thanks again for being here with me. I wouldn't have wanted to be alone. Keep the faith, Tyler.

"Wait!" Tyler cried out. "No! No!"

The nurse and a doctor came rushing in, and after a flurry of effort that no one expected to revive the patient, the nurse gently told him what he already knew, that his "friend" was dead. Tyler knew she mistook his stunned reaction for grief. With shaking hands, he gave her the bank and burial plan information for Horace Dillon's niece.

"Don't you want to wait for her?" the nurse asked.

"She doesn't know me," he said, and left.

He was never sure afterward how he found his way back to the van, because he was lost in a fog of disbelief. He crawled into the back of the van, knowing it would not be safe—for others—if he drove in this state. Shade watched him anxiously.

"Did you know?" Tyler asked as Shade moved closer. "Did you know from the start that I was supposed to hand this—this misery on to her?"

Shade made a soft keening sound.

Tyler put an arm around the great dog's shoulders, burying his face in his fur. "I can't," he whispered. "I can't damn her to this."

34

As she showered and dressed, Amanda decided that as much as she wanted more than slumber parties with Tyler, sleeping near him had left her feeling surprisingly contented.

She found a book about the Napoleonic Wars in Tyler's library, and took it to Brad's room, where she offered to relieve Ron and Alex from their watch over her cousin.

They thanked her and smiled at her in a way that instantly made her believe the whole household was probably aware of the fact that she had spent the night with Tyler. Amanda quickly dismissed any thought of explaining that they were probably assuming too much. Let them assume.

Brad's bruises had emerged, changing to dark purple, making his condition look even worse than when she had checked on him the night before. But the swelling was going down and Alex assured her that he had been sleeping quietly.

She had been sitting there for two hours, so lost in thoughts of the previous evening that she had not made much progress in the history book, when she heard Brad murmuring in his sleep. His eyebrows were drawn together, and his body began to twitch beneath the sheets. He made small sounds of distress, as if he were caught in an unhappy dream.

"It's all right," she said softly, trying to soothe him without waking him.

His eyes opened, but for a moment he did not seem to see her.

"It's all right," she repeated, setting the book aside.

"Amanda?" He seemed surprised to see her, then looked around the room, puzzled.

She kept her voice low and gentle. "You're at Tyler's house. Remember? I imagine you must feel really stiff and sore today—in fact, you probably feel worse today than yesterday, but I can call someone to help you take a hot shower—that might loosen you up a bit—"

But before she could say more, he had recalled his situation. To her dismay, he burst into tears. "Oh my God . . . oh my God . . . Amanda, I'm so sorry—"

"Don't start that again," she said sharply.

It brought the sobs to an abrupt halt. He looked up at her in surprise.

"I mean it, Brad. Quit it. I had all the remorse I needed from you yesterday. More than enough."

She handed him a tissue, and he wiped his face with it. She studied him for a moment as he calmed down. She was glad to see that his pupils looked normal, that the glazed look was gone. And other than the problems caused by his lips being cut and swollen, his speech was clear—all good signs.

"That's better," she said. "Listen to me. What's most important is that you recover, and you aren't going to do that by getting upset. I'm fine. Better than fine, in fact, and I probably owe some of that to you."

"Amanda, listen to me—I've put you in terrible danger."

"If you're talking about holding that knife to my throat—I guess I didn't believe you really wanted to hurt me. Where were you supposed to take us?"

"Somewhere in the Valley. I was supposed to call to get instructions after we drove over the pass. Evan and Daniel were going to meet me. I—I'm so ashamed, Amanda. I don't know how you can forgive me."

"You were scared. You'd been hurt. You weren't yourself. That's how."

"But, Amanda, about the knife—that's not what I meant about putting you in danger."

She raised her eyebrows.

"Well, yes, that was putting you in danger, but that's not the worst of it. They asked me why Tyler had left the party, and I told them it was because of you."

"What? That's so not true."

"Yes, it is!" he protested. "When you took off, he started to follow you out the door. Called out to you. Rebecca tried everything she could think of—including practically wrestling him into staying. But he wasn't there for more than a few minutes."

She thought this over. "He didn't follow me. He rode ahead of me on his motorcycle."

"Maybe he didn't want you to feel nervous. It's not as if there's anyplace to go off that road other than the freeway."

She decided not to tell him about Tyler's desert retreat.

"He had to know you were headed back home," Brad said.

"Hmm. I'll ask him about it."

"Whatever! The thing is, Amanda, now they know about you."

"Don't blame yourself, Brad. If they're after Tyler, they would have connected me to him sooner or later."

"What's going on between you two?"

"We're friends. Maybe more than that. I don't know."

"I knew he liked you, but you didn't seem that interested in him. Tyler said you were staying here for your safety, but it sounds as if—"

Before he finished his sentence, the bedroom door opened. Rebecca stood in the doorway, a look of shock on her face. She hurried to Brad's bedside. "God almighty, Brad! Did Tyler do this to you? I swear I'm going to call the cops!"

"No!" Brad said. "Don't you dare call the police! It wasn't Tyler!"

"Rebecca, calm down," Amanda said quickly. "Brad needs peace and quiet, not drama."

Rebecca turned on her. "Oh? And who died and made you Nurse Ratched?"

Before Amanda could answer her, Alex came into the room and said quietly, "Leave this patient's room immediately or I will personally throw your bony ass over the front gate."

Rebecca seemed utterly dismayed. Amanda wondered if it was because Rebecca was, for once, the second most beautiful woman in the room, or if it was the fact that Alex clearly was relishing the possibility of the gate toss. Rebecca turned toward the bed and said, "Brad?"

"It's okay, Alex," he said. "Just a misunderstanding."

"All right," Alex said, "but Tyler left very clear instructions that if your sister arrived here and her visit was upsetting to you, we should escort her off the premises."

"Maybe you should come back later," Brad said to his sister.

Rebecca's expression changed. "No, please—okay, look, I'm sorry. I'm just worried and upset! Which I think would be totally understandable! Please don't make me leave, Brad."

"Okay, but get a grip, all right?"

She looked ready to object, forced herself not to speak, and nodded.

He said to Alex, "We'll be okay now."

"Yes, I'd like to be alone with my brother," Rebecca said.

"No way in hell," Alex said with a smile.

"I'll stay with them," Amanda offered. "It will be all right."

Alex hesitated, then nodded. "All right. If you need me, call. I mean that. Tyler won't be happy with me if Brad suffers some kind of setback."

"I'm his sister!" Rebecca said.

"Right," Alex said, "the one who was too drunk to notice he was missing for a couple of days." With that parting shot, she walked off.

Rebecca did have that puffy, day-after-the-party look. Not at her best. She was probably massively hungover.

"So what happened to you?" Rebecca asked when the three of them were alone.

Brad looked down at the bedding and began to fidget with the comforter. Without looking up, he said, "Some people I know turned out not to be so nice."

"Who?"

"You don't know them."

"Who?" she persisted.

"These people aren't playing around, Rebecca! I don't want you to go after them!"

"It won't be necessary for Rebecca to go after them," a low voice said. Amanda turned to see Tyler standing in the doorway.

35

Tyler!" Amanda said with relief. But as she looked at his face, she sensed that something was troubling him. She wanted nothing more than to take him aside and ask him what was on his mind.

"Tyler!" Rebecca said, and launched herself toward him, pulling him into an embrace.

He managed to evade a kiss. He gave Amanda a look of such helplessness, she couldn't stifle a laugh.

He disengaged himself from Rebecca—not without a little difficulty—and came to Amanda's side. "You all right?" he murmured, and put an arm around her waist. He held her close.

Now what does this mean? she wondered. Was he just trying to get Rebecca to back off? But he seemed anxious about something, and she doubted it was Rebecca. So she smiled up at him and said, "Absolutely fine. But I'm worried about Brad."

"How are you doing, Brad?" he said.

"I'm feeling a lot better," Brad said. "I—maybe everyone could give me a minute to shower and get dressed, and we could talk in another room?"

"Certainly," Tyler said. "But are you feeling up to that? It would probably be better for you to move around a little if you're feeling strong enough, but don't push yourself. We still haven't learned what substances you were given—the doctor said that may take some time."

"Substances?" Rebecca said.

"Yes," Brad said. "I was drugged. Actually, while I didn't enjoy it, that was the best part of what they did to me. It eased the pain a little."

"Brad—"

"I know you have a lot of questions, Rebecca. Everyone else does, too. But why don't all of you get out and let me dress, and we'll talk more in a few minutes."

The wait for Brad was tense but did not result in violence, Amanda was pleased to note. Ron and Alex sat close to each other on one sofa. Tyler and Amanda sat next to each other, if not quite so close, on the sofa directly across from it. Shade lay at their feet. Amanda still sensed some uneasiness in Tyler, but this was not the time to ask about it.

Rebecca paced, arms folded, and scowled at Amanda as she walked in one direction, at Alex on the return.

Brad arrived, and Rebecca watched as he moved slowly and stiffly into the room. He eyed a big soft chair with misgiving. Tyler said, "Would you prefer a wooden chair?"

"Yes, thanks. That one looks as if it would be wonderful until I tried to get up out of it."

Tyler stood up and moved a wooden chair forward, and helped Brad ease himself carefully into it.

Rebecca, back to looking more worried than angry, brought Brad a cushion for his back and pulled up a second chair to be at his side.

Amanda asked for some notebook paper, which Tyler brought to her before returning to sit beside her, again not quite touching her, as if he was determined to concentrate on what Brad was saying without distraction.

So she took notes, as did Alex. While Brad told his story of meeting a man named Eduardo Leblanc, getting help with his gambling debts, and all that followed, no one interrupted him. But when he described the bizarre events in the basement, Rebecca tried to convince him that he must have hallucinated all of that as a result of the drugs he had been given.

Amanda wasn't so sure. Brad's terror about that was certainly real—at one point he had grown very white faced and started shaking. When he refused Tyler's offer to discuss this another time, saying that he wanted them to know what they were up against, Amanda began to think that she had underestimated her cousin in a number of ways.

"What did this man in the basement want?" Tyler asked.

"I'm not sure it was a man. Human, I mean." Brad shut his eyes tightly.

"Oh for—"

"Let him tell it as he experienced it, Rebecca," Tyler said, and she subsided.

"I don't know how he did it. With his mind, it seemed to me—as if he could get inside my head! I never felt him touch me, but—my God, the pain . . ."

He started shaking.

"Let's move on to something else," Amanda pleaded. "He can tell us more about that later."

"Tell me more about this Eduardo," Alex said.

"Everyone knows Eduardo," Rebecca said before Brad could reply. "He can't have any connection to this. He's fabulously wealthy. He's always at parties."

"Was he at yours?" Tyler asked.

"No," she said, pouting a little.

"He hasn't been around lately," Brad said. "And his cell phone is disconnected."

"When was the last time either of you saw him?" Alex asked.

They thought for a moment. "A week or so before we met you, Tyler," Brad said. "After that, I only had contact with Daniel and Evan."

"So you never discussed Tyler with Eduardo, but Evan and Daniel asked you for information about him?" Alex asked.

"Right. The first time, all I was supposed to do was to call them when Tyler was out of town."

"The break-in!" Amanda said.

"They robbed your house?" Brad asked in dismay.

"No," Tyler said quickly. "They did break in, but nothing was taken."

"I was so stupid! I'm—I'm so, so sorry."

"Apology accepted," Tyler said. "It was really not a problem. So forgive yourself for that."

"Not so easy," Brad murmured.

"What else did they ask you to do?" Alex asked.

"Just one other thing—it had to do with the party. I was supposed to try to make sure Tyler came to it, to let them know when he got there, and to call if he left before they showed up."

"Do you know that they tried to killed Tyler that night, and almost killed Amanda, too?" Ron asked. "There was an accident—"

Brad's face showed shock. "What?"

"We're both okay," Tyler said, shooting a warning look at Ron. "Please don't add that to your worries, Brad. I think we should probably thank you, really."

"Thank me? For almost getting you killed?"

"But we weren't killed and we're both fine," he said. "We got to know each other because of that accident, so yes, thank you."

Brad seemed to withdraw into his own thoughts. Amanda could see that Rebecca was both unhappy and curious. Fortunately, she stayed silent.

"This Evan and Daniel weren't participating in the party itself, right?" Alex asked.

"Right."

"Tell me what went on right before they took you."

He described going out for a walk around the grounds on the evening of the party.

"Is there anyone else who might have seen the men who took you?"

"Only Colby."

"Colby . . . ," Amanda said, and looked at Tyler, who was frowning.

"Yeah," Brad went on. "He was out by the guesthouse, smoking a cig. He was getting ready to leave."

"You and Amanda know this Colby?" Alex asked Tyler, not having missed the exchange of glances between the two of them.

"Yes. He will be difficult to contact."

"Could he have something against you?"

"We've known each other a long time," Tyler said evasively. "This isn't his style. Brad, is there any way he would have known you would be walking around outside just then?"

Brad thought, then shook his head. "No, I didn't tell anyone I was going outside, and he couldn't have followed me from the main house because he wasn't there when I left it. I don't think he had been standing there that long. He had been busy with some ladies in the guesthouse."

"I still don't like it," Alex said.

"I'll pursue Colby on my own," Tyler said. "Brad and Rebecca, do either of you know Eduardo's address?"

Brad and Rebecca exchanged a look. "No," Brad said. "I haven't been to his place. But—well, you know, you see someone at one party, and invite them to the next, or you text or call or e-mail."

"Who introduced you to him?"

"I'm sure someone must have," Brad said, but he couldn't remember who it might have been.

"Brad, you borrowed thousands of dollars from someone you didn't know any better than that?" Amanda said. "What if he was some sort of criminal? And why didn't you come to me? I would have helped you."

"Well, obviously he is some kind of criminal. But I didn't go to him, he offered it to me. And it was just until my next payment from the trust came through," Brad said. "And as for borrowing from you, I figured you were having similar problems."

"What! Gambling?"

"No, but—but your clothes! And you drive an old car and—"

"Not because I can't afford a new one! And some of us are not shopaholics."

"Let's get back to this Eduardo," Ron said quickly. "You haven't seen him for a while?"

"No. Like I said, I last saw him just before I met Tyler. That's when I met Daniel and Evan." He shifted uneasily in his chair.

"Are you all right, Brad?" Amanda asked. "Do you need to lie down again?"

"No, I'm okay," he said, but she thought he looked uncomfortable, and not just at the reminder of the robbery.

"Maybe whoever hurt Brad did the same to Eduardo," Rebecca said.

"Perhaps," Tyler said. "But if he introduced you to Evan and Daniel, I have my doubts. Alex, what do you think?"

"Hard to say. He paid your debt in cash, Brad?"

"Yes."

"Let me get that cell phone number from you and I'll see what I can do. Also—if you and your sister can give me the names and numbers of other people who knew him—"

"Certainly not!" Rebecca said. "I don't think our friends would appreciate it very much if I gave out their numbers to a snooping—"

"I'll help you with that," Ron interrupted. "I know most of their friends, and I couldn't care less about what they'd 'appreciate.'"

"Thanks, Ron," Alex said, smiling at him.

"I'll ask around, too," Brad said.

"Thanks," Alex said, "but I think you should lie low for the time being. It will help us to protect you while you're recovering. Tell me again what you were supposed to do if the kidnapping had gone better."

Amanda could see Brad blush under his bruises. "I was supposed to make Amanda drive. We were supposed to get on the freeway heading toward the Valley. He—the thing in the basement—said when we got to the freeway, to call to get instructions on how to get to the next place. He said Tyler had something that belonged to him." He glanced uneasily at Tyler.

"Did he say what that was?" Tyler asked.

"No. I asked and—he said I was 'impertinent.'" He shivered. "He punished me for asking. That was the worst—the worst I've ever felt. So I didn't ask anything more, and then—I don't know, I remember Daniel came back to the cellar, and the thing gave him some orders, and he mixed something up, and made me drink it. Mostly what the thing in the basement wanted was for me to bring Tyler to him. And he wanted to know if Tyler and Amanda were in love."

"What?" Amanda said.

"I told him I thought you were fighting, you know, because you left the party and all. That seemed to amuse him." He shivered again.

"You say he gave you a phone number to call," Alex said "Tell me that number, too."

He did. Brad was clearly tiring, and this time when Amanda suggested that they let him sleep for a while, Tyler quickly agreed that it would be best. Brad made a token protest but allowed Rebecca to talk him into taking a break.

"I'll sit with you, if you'd like," she said.

Amanda wasn't sure that would be restful, but Brad seemed happy to know he wouldn't be alone.

"He's still afraid," Ron said when they had left the room.

"He probably will be for some time," Alex said. "They really worked him over."

"He didn't owe them all that much," Ron said.

"Oh, I don't think this ever had anything to do with money," Alex said. She looked at Amanda and Tyler. "I'm just trying to figure out if these guys are really after Tyler or Amanda, or both of you—and why."

36

Daniel put the broom away and took out the mop and bucket. He filled the bucket with a pine-scented cleaner and hot water, and went to work on the kitchen floor he had just swept. He repeated the process three times before he felt there was a slim possibility that he might eat in this room again.

The night after the small beetles arrived, it had been cockroaches. They were bigger than the other beetles—and faster. They had made a rattling sound, like a thousand castanets, as they surged together toward the cellar door.

Last night, he would have welcomed the cockroaches back. Crickets had been called to the house. Multiplied thousands of times over, their high-pitched chirps maddened Daniel and Evan. Cleaning up a big load of cricket frass was not the worst thing he had ever been assigned, but he wished his lordship would stop bringing insects into the house.

Daniel thought nearly constantly of escape, without being able to bring himself to make the attempt. Still, as each night went by, he knew "Mr. Adrian" was growing stronger. If he didn't leave now, would he ever be able to evade his lordship?

He thought of Eduardo, who had been destroyed by the dog. Many times, Daniel wondered if Eduardo had intended it to happen.

The day of the attack, Eduardo had told Daniel a story, confided in him as never before. He spoke of being hired on to the dive crew of a ship that worked mostly in the Caribbean. Treasure hunters.

He told him what had been discovered in the wreckage of the *Morgan Bray,* that the voice in the chest he'd recovered had ordered him to travel to the Turks and Caicos Islands.

The voice continued to speak to him, a voice he knew only he could hear. It said it was the spirit of a man who had been a pirate for a time, and sailed those seas. It guided him to a place on one of the Caicos and told him to dig. Just as the voice had said, he found a cache of jewelry and gold coins.

His discovery made him a wealthy man, and the voice led him to even greater wealth. But soon he began to realize that leaving was not an option. Any attempt to leave "his lordship" resulted in a crippling pain that ran down his spine like a rod of fire. If he was foolish enough to attempt further resistance, within seconds his testicles would feel as if they were being crushed by an iron hand, a vicelike pressure would be felt at his temples, and his throat would constrict. In less than half a minute, his lordship would easily have Eduardo on his knees, begging forgiveness.

So Eduardo did all he could to make his own life comfortable. He learned that if he was complacent and obedient, he could live in luxury. Although the tuition was often painful, his lordship taught him how to behave in a way that made him an acceptable guest in any household. In effect, he became a jet-setter.

For nearly a decade, his lordship urged him to travel, seeking a certain man who might or might not be calling himself "Tyler Hawthorne." They began in England, researching old records, and then moved on to the United States. Eduardo spent a great deal of time describing the world around him, as if to a blind man, a blind man who had slept for two hundred years.

They searched for any mention of anyone named Tyler Hawthorne, and found many persons with that name, but none was the one his lordship sought. Eduardo found several graves bearing such a name, but his lordship insisted this man would be alive.

In the ninth year of their searches, they learned of a Tyler Hawthorne who had bought an expensive property in Los Angeles.

His lordship commanded that they move nearby. "Not too close, mind you—he may be able to sense my presence, and I want this to be something of a surprise."

His lordship also required a basement, so it took Eduardo even more time to find a home that would suit his needs, because not many homes in Los Angeles had rooms belowground. Finally, though, they had found this house.

His lordship then told Eduardo to recruit two helpers, and described to him his necessities. These must be men who were strong in body but weak in integrity. They must be both desperate and greedy. They must be utterly unattached to family or friends. They must be able to fight, but also be capable of living peaceably in close quarters with others. They should be ignorant, but not stupid. They would, in fact, be much like Eduardo, he said, with one exception. They should have skills as burglars.

When Eduardo told him this part of his story, Daniel had felt angry. But by that time, all the fight had gone out of Eduardo; he took no offense at being called such names. A decade in his lordship's company had left Eduardo as little more than a smiling, obedient husk.

A handsome husk, though, and able by then to make himself at home among the wealthiest in Los Angeles. He was still in his twenties and welcomed at parties. He befriended a young man who was visiting the house nearest Tyler Hawthorne's. He could easily see that Bradley Clarke was insecure and troubled. He soon learned that Bradley had gambling problems. Nothing could be better. Eduardo quickly freed him from financial debt by putting him into another kind of debt entirely.

Daniel and Evan had been easy to recruit. Both were eager to live the promised life of ease in exchange for a small amount of dirty work. If it seemed strange at first, comfort and enormous wages made them willing to overlook the odd requirements of their bizarre employer, a man who took them down to the basement, leading them by candlelight, telling them he was getting messages from an iron box.

Those misunderstandings were soon cleared up.

They learned from Eduardo that his lordship was not pleased with them, since he could not enter their minds as completely as he did Eduardo's—it seemed that only a very few individuals would be subject to that particular horror. However, a new chapter in his lordship's existence was about to begin. After a decade out of the sea, he had found a place where he could, as he phrased it, "begin regeneration." Evan and Daniel were put to work removing the locks.

"Go to the stairs," Eduardo said when the locks were off. "Take the candle with you."

In the far corner, in the darkness, Eduardo opened the iron chest.

The stench was immediate and overpowering, so sharp that it made their eyes water.

"Leave me!" a voice shouted.

It didn't have to ask twice.

Back then, Daniel was never sure what it was that Eduardo brought into the cellar every few nights, but the stench worsened. He mentioned to Eduardo that he was sure someone would call the cops about it.

"He's shielding the house," Eduardo answered dully. "Don't you realize that you only smell it if you open the basement door? It's the same with the screams. No one hears them outside the house."

Daniel knew all about the screams. His, Evan's, Eduardo's.

Now that his lordship could address them directly, he had more power over them, it seemed. Daniel had tried once, when he had been sent miles away on an errand, to go even farther away, to make a run for it. He had not gone far before he felt a kind of craving unlike anything else he had ever known. It was as if his cells had become magnetized, and his lordship was exerting a pull on them. He could think of nothing else, do nothing else, but return.

He had paid an awful price for that experiment. He had not been able to leave his bed for three days.

He thought of that experiment now, of how this bargain had cost him his freedom in a way prison never had. Eduardo had taken the only escape route.

He would never forget the night Eduardo had been killed by the dog.

That dog had surprised Daniel and Evan, but now Daniel wondered if Eduardo had known about the dog all along.

His lordship had been displeased with them when they came back and reported what had happened, although what they could have done differently, Daniel did not know.

Just as now, he did not know what he could do—short of sacrificing himself to the dog—to leave his lordship's employ.

No human could help him, although he found himself wishing one could. Earlier, he thought he saw a man standing at the top of the drive, smoking a cigarette, and he found himself wishing someone—anyone—would notice the smell of the basement or hear the sounds coming from it, or see all the damned bugs running toward it.

But in the next moment the smoker was gone, and he began to wonder if he had imagined him being there in the first place.

Late that night, the voice from the basement called to him, telling him to open the back door.

The spiders wanted in.

37

Five days after Rebecca's arrival, she announced that she would be staying at "the family's house," and although Brad had berated her—saying that it was, as Rebecca knew, Amanda's house, and that Rebecca should apologize and ask Amanda's permission—Amanda quickly cut off what was bound to escalate into another prolonged battle between the two of them, saying that she needed to make a trip back to the house and would be glad to accompany Rebecca there.

Amanda told Tyler of these plans. After seeing that all his objections were having no effect, he said, "All right, then Alex will take you."

"Rebecca will want her car."

"Fine. Alex can drive you down, following her."

Amanda hesitated, then said, "I'm going to make arrangements for a rental car to be delivered."

"You may use the Cooper or the van anytime you'd like."

"To go somewhere alone?"

He didn't answer right away, and she wondered if she had angered him, but she saw no sign of this on his face or even in the way he held himself.

He said, "If you think about what Brad has been through, I doubt you will decide I'm being overly protective when I say that I would prefer—would beg you, in fact—not to go out alone until we discover more about his attackers. However, I would never want you to feel as if you are imprisoned here. My deepest apologies if you have been eager to escape me."

"Escape you! If anyone has been an escape artist lately, it's you."

"If you mean I haven't been here much, I admit that's true. And you know why."

Amanda took a deep breath and let it out slowly. What was she complaining about? The people he helped were dying. He was their last chance to communicate with their loved ones. What need of hers could be greater than theirs?

The last few days had left her unsure of where she stood with him. Even though he was gone most of the day and until late at night, she continued to sleep in his bed, Tyler keeping watch beside her. Twice they had switched places—his work had caused him to become ill with fever and she had refused to let him sleep on the floor. She did her best to comfort him, although each time it passed within an hour or so. He said these episodes had been mild.

Occasionally he had been affectionate—taking her hand, putting an arm around her shoulders, giving her a light kiss on the forehead—and if beneath that affection she had felt some restraint, she only needed to think of her own restraint in the presence of the ghosts. She should be grateful to him—and to Shade—because, until now, the ghosts had made her doubt her own sanity.

But thinking this made her realize that it might be time to trust her own perceptions for once. She looked at him and thought about his past. And his expertise in keeping secrets. Over all those years, what chance did he have to get close to anyone, to confide in anyone?

"Tyler, what became of your valet, Merritt?"

Startled by the change of subject, he said, "He died."

"I had assumed that much. One of the worst aspects of what has happened to you, I am sure. You've had to watch everyone you've loved or cared about die."

"Actually, I have seldom been at the deathbed of a friend. I wasn't at Merritt's. I was in America by then."

"He didn't come here with you?"

"No. We spent almost a year together in England after Lord Varre's death—the death of Marcus deVille, that is. By the end of that time, because of the papers Varre had left to me and the things he had said, I had given more thought to the complications of appearing to be twenty-four forever. To avoid some of those complications, Adrian had either dismissed or murdered his servants after they had been with him a few years—more often the latter. I didn't want to become anything like him."

"You *aren't* anything at all like him!"

He smiled at her vehemence. "Thank you."

Much as it comforted her to see that smile, she knew something had been bothering him lately. But what?

"So," he went on, "having heard tales of this country, I decided to come to America, where English was spoken but I was not known, where I could move often and live without servants. A place with a vast wilderness to recommend it."

"Merritt didn't want to join you?"

"When I first mentioned it, he begged me to take him along. I'm afraid I was a bit underhanded. I purchased a home near that of Widow Makins. I sent him on many errands to ensure that she was being well cared for."

"He married her?"

"Yes, when a decent period of mourning had passed. In those days, that was required. During that year, I considered what I must do regarding his employment. I had already realized that he was an excellent judge of horses and an expert in their care. So I asked him to stay in England as a business partner, and eventually he agreed to do so."

"You never saw him again?"

"Oh, in the first few years, I traveled back to England fairly often." He paused. "But after ten years or so, I heard more and more comments on my youthful appearance. I reached the point of realizing that I needed to say good-bye to my friends and family there. Merritt was happily married and had made a great success of our business, and my brother and his wife were happy with their family. I decided I wanted to remember them in that way, and stopped going to England until the twentieth century, by which time anyone there who had known me had died. In the decades before that return, I wrote to them and tried to be content with staying connected to them through our correspondence."

"That can't have been easy."

"The years when those people were dying were the most difficult time, I think, because I had to let go of relationships that I had formed naturally. By that I mean I had grown close to those people without knowing that I would become such a changed creature. Anyone I met after I first visited the estate of Lord Varre—well, if I met someone new, I was fully aware of what was at risk."

He fell silent, and put his head in his hands.

"So you kept your distance."

"That was for the best," he answered absently.

"Did you grow homesick?"

"Hmm?" He looked up at her and said, "Sorry, I was lost in memories there for a moment. What did you ask?"

"Did you miss England?"

"For a time. When I returned, the England I had known was gone. People, times, places—the world does not stand still. Nothing remains unchanged." He gave her a wry smile. "Other than yours truly."

"I don't believe that's true. Physically, you may be the same, but you can't tell me that you've remained unchanged."

"You're right, of course."

"You've adapted remarkably, really—you know how to use a cell phone and computers and other modern things."

He laughed. "It isn't as if I'm a time traveler, you know. I wasn't suddenly taken from the nineteenth century and dropped into this one. Besides, I confess to a fondness for gadgets. And you are forgetting the desert house."

"No, I don't think I'll ever forget the desert house." She moved closer to him.

He watched her, almost warily, she thought. She took one of his hands.

She stroked his fingers. He seemed to relax a little.

She studied those fingers, and said, "In the papers you gave me, your history—you said you couldn't remove the memento mori—the mourning ring."

"For a long time, I couldn't. Then I found a way."

"How?"

He hesitated, then said, "Colby hinted to me that it was possible. So I started to search for a method. Among Adrian's papers, I found a great many works on sorcery and necromancy. Most of those writings seemed to me to be utter nonsense. But now and again—very rarely, mind you—I came across something that . . ."

She waited, trying to make herself still and quiet so that he would continue. After several moments, he said, "Now and again I would find a passage that almost seemed to call to me. Whatever language it was in, I could read and understand it. You might show me another page in the same work, and I would find it unfathomable.

"One of these passages concerned the removal of the ring. I said the chant, not knowing exactly what might happen once the ring was off. Would I age? Fall down dead? I would have considered either a good outcome. As I said the final words, the ring slid easily from my finger. I felt a great relief—but I was dismayed to learn that removing the ring did not change my situation in the least."

"Did you destroy it?"

"No. It's hidden."

Before he could say more, she held up a hand and said, "I won't ask!"

"Thank you, Amanda. The ring is so dangerous, you see."

"I understand."

He smiled. "As no one else does." He studied her for a long moment, then said her name as a whisper.

They heard Shade growl and they broke away from each other.

"The chaperones?" Tyler asked, looking in the direction the dog was staring.

"Yes," she said. She sighed and stood up. The ghosts disappeared.

"Maybe we should have a talk with them," Tyler said, standing beside her.

"I suppose you're right. Tonight?"

"Yes—although—"

"If you have to work, I'll just wait for you."

He looked toward the dog. "Shade's not growling now, so I take it they aren't looming too close?"

"No. They're over by the fireplace now."

"Just being protective, I suppose." He seemed lost in some kind of troubling thought.

"Tyler?"

"You won't mind if Alex drives you down to your house today, will you, Amanda?"

"No, not if it will make you feel better."

"Thank you—I would be worried otherwise."

"You still seem kind of tense to me. What else is on your mind?"

She heard him swallow hard. "Once you're there—you will come back?"

She looked up at him. Was he oblivious to how she felt about him? She wasn't the one who had become distant. *Men.* "Yes, I'll come back."

She saw the relief go through him, but then he said, "I—I understand that I've seemed, well, *reticent.* And if that reticence has hurt you, Amanda, I'm so sorry. It's just—this is something new for me. I wasn't expecting this. I want to be sure I'm not putting you in danger."

"If you think I'm going to let those thugs who beat up Brad rule my life—"

"No, no. Of course not."

"Well, I don't mean to say you're afraid of them either."

She saw him tense.

"I've said something wrong, haven't I?" she said.

"No, but remember—courage is one of the many virtues I can't lay claim to."

"Listen to me, Tyler—I'm serious about this. How many people could cope with half of what you encounter in the average day? Or have the strength of mind to adapt over centuries, or to face loss after loss, and solitude, and all the other things that are part of your life? So don't ever tell me you lack courage."

He smiled. "See what comes of knowing my secrets, Amanda? You've been burdened with my complaints."

"Not at all. I like learning more about you."

He traced a finger over her eyebrow. "Just be patient with me, if you can."

"Likewise."

"I want to learn more about you, too. Perhaps we could use this time—until we can figure out how to rid ourselves of our chaperones—to get to know each other better."

"Yes. I like that idea."

"Good."

He was, she thought, caught between his attraction to her and a nearly two-hundred-year-old habit of not allowing himself to get too close to anyone. Talk about commitment challenged! This was not going to be easy, but hell if she was going to give up on him.

The intercom buzzed. Tyler answered and listened. "Excellent. We'll meet you in the library."

When he hung up he said, "Alex has a report for us on Eduardo Leblanc."

38

None of Brad's friends has seen Eduardo Leblanc recently," Alex said to the group gathered in the library—Tyler, Amanda, Brad, and Ron. Rebecca was a no-show. "In fact, Brad seems to have been the last person to see him."

"You think he's moved?" Amanda said.

"Or is dead," Ron put in. "These people obviously play rough."

"Hard to say," Alex said. "For all I know, Eduardo's still alive." She handed a photo to Brad. "Is that him?"

Brad studied it. "Wow. He's younger in this photo, but yes, that's him."

She handed the photo to Tyler. The photo had been taken on a ship. A handsome, dark-haired young man smiled at the photographer. It was hard to gauge his build—cradling a dive helmet in his arms, he was dressed in a deep-sea diving suit.

"Eduardo Leblanc has a habit of showing up in places and then disappearing for a while," Alex said. "He's traveled throughout Europe, especially in England, Spain, and Italy."

Tyler passed the photo to Amanda. "You have a list of places he visited?"

"Some." She consulted her notes. "London, Bristol, York, Chester. Paris, Marseilles. Rome, Florence, Ferrara, Milan. Barcelona, Madrid,

Valencia. He spent time in Navarre—a little longer than the other places. I also have reports that in each of these places, he often vanished into the countryside for days at a time."

Tyler frowned. "I'll give you a list of some properties near each of those areas. I'd like to know if he visited any of them."

"Yours?"

"No," he said, "but if my list matches his travel pattern, I have an idea why he may have visited those areas." From the time Horace Dillon, the homeless man whose deathbed he had attended five days ago, had mentioned "an old enemy," Tyler's suspicions had lain in Colby's direction, even though he had never truly considered Colby as such—probably because he was irritated by Colby's attention to Amanda. Now, he saw his mistake.

All of the cities Alex had named were places where Adrian deVille had lived. In outlying areas some miles from each of them, Adrian had built small cottages, places where he might safely reappear. Tyler had spent a great deal of time discovering these retreats and systematically destroying them. Had he found them all?

He could only imagine Adrian's wrath at discovering that his refuges no longer stood.

Alex said, "I asked if they were your properties, because Eduardo was apparently looking for you."

"For me—by name?"

"Yes. He asked about you in each place but didn't get any help."

"Tyler . . . ," Amanda said faintly.

He smiled, trying to reassure her. "Shade is still with me, remember?" He turned to Alex. "What's his source of wealth?"

"That's a little difficult to determine, but I have some guesses."

"Is sunken treasure one of them?" Tyler said.

She stared at him in astonishment. "How did you know?"

"Let's say I made a good guess. Otherwise, I begin to believe I have been remarkably stupid about all of this. Tell me what else you've learned about Eduardo."

"Eduardo Leblanc is indeed his real name. Cuban American, born and raised in Florida. He has been estranged from his family since he was a teenager—his dad owned a dive shop, and Eduardo was a good diver, by all accounts. Eduardo turned eighteen, dropped out of high school in his senior year, went to work as a diver for a salvage company. Seemed happy with it until one disastrous dive."

"They found the *Morgan Bray*."

"The *Morgan Bray*—," Amanda said.

"You know about it?" Alex said, openly puzzled.

"I knew someone who lost an ancestor on it," Tyler said. "And, as it happens, I recently spoke to Amanda about that. It was a famous ship-wreck in its day. Said to be cursed."

"Well, that sure fits what happened to this expedition," Alex said. "It nearly drove the company out of business. The owner said he had never experienced anything like it, and Eduardo was not the only diver who quit after that day. He and another diver were attacked by sharks—"

"Two divers?" Ron said. "Shark attacks on humans are really rare, and it's almost always a lone diver or a surfer."

"The owner of the dive company said much the same thing. He had worked in the Caribbean for decades, completed hundreds of dives, and had never seen sharks behave as they did. It was unheard of. But that wasn't the only thing that went wrong. Other members of the dive crew suddenly fell ill. Tens of thousands of dollars' worth of the ship's special-ized equipment malfunctioned or was damaged."

"They don't blame Eduardo for all of that, do they?" Brad said.

"No, of course not."

After a moment, Tyler asked, "Do you think the ship owner would let you see a list of what they recovered from the *Morgan Bray*?"

"I'll ask. He told me they had just started work on it when this di-saster happened, and it took years for him to rebuild his company—the legal fees alone nearly did him in. But his company had the salvage rights, and he returned. He said they had no problems whatsoever after that." She paused. "I got caught up in his story, but he gave me most of the information I was looking for early on—that Eduardo Leblanc had worked for him, but quit and never returned after the problems with the *Morgan Bray*."

"I may not need the list after all," Tyler said. "Tell me what else you've learned."

"Eduardo made his wealth from a treasure, it seems, but this former boss doesn't believe that Eduardo did it legally. Because he started hearing rumors that Eduardo had made a discovery so soon after he left the company, at first he worried that Eduardo had stolen something from the *Morgan Bray*. When he investigated, though, he learned that the items Eduardo sold were two hundred or more years older than anything recovered from the *Morgan Bray,* and were mostly Spanish and Portuguese. The *Morgan Bray* was an English ship, not carrying anything in the nature of those items."

"He's had a silent partner," Tyler said. "And I'm sure whatever wealth he acquired after that was by subtler means."

"That fits," Alex said. "I had suspected as much. What little information about his wealth I could track down didn't match up with the expertise one would find in most twenty-one-year-old salvage divers. Every description of him before that dive was of an impulsive, rough-edged, and rather immature young man. Energetic and smart, but uneducated."

"And after?"

"I can answer that," Brad said. "If I hadn't seen that photo, Alex, I'd swear the Eduardo I met was a different person. The Eduardo I knew was sophisticated, unassuming, soft-spoken . . ."

"Worldly-wise?"

Brad hesitated. "Yes, but world-weary, too. Cynical to the point of seeming depressed."

They were interrupted by the entrance of Rebecca.

"Amanda, are you ready to go?"

"Alex?" Tyler asked.

"Sure. If Amanda's ready?"

"Alex is not coming with us!" Rebecca said.

"Yes, she is," Amanda said. "But—Tyler, do you think Rebecca should leave?"

"Not this again!" Rebecca said. "I refuse to be held prisoner here!"

Tyler sighed. "No one wants you to stay here if you don't want to." To Amanda he said, "I've tried to warn her. She refuses to hear what I have to say."

"Rebecca, you do understand that you could be in danger?" Amanda asked.

"In danger of what?"

"The people who attacked Brad might attack you."

"Nice try. Look, if you don't want me staying at your house, I'll just go home to the desert. But I am not staying here." She stalked out of the room.

"If you'd like, I'll have someone patrol there every hour or so," Alex said. "We're stretched a little thin right now, but in a few days the people who've been tracking down Eduardo can be back here, and I can have someone there twenty-four/seven after that."

"Thanks," Tyler said. "I think that would be a good idea, if Amanda won't mind?"

"Not at all. Thanks." Amanda sighed. "I guess we'd better get going, or she's going to get down to my house and discover she doesn't have a key to get in."

"Hurry up then," Brad said with disgust, "or she'll break in a door."

Half an hour later, Amanda stood on the small balcony outside her room. Alex had sensed that she needed time to herself, and left her alone on the pretext of checking the house to make sure it was still secure. Amanda had already packed up what she needed, and now she simply tried to calm herself, to overcome the feeling of foreboding that had been pressing in on her from the time she had heard that the wreckage of the *Morgan Bray* had been discovered. Was Adrian deVille alive again?

She looked up the hillside, toward Tyler's house. She saw Shade standing on the deck, watching. She caught herself just before she waved to him and smiled. That didn't seem such an odd thing to do, now that she had come to know the dog better. Not long ago the sight of Shade would have frightened her. Now, he made her feel safer.

She remembered the story of the long-ago ancestor of the deVilles, the woman who had stood up to Adrian and befriended Shade. Shade would keep them safe.

She heard the rustling of leaves beneath the balcony.

She looked down and saw Shade.

Startled, she looked toward Tyler's house. Shade was still there.

She looked between the two dogs, and although Shade was at some distance from her, she knew him well enough now to be able to see differences in the two dogs. Although also a very large dog, this one seemed to be a little less muscular than Shade, to have a slighter build. She stared, and her stare was returned unflinchingly. The dog seemed as fascinated with her as she was with him.

Him? Her? She couldn't tell from here. She had the oddest feeling about it, as if she should hurry downstairs to be with it.

Not every big black dog was Shade, she reminded herself sternly, and her hand came up to touch her scar.

Suddenly the dog's head turned, as if it had heard a distant sound, and it moved out of sight.

"Amanda? Did you find the spare key?"

Rebecca's voice snapped her out of the spell the dog seemed to have cast on her.

She turned to see Rebecca standing in the bedroom doorway.

"Yes," she said. "Yes, of course."

On the way back to Tyler's house, she thought of the night she and Alex had driven past the woods. Amanda had been distracted by seeing the ghosts, but Alex had said that she thought she had seen Shade.

It seemed likely that this other dog was the one that had been coming around her house. But was it another cemetery dog? Could there be more than one at a time? Was there someone else like Tyler, nearby? She recalled something in the pages Tyler had given her to read—a claim by

Adrian that he didn't need Shade, that he would find another cemetery dog.

What if Adrian found this dog? What if he had already found it, and the dog was his?

She shivered. She would ask Tyler what to do.

But when she got back to the house, she learned that Tyler had just left.

Ron said, "He asked me to ask you to please—I was supposed to emphasize the 'please' part—stay here until he gets back."

She agreed to do so and decided to spend some time in the library.

The ghosts were waiting for her there.

39

The pill bugs—Evan called them sow bugs—arrived during the morning, and in the afternoon an insect Daniel thought to be one of the most butt-ugly living creatures he had ever seen. When he dared to ask what it was, Adrian told him it was an ant lion, the larva of a dragonfly-like insect.

"They're quite beautiful in the adult stage," Adrian had said.

Daniel found that difficult to believe.

To his growing list of reasons for hating Adrian, he added ant lions.

Adrian was probably completely screwing up the environment, Daniel thought. Daniel wasn't a scientist, but you didn't need to be one to figure out that if a thousand of something got eaten up in the cellar, whatever usually ate that something was going hungry.

He was wondering if a thousand ant lions could be missed by anything or anyone when Adrian called Daniel and Evan to the basement.

He braced himself and followed Evan down the stairs. They were allowed to turn on the basement light now, but Daniel really wished they were back to the candle days. The only advantage was that they could now see what to avoid on the floor.

Adrian himself was worse than an ant lion. Far worse. Daniel knew that if they avoided looking at him, they would be punished, but the sight always turned his stomach.

Adrian had no skin. In some places—such as along the place where a man's rib cage would be—he had something like an insect's shell. His arms and legs were thin sticks, little more than muscle-covered bones. His feet were thin and long, and seemed almost too narrow to support him. His toes were fused together. His hands were pincers. Over his visible muscles, ligaments, and tendons, a thick mucus glistened.

Only his head seemed to be mostly human. He had no visible ears or nose, but he had dark eyes and hard, insect-shell eyelids now. Otherwise his mouth and other facial features seemed to be those of a man. A fleshless man.

The basement held a new odor, something like mustard, and although there was still an underlying scent of decay, the new stench masked it.

To Daniel's relief, Adrian was focusing on Evan tonight.

"Do you know, Evan," he said, "I had not realized previously what a handsome fellow you are . . ."

Evan blushed, but Daniel thought it was true that Evan was good looking, and what's more, that Evan knew it. He had used those looks to get over on more than one woman. Evan wasn't tops in the brains department, but women didn't seem to mind.

Still, he didn't blame Evan if it made him uneasy to hear Adrian talking like that.

"How old are you?" Adrian asked.

"Thirty-six, my lor—I mean, Mr. deVille."

"Hmmm."

Adrian's eyelids make a clicking sound as he blinked, like the shutter of an old camera.

Adrian turned to Daniel.

"I have work for you to do."

Daniel waited.

"It will be so much better when I have finished my transformation. I will be able to attend to these matters myself." He sighed. "Evan tells me that Hawthorne's lover may be back at her home. I want the two of you to make another trip there tonight, to confirm this. If it's true, I want you to bring her to me."

There was only one possible response, and Daniel made it. "Yes, sir."

40

Tyler stood at the bedside of Mrs. Mary Cleeves, who was about to die in Olive View Hospital, in Sylmar. He had helped her communicate with her daughter, who stood on the other side of the bed, weeping. But Mrs. Cleeves's next words were for Tyler.

You're troubled, aren't you?

Is Adrian back? he asked.

You already know the answer to that question.

What does he want?

You know the answer to that, too. She paused, then said, *It's so difficult to make decisions when one's loved ones are in danger, isn't it?*

Amanda's in danger?

Everyone who lives is in danger, Tyler Hawthorne. Even you.

Wait! What danger is she in?

I think you already know. Here's something that will help you: Take good care of that dog. Now, I've got to be going. Thank you for helping me and all the others.

She died. Her daughter began to cry harder.

Would it be too much to ask, Tyler raged silently, *to allow one of these people to give me a complete message?*

Silence answered him.

*   *   *

He left the hospital, greeted Shade warmly, and bestowed praise and attention on him. He let him out of the van on a leash—an unnecessary device in Shade's case, one Tyler used only to prevent legal problems, and to provide some comfort to people who feared large, black, rather ferocious-looking dogs. Near the hospital, Shade briefly took an interest in an area that Tyler knew had once been the site of a tuberculosis sanitarium.

They got into the van, and Tyler called the house. Alex answered and said that Amanda had been in the library most of the day. "Want me to transfer the call to her there?"

"No, I don't want to disturb her," he said. "Just . . ."

"I'm keeping an eye on things, Tyler. I won't let you down."

"I know. You've done a remarkable job all the way around—and under difficult conditions."

"Not at all. You'd be surprised by how peaceful it is around here this afternoon. Especially now that Rebecca's out on her own. Ron and Brad keep making up rude nicknames for each other, but that's all by way of male bonding."

"You're very understanding."

"Me? I grew up as a tough guy's only child. One-hundred-percent tomboy."

"I have a feeling that Ron would say, 'Not quite one hundred percent.'"

She was still laughing when they ended the call.

He drove Shade to the corner of Bledsoe and Foothill, where a cemetery dating from the 1870s stood. They walked around the outside fence for a while, but again Shade seemed only mildly interested. He gave Tyler a look, one that seemed to say, "Are we done here?"

"All right, but I'm just trying to follow orders. 'Take good care of that dog.' Not that I find the duty unpleasant, mind you. And I'm sorry if I've been distracted lately."

Shade looked off at the horizon, avoiding Tyler's gaze. Nearly two centuries in the dog's company led Tyler to interpret this as a signal of disappointment or disapproval.

"Forgive me, I'm just a stupid human."

Shade looked at him and wagged his tail.

"You really don't need to agree so readily to that."

Shade wagged his tail harder, then romped over to the van.

"Home it is, then," Tyler said.

As they got into the vehicle, Tyler asked, "Should I tell her?"

Shade gave a sharp bark.

"Easy for you to say. I don't know how to begin to talk to her about this."

Shade stared at him.

"All right, all right. I didn't say I wouldn't do it, just that it would be difficult."

Tyler found Amanda in the library, perched on a rolling shelf ladder, removing a slender volume from one of the upper rows of books. A stack of some of his oldest books was piled on a table. Shade's reaction when they entered the room told him the ghosts were present, apparently hovering in midair somewhere behind her.

Amanda looked down when she heard him enter and smiled, her pleasure in seeing him written plainly on her face. This was, he thought, part of what attracted him to her—she did not hide her feelings from him.

All the turmoil he had been caught up in over the last week eased for the moment. He stood just inside the doorway, watching her, savoring his own sense of happiness and well-being. When was the last time he had felt anything close to it?

She was glad he was home, and he was equally glad to be here with her. A simple thing, he supposed, but a pleasure he had not shared with another person before Amanda had come into his life.

"Sorry I was gone so long," he said. "What are you doing?"

"Research, in my limited way." She made a face and began her descent. "I'm not sure it could even be called *researching*." She sat at the table and gestured to him to take the chair next to her. "I can't even identify the languages half of these books are written in. But the pictures in them make me think the ghosts were right about them."

"Back up a moment—researching what?" he asked.

"Dogs. Cemetery dogs. I asked the ghosts for help. They're really excited about this one," she said, holding up the book she had just retrieved. "It took me a while to figure out that they wanted me to go up the ladder."

"I'm sure Shade must be flattered that you're going to all this effort."

"Oh, well—forgive me, Shade, but I was trying to see if there was something about the new dog."

He froze. "New dog?"

"Yes! The one that's been coming around my house."

He felt himself pale.

"Tyler? What's wrong?"

"You've seen the dog? It looks like Shade?"

"Could be his twin. Slightly smaller than he is, I think, but not by much." She described seeing the two dogs at the same time. "But it ran off into the woods."

"We have to find it," he said, coming to his feet. "We should look for it immediately."

"Tyler—wait. Please, tell me what's wrong. Do you think Adrian wants that dog?"

"That's just one of my fears. But yes—it's possible he knows there is another cemetery dog in the area, and if he does, he will definitely try to make it his own."

He started for the door, but Shade suddenly blocked his way.

"Shade, what is it?"

"Um . . . the ghosts keep pointing toward the books," Amanda said.

Shade wagged his tail.

"Now?" he asked. "Under the circumstances, don't you think books can wait?"

Shade stared at him.

"All right, all right." He went back to the table.

Amanda handed him the book from the upper shelf. "Do you know what this language is?"

He sat beside her and looked at the text. "I think it may be Euskara."

"Of course. I should have recognized it right away. What the hell is Euskara?"

"Basque. Linguistically unique—it doesn't seem to be related to any other language."

"Do you read it?"

"No."

"Oh. But you told me about being able to read texts to break the curse on the ring . . ."

"Let's hope that works again. Perhaps it depends on the book rather than the reader," he said, slowly turning its pages.

"Magic books, eh? Well, why not? This one is amazing—I glanced at the illustrations. The book is full of beautiful woodcuts. I could swear some of them are pictures of Shade."

"I think that's why I bought it. I admit I haven't looked through it since then, though."

"Do you have a Basque dictionary?"

"Sorry, no."

"Basque country is near the border of Spain and France, right?"

"Yes, although the Basque have been scattered across the world."

"I just wondered—well, for a couple of reasons. Alex mentioned Navarre as one of the places Eduardo visited."

"Right—and she mentioned that he had stayed there a little longer than elsewhere." He looked at the book with new interest.

"I also wondered about the book—because it seems as if it was published privately, by someone in Los Angeles."

He glanced at the title page. "Yes. But that's not so strange. There have been Basque enclaves in Southern California for many years. In Los Angeles, Orange County, Bakersfield, and other places. Similar to hundreds of thousands of other people, lots of Basque men came to California during the gold rush."

"So they were miners?"

"Some were, but many then turned to raising sheep and cattle—they fed the miners. You could usually make more money selling supplies to the miners than being one."

"Were you a miner or a supplier?"

He smiled. "I tried both, but I spent most of my time in the West as a doctor."

"A doctor!"

"Don't look so impressed. I wouldn't try my hand at it now. When I first came to America, the requirements for a medical education were quite different from what they are today. Then, it just took a few months of study and an apprenticeship. I had decided on the profession even before I immigrated."

"I suppose a doctor could move around a lot?"

"Yes. And I was often called to the bedsides of the dying."

"This was before anesthesia, right?"

"And so much more. I tried to help my patients as much as possible, but when I think back . . ." He shuddered. "Let's just say things have come a long way since then."

"Something else to be thankful for."

He tried to let go of his anxieties about her, about the new dog, about the ghosts, tried to open his mind to whatever the pages might offer. Shade insisted he stay here—why? Because of Amanda, the ghosts? No, he told himself, feeling worry return—relax, let go.

Shade moved beneath the table and laid his head on Tyler's feet. The ghosts were gone, then. As he studied the pages, he realized Amanda was right—the animal in the prints looked a great deal like Shade.

A familiar sensation came over him, and he began to understand the sense, if not the word-by-word meaning of the text. "This seems to be presented as a folktale. It's about a ghost dog known as 'Wraith' that was seen in local cemeteries. There were many indications that the dog was a ghost. No one could get close to it. Its black coat allowed it to disappear into darkness. No one knew who fed or cared for it, or where it lived during the day. But at night, it was known to protect graves from any who would try to rob or vandalize them. It was thought to have a special friendship with the dead. Once or twice it was seen in a home or a church. Some said that its appearance outside a cemetery presaged a death."

"I knew it was about a dog like Shade! I mean, they obviously made some stuff up, but it's a dog like him, isn't it?"

Shade got up and sniffed at the book.

"Well, Shade, did you ever know this Wraith?" Tyler asked.

Shade wagged his tail.

"I guess we needed to know this other dog's name," Tyler said, then frowned. "Which can only mean there's no human, no Messenger available, to introduce us to it—it's without a companion."

"I wonder what became of that person?"

"Hard to say. All I know right now is that Adrian wants that dog."

"And he also wants that ring back?" she asked.

"Yes, without a doubt. Given what Brad said about him, I suspect Adrian's not yet mobile. He would have no need of these henchmen, and he wouldn't be hiding in a foul-smelling basement."

"So the dog isn't his yet?"

"No. He'd be preening in broad daylight. But very likely he did send Daniel and Evan to look for the ring, and perhaps to search for some of his other former belongings."

"Former? Will he see it that way?"

"I don't care. Adrian's descendants and others who lived on his estate paid a high price to ensure that he couldn't reclaim those items."

Amanda paced. "I wish I had known all this when I saw the dog this afternoon."

Tyler carefully turned a few pages in the book, then took a long look at one of the prints, which showed a woman standing beside the dog. The woman appeared to be slightly disfigured by a mark or scar near one eye. Almost a replica of the scar on Amanda's brow. He waited, hoping that some part of the accompanying text would become clear to him. It did not.

He turned the page, unsettled. Shade protected him. Was he keeping Amanda from her own protector? Keeping Shade from a companion of his own kind?

"Shade has been watching the woods at night," he said. "I thought it was because of ghosts—even before you told me about your ghosts, Colby mentioned that the woods were haunted. Now I wonder if the dogs have been trying to get together."

"But the fence stopped Wraith?"

"If it's a cemetery dog, fences are no real barrier."

She shivered, then straightened her shoulders. "Well. Let's go looking."

"Are you afraid? Would you rather I looked for it alone?"

"A little, I guess—but I want to come with you. I'm more curious than scared."

"As you probably know, there's a gate leading from the fence into the woods. I'll get a pair of flashlights and we can look around. Whatever we do, we have to make sure Adrian doesn't get his hands on that dog."

41

As he drove, Evan complained about Adrian, which was nothing less than what Daniel expected. Still, it added to his depression. He looked out of the passenger-side window, hoping Evan would get the hint and shut up.

He had no real hope of that. Or of anything else, he realized. Even when he had been in prison, he had not felt so trapped. There, at least, he knew he would eventually get out.

As they continued up the now familiar road, he began to think of this woman they were after. What would become of her?

He shook himself, as if to throw off the thought.

Why should he care?

Hadn't bothered him to beat the crap out of Brad. That rich little snot. This was just another superwealthy useless bitch.

He heard Evan mention the word "gun" and refocused his attention. "What did you say?"

"Brought a gun. Picked it up this afternoon while I was running errands for His Royal Roachness."

"Are you nuts? You know what he said about guns! They're too noisy, they're not subtle enough. You can take a girl without a gun, can't you?"

"I know Adrian wouldn't approve, but hell if I'm gonna try to stop that dog with a knife."

"Guns make noise," Daniel repeated.

"I'll risk having to explain a few pops out of a gun if it keeps that dog from setting me on fire."

Daniel knew Evan well enough now to realize that argument would be useless.

Daniel wondered if a bullet could stop the dog. If the dog came charging after him, he wasn't so sure he would try to resist meeting Eduardo's fate. Let the dog come at him. Let it free him.

As Daniel thought this, Evan made the turn up onto the canyon road where the woman lived. In a few miles, they would be near the place where Eduardo had died.

He felt a jolt of fear. Daniel quickly began to murmur a prayer, then stopped as he became aware of what he was doing. He took a deep breath and let it out slowly. Strange. He hadn't prayed since he was really little. Where had that come from?

He glanced nervously at Evan to see if he had noticed his reaction, but Evan was still talking about how much he hated the way Adrian looked now.

A Lexus passed them. Evan called the driver a dickhead, but the car was too far ahead by then for the driver to have heard him.

Other cars came down the canyon road. "Lot of traffic," Daniel said.

"Too many cars. We'll never pull this off with this many people around. As usual, he's screwed up the planning. He has no idea what the outside world is really like. We'll have to wait. If he wasn't such a control freak . . ."

Daniel tuned out the complaints and focused on their surroundings. They had previously scouted out most of this road, so when they came to a narrow strip of asphalt marked PRIVATE DRIVE, Evan turned down it and stopped just out of sight of the road. Farther down the drive, still nearly hidden from their view by tall eucalyptus and pines, was a darkened house.

Evan parked, lowered the windows, and turned off the engine. He turned off the headlights and the two of them sat listening, watching for any sign of life from the house. It remained silent and still, and no lights came on. Daniel pulled a map of the area from the glove compartment. They didn't need it, but if someone should ask what they were doing there, they would claim to be lost, looking for a street in the next canyon over.

After a few minutes, Evan lit a cigarette.

"I thought you quit," Daniel said.

"I did. Started again today."

"You know that'll kill you."

"I can only hope that's true, but I doubt it. I'd prefer cancer to whatever Adrian has in mind for us."

"You think maybe he's going to try to kill us?"

Evan rolled his eyes. "*Maybe? Try?* I have no doubt that's exactly what's going to happen to us."

"He needs us as his slaves."

"Does he? Once that creepy-crawly thing has strength in his legs and a little bit of skin on him, we're goners." He took a deep draw on his cigarette and stared ahead in moody silence.

Daniel went back to his own thoughts. He could not shake the memory of Eduardo and the dog.

42

Tyler and Amanda made their way down the steep slope below the deck and reached the gate without any sign of the dog, which they referred to as Wraith. Shade made his way alongside them, although at times Amanda could not see him in the darkness.

Tyler unlocked the gate and they stepped through it onto more level ground. Amanda could now see her house. Every light seemed to be on, including the outdoor floodlights. "I guess Rebecca is all for global warming," she said.

"Perhaps she feels afraid, being there alone." He glanced at his watch. "Alex will be sending someone to patrol in a few minutes."

Between the lights from the house and the light of the moon, Amanda's eyes adjusted quickly to the darkness. She only used the flashlight because she didn't want to trip over a root or step in a hole. Which, she reflected, would be just like her.

The day had been warm, and the trees and shrubs that grew throughout this little patch of woods gave the air a sweet scent. As she looked out at the sea of lights that was Los Angeles, she sensed something odd. It took her a moment to realize what it was. "I wonder why the crickets are so quiet."

Tyler, who was a few feet away, stood still, as did she, listening.

"It's as if there aren't any," he said, frowning.

When they started walking again, Shade began to circle them, as if trying to get them to move closer together. Once they were next to each other, they stood still.

"What is he doing?" Amanda said.

"Herding us." He looked down at the dog and said, "All right, Shade, we're together. We're staying right here."

Shade sat and stared up at him.

"What is it?" Tyler asked.

The dog looked from Tyler to Amanda and back again.

"Now?" Tyler asked. "Out here?"

Shade barked, making Amanda jump.

"You're scaring her," Tyler said.

"I think I'm over being scared of him," she said. "He just startled me."

Shade continued to stare at Tyler.

"What's going on?" Amanda asked.

"I believe he's requesting—or insisting—that I have a conversation with you."

Shade wagged his tail.

"I don't understand," she said. "We've been talking to each other all evening."

"Yes, well . . . he wants me to have a particular conversation." He turned to the dog. "Not now. Your timing couldn't be worse."

Shade didn't budge. When Tyler tried to take a step forward, the dog blocked his way.

Amanda found she hadn't completely overcome her fear of Shade after all.

"Is the arrangement," Tyler asked Shade in a low voice, "that you command me? Or even that I, in reality, command you?"

Shade looked away for a moment, glanced back at Tyler, then moved out of their way.

"Thank you," Tyler said. "Now, if you don't mind helping us find Wraith . . ."

But Shade kept moving, and trotted back toward the house.

"Shade!"

The dog ignored him. He soon disappeared in the darkness.

Amanda stared after him, then looked up at Tyler. She could just make out his features and thought he looked bereft. She moved closer to him and took his hand. "Maybe we should go after him. The ghosts . . ."

"No, he'll come back to me if I'm in real need, or when he's decided he wants my company again. If he doesn't care to be with me right now, we'll spend the whole night running through the canyon trying to catch up with him."

"Has this happened before?"

"Yes, but not very often. I suppose he needs a break from me now and then."

They were distracted from their conversation as, below them, the lights outside Amanda's house were turned off. Next the indoor lights went off, downstairs first, then upstairs, until only one remained on. Oblivious to their presence, Rebecca was calling it a night.

"Do you want to wait for Shade to come back?" Amanda asked.

"This would undoubtedly be easier if he helped, but since he's on strike or pouting or whatever, let's do what we can on our own. Are the ghosts here?"

She looked around. "Not at the moment."

"Well, we'll do what we can. Let me know if you see them."

"Do you mind if we search up here first, away from my house? I want to give Rebecca a chance to fall asleep—I'd rather not have to explain to her what we're doing out here."

He agreed to this. He kept hold of her hand as they walked. Not perhaps the most efficient way to search, she thought, but she was glad to have him at her side. She could not shake a feeling of foreboding.

That feeling, she realized, probably had to do with this "conversation" Tyler had mentioned. She didn't want to bring it up—if he was willing to be at odds with Shade over it, he clearly didn't want to talk about it now. Not a good time to push.

They found fresh tracks—prints made by a large dog—leading toward Tyler's house, then realized they'd probably been made by Shade.

They were again distracted, this time by the Danton's Security car going down the driveway at Amanda's house. They heard rather than saw the guard get out of the car, and the lights in and outside the house started going on again. Rebecca must have stepped outside to talk to the guard, because although they couldn't make out what was being said, they could hear male and female voices.

When traffic let up, Evan and Daniel drove the truck closer to the house but parked at the side of the road when they saw a security patrol car leaving the driveway. They got out of the truck and made their way on foot, even though both of them feared being so vulnerable to the dog. Lights were on all around the house—not good for their purposes.

But almost as if they had wished for it, the lights started going out again.

"Let's not sit around out here waiting to get caught by that dog," Evan said.

Several of the windows upstairs were open, and Daniel could have entered by any of them, but sooner or later they would need to use a door, so he went to the alarm box. Setting up a bypass on the alarm system, which would make everything appear to be in fine order to the security company, took only a few minutes, and the lock on the kitchen door even less time. This was their old profession, and Daniel felt some comfort in returning to it.

The woman was upstairs. Evan signaled that he would get her, for Daniel to keep a lookout. Daniel started to protest, then decided even Evan wouldn't be such a fool as to do damage to a woman Adrian wanted for himself. Let him be the one to haul her down here.

Tyler told himself that he had made the right choice in not talking to Amanda just yet. If Wraith was meant to be hers, then nothing he said or didn't say would make a difference. He had been told, though, that he had a choice, and he would never choose to make her into what he was.

Still, he began to wonder what would happen if she called to the dog.

They stood on the slope, watching as the lights at Amanda's place started to go out again.

"The ghosts haven't shown up yet, have they?"

She looked around and tensed. "Oh, no," she said, "Tyler, they're nearby! Maybe you should call to Shade—something strange is going on . . ."

"What?"

"My mom and dad are here. My aunt and uncle aren't. They've never split up before. My dad is pointing toward the house. They seem to want us to go down there. Wait—they're gone again."

In the next moment, they heard a sound—not quite a scream—coming from Amanda's house.

43

"Amanda!" Tyler said, grabbing her arm to keep her from running toward the house. He moved with her to a hiding place behind a large tree. "Let's not give them three hostages instead of one, all right?"

Reluctantly, she agreed. "Do you think it's Evan and Daniel?"

"In all likelihood. But they must have approached on foot, which gives us an advantage."

He took Amanda's hand and began to cautiously move from tree to tree, until they were at a vantage point from which they would be able to see anyone leaving by either the front or the back door of Amanda's house.

"The back door's open," Amanda said.

Tyler's cell phone rang.

Daniel heard the sound of terror the woman made, which Evan apparently quickly cut off.

Daniel rushed up the stairs and found Evan struggling to hold her still. Daniel grabbed her feet. Evan took out his gun, and for an awful moment Daniel thought he might shoot her, but before Daniel could protest, Evan rapped it against her head. Her struggles ceased.

"You moron!" Daniel whispered. "You hit someone on the head, you can kill them!"

"She's not dead, she was screeching before I even stepped into the room, and she won't be out for long, so help me make sure she doesn't yell her head off when she comes to—moron!"

Daniel took a closer look at the woman. "This isn't the one!"

"What do you mean, this isn't the one?"

"The one we want has dark hair, remember?"

The woman moaned. Her eyelids fluttered.

Evan swore bitterly. "Well, I still don't want her screaming when she wakes up. Damn it, Adrian's going to have my hide!"

They quickly bound and gagged her.

"Who the hell is she?" Evan asked.

Daniel spotted a purse and rifled through its contents. "Rebecca Clarke. Damn. This is Brad's sister."

"Maybe we can use her to get the other one down here."

"Maybe . . ."

Hoping the details of a plan B might come to them, they stared in silence at the blonde, who continued to moan softly. Her eyes opened briefly—she seemed to be trying to rouse herself.

Daniel heard the sound of a cell phone somewhere outside and moved to the window. He carefully parted a curtain. "Someone's coming!"

Tyler muted the ringing cell phone in frustration, and nearly didn't answer the phone, but then he saw that the caller was Alex.

"Tyler—I thought I'd better let you know—Rebecca was all bent out of shape because supposedly Shade was nosing around Amanda's house, and she asked my guard to take your dog back home—and he agreed and put it in his car and brought it here. Problem is, it wasn't Shade. And now there are two dogs here—two Shades."

"The second dog is up there?" He breathed a sigh of relief. "It's fine. Its name is Wraith, I think. Can you tell them apart?"

"Well, yes, very easily. The new one—Wraith?—is a female."

"Oh."

"Yes," Alex said. "She's big for a bitch, nearly Shade's size. They look almost identical otherwise. Rebecca apparently didn't notice the dog's sex."

"Alex, listen to me carefully. This is extremely important."

"All right . . ."

"Do not let that dog—or anyone from the house—come down here. Lock the gates, shut the dogs in—and don't let anyone out, no matter what you hear down here."

"Tyler, what's going on?"

"I'll explain it later. Don't let any stranger who claims his dog is missing take Wraith. In fact, absolutely no one else enters or leaves until one of us calls you and uses the code word 'ring' in a sentence to let you know we're not calling under duress, all right?"

There was silence, then Alex said, "Are you sure this is wise?"

"Alex, as of this moment, I can't give you a more important job than making sure that those dogs do not fall into the wrong hands."

"Someone wants to steal Shade?"

"Yes. And Wraith. So keep them there. They'll also protect you and Ron and Brad."

She laughed. "Thanks for the vote of confidence . . ."

"I didn't mean it that way. Of course I'm depending on you to protect everyone there. I think the people who attacked Brad may be at Amanda's house, so keep an eye on things for me where you are, all right?"

"Sure. Call me if you need me down there."

He hung up and gave the phone to Amanda. "I want to rescue Rebecca, and you know I can do it—I'm able to defend myself, and they can't really harm me. But I can't be worrying about you, Amanda, which I would, and you'd just be—"

"In the way."

She looked away from him, and he knew he'd hurt her. "I know you want to help, to be useful, but if anything happened to you—"

"I'll stay here and call Alex if you aren't out in a few minutes," she said with a kind of determined calm. "I remember the code word."

"This is important—if you really think I've been . . . taken out of action, ask Alex to release Shade. Run back to the house and stay there. And no police, right?"

"I understand," she said. She hesitated, then hugged him hard and whispered, "Tyler, please be safe. I have such a bad feeling about this."

" 'Be safe,' huh? Not a wish I usually think of needing, but I'll do my best."

"Hurry—I don't want them to hurt her. Yell if—well, if you think I can be of help."

"I will. And if you see them taking her out by the front door as I go in the back, scream bloody murder, then run to a new hiding place." He gave her a quick kiss and ran toward the house.

Daniel said, "It's Hawthorne and the girl!"

"Wherever he is, that dog's not far behind," Evan said. "Let's get out of here."

They moved downstairs as quietly as possible, abandoning the blonde, and watched for a chance to leave.

"They're moving closer!" Evan said.

"I don't see the dog with them."

"So what? Remember the last time? That thing disappears in the dark."

"Hawthorne's the one Adrian really wants," Daniel said, "or his ring anyway. Why bother with the girl?"

As if to provide for Daniel's plan, Hawthorne started moving closer to the house—without the girl, and with no sign of the dog.

"Fine," said Evan, pulling out the gun again, "but I'm not taking any chances."

"Don't be stupid! The two of us can take him without all that noise." Evan ignored him.

They hid behind a large couch and watched as Hawthorne carefully peered around the back door. No sooner had Hawthorne stepped silently across the threshold than Evan fired three times in quick succession.

44

The report was deafening in the confined space of the house, but Daniel saw that Evan's aim was true—Hawthorne crumpled to the floor. They hurried forward.

Although he was a fair shot himself, Daniel preferred not to use firearms. Gunshots were loud and messy. But looking at Tyler Hawthorne, whose eyes stared up, unseeing, Daniel couldn't argue with their effectiveness. Hawthorne's bloodstained fingers clutched weakly at his side. He strained to draw fading, burbling breaths. Evan had wisely aimed for his body—in the dark, a head would be a hard target to hit.

Hawthorne coughed softly once, blood pouring out over his chin and neck as he did, then closed his eyes. He didn't draw another breath.

"Get the truck," Evan ordered. "Hurry. We have to get our asses out of here before that damned dog comes after him."

"Or the police," Daniel said, stepping over Hawthorne's body. "The girl is probably calling the cops right now."

The truck was nearby, but Daniel ran as if the devil himself were after him, which, he thought, might not be far from the truth.

Amanda stifled a scream as she heard the gunfire, and fought an urge to run toward danger.

He can't be killed. He can't be killed.

But what if Adrian, with all his dabbling in the occult and centuries' greater experience, knew some secret weakness of Tyler's? Perhaps the bullets were coated with some poison or were made of silver or something. Wouldn't it be just like Adrian to have had, from the very beginning, some way of killing Tyler? He wouldn't leave the ability to reclaim his immortality to chance. He would make sure he could get his powers back from Tyler.

She saw a man run from the house, but he didn't have Rebecca or Tyler with him. She forced herself to wait.

Then she saw a familiar truck roaring down the driveway, the one she had seen in the desert, the one that had struck Tyler. She fumbled the cell phone open and called Alex.

"Tyler?" Alex answered. "What the hell is going on? We just heard gunfire."

"It's Amanda. Um . . . thought I'd ring. Tyler said to tell you to let Shade loose."

"Good, because just now, with the help of two of my biggest men, I barely managed to stop him from smashing through a window." She yelled to a guard to let the dog loose.

"Also," Amanda said, "no police. That's really important."

There was a brief silence, then Alex said, "Okay, but I can't guarantee that someone else in the canyon didn't already call them."

"I know. Thanks. I have to go."

She hung up, then watched in alarm as a tall man emerged from the house, carrying Tyler over his shoulder. The man hastily took Tyler's lifeless body to the truck, then ran back toward the house.

No . . . dear God, please let him be all right! Let him live . . .

She heard a rustling sound behind her—Shade was running flat out, moving with amazing speed. He passed her as a black blur. She followed him as quickly as she could.

Evan dropped Hawthorne to the ground at the back of the big pickup truck and lifted the camper-shell door. He then lowered the tailgate and tossed Hawthorne in the back. He thought he heard Hawthorne groan—but that was impossible. He had felt for a pulse before taking him out of the house—the guy was dead.

Daniel hadn't left the cab of the truck. Lot of help he had been with all of this. Evan shut the tailgate and hurried back into the house. Hell if he was going to leave any witnesses behind.

Amanda had just reached level ground when she saw Shade gather himself and leap over the tailgate of the truck. Slowly, the truck began to move.

"Stop!" she shouted, but the truck picked up speed.

Evan would be safe, Daniel thought, now that the dog was in the truck. Even with the camper door up, the dog wouldn't leave Hawthorne, and although Evan probably wouldn't figure out that Daniel had just saved his life, he'd find a way home. If Evan had done what he was supposed to do and climbed back into the truck, they could have driven off without the dog as a passenger.

Adrian would know what to do with the animal.

Adrian would protect Daniel from the dog.

Something within him argued that he was a fool to believe this was true.

He looked in the mirror and saw the girl running after the truck.

He sped up.

45

Amanda broke her stride and stumbled as her parents' ghosts appeared in front of her. She just managed not to fall. Her father motioned her toward the house, but her attention was on the fading taillights ahead of her. She lost sight of them as the truck turned onto the road.

"Do you mean to harm him? To have him become a ghost?" she asked, trying to catch her breath.

They shook their heads no, then pointed at the house again.

"If you love me," she said, "if you have ever loved me, follow him. Find out where he's being taken."

Her parents glanced at each other, then turned to her. They pointed toward the house.

"All right, all right! But please . . . please . . . help me!" She drew a hard breath, fighting back panic and frustration. "I need you."

With a speed that astonished her, they moved in the direction of the truck, then disappeared.

Could she trust them? She wasn't sure, but Shade was with him.

She ran toward the house, wondering how, without Shade's help here, she would stop a man with a gun from whatever harm he intended.

* * *

Evan heard the truck drive off and ran to a window. He was just in time to see a young woman running down the drive after it. He swore that if he saw Daniel again, he'd kill him. Then he'd find out if Daniel's mother was alive, and if she was, he'd kill her, too, just for raising such a damned fool.

Although his own estimate of his intelligence was high, he could not decide what he should do now. Go after the girl outside, before anyone saw her out on the road and asked her what was wrong? Before she called the police? Or should he go upstairs as he had planned, finish that one off, and then kill the other one? It wasn't as if either girl knew who he was, though, so maybe he should get out of here and save his bullets for the dog.

He scratched absently at the parts of his skin dampened by Hawthorne's blood.

Maybe he should go outside and catch the girl and take her back to Adrian. After all, that was what they were supposed to do. Adrian always got mad if they did anything other than what he ordered them to do.

Completely ignoring the fact that he carried a firearm in defiance of his master, he pictured himself showing Daniel up by delivering the real prize. But, even without the girl, how was he going to get back home? He checked the garage. A Jag was parked there. Sweet. It was about to become his new ride.

Daniel had a lot to answer for. Evan decided he would catch the other girl and take her with him. Bring the blonde along as a bonus. That plan, he decided, would be best.

By the time he had worked through his plan, he saw the brunette turn toward the house. Now what was she up to?

Amanda remembered that the back door was open. When she neared the house, she began to move more cautiously. One of the men was gone, and so was the truck, but Tyler's other attacker was probably still in the house. The idea of encountering him frightened her, but she didn't want to leave Rebecca in his power for another minute—he might be hurting her even now.

Although her eyes had adjusted to the darkness outside, as she stepped into the kitchen, it was harder to see.

She knew her way around the house, though, and walking as quietly as she could, she made her way to the living room.

She listened hard but could hear no sound other than the hum of the refrigerator and the ticking of the grandfather clock. She reached the foot of the stairs and carefully began her ascent.

A night-light in the upstairs hallway allowed her to see that the door of the guest room Rebecca used was closed. Amanda had just taken a creeping step toward it when the ghosts of her aunt and uncle appeared. She drew in an audible gasp but managed not to trip or knock anything over. She was just feeling relieved about this when Aunt Cynthia motioned toward something over Amanda's left shoulder.

The hall lights came on as she turned. The man who had carried Tyler to the truck was pointing a gun at her.

"Just step into that room," he said.

Shade lay beside Tyler and breathed softly on his face.

Tyler's eyes opened, but he squeezed them shut almost immediately, warding off pain. He felt the burn of fever spreading through his body, and fought to keep track of the words he wanted to say. After a moment, he managed a dry whisper. "Shade, I beg of you—protect Amanda."

The dog didn't move. Tyler forced himself to open his eyes. Shade seemed suddenly alert, staring at something behind the truck. The dog came to his feet, seeming to need no effort to maintain his balance as the truck swayed with the curves of the road.

"Please, Shade. Please help her."

He looked at Tyler, came close to him once more, and again breathed softly on him.

The pain lessened immediately.

Shade stared hard into Tyler's eyes, as if he wished to convey some message of his own, then turned, and in a single leap was out of the truck.

In his delirium, Tyler thought an elegant couple in evening dress joined him almost as soon as Shade was gone. They seemed familiar, but he couldn't recall where he had met them. He could have sworn the woman looked at him in sorrow, and placed a pale, cool hand on his forehead, soothing the fever and bringing him sleep.

46

Amanda obeyed the man with the gun. He turned the light on, and she saw Rebecca, bound and gagged, lying awkwardly on the floor. Her face was scraped and she was bleeding from a cut on her chin. Seeing her cousin mistreated, knowing this man had shot Tyler, seeing Tyler's blood on his hands and clothing—all combined to make Amanda feel suddenly more angry than afraid.

Rebecca, pale and wide eyed, looked relieved to see Amanda until she saw the man just behind her. Amanda hurried to her cousin and tried to move her to a more comfortable position. With some effort, she managed to help her sit up. Rebecca seemed woozy. She leaned against Amanda.

"What did you do to her?" Amanda asked.

"Shut up!" he said.

Rebecca made a little screeching sound behind her gag, but she wasn't looking at either Amanda or the man with the gun. When Amanda followed the direction of Rebecca's gaze, she saw her aunt and uncle hovering nearby.

"Shut up, I said!" their captor repeated.

"Are you the one called Evan, or are you Daniel?"

He was shocked to hear her mention their names.

"You told your names to Brad, remember? Uncle Jordan and Aunt Cynthia, is this Daniel?"

"You aren't fooling me with that old 'someone is behind you' stunt," he said.

But behind him, the ghosts were shaking their heads. Rebecca cowered against her.

"Evan it is, then," Amanda said.

"Look, you, I don't know what kind of trick you're trying to pull on me, but I told you—"

She saw his uncertainty, his fear, and decided to keep him off balance. "Are your parents living, Evan?"

Evan was so taken aback by this question, he answered, "No. Dead for years."

"Well, if their ghosts suddenly appeared in this room, wouldn't you screech?"

"Leave them out of this. You don't know a thing about them!"

"True, although I'm sure they're both very disappointed in you, wherever they are. The point is, the ghosts of Rebecca's parents are right here, right now. Just behind you."

He glanced nervously in the direction of Rebecca's gaze and took a step sideways.

The ghosts seemed suddenly distracted and turned their heads as if they had heard a noise. They disappeared.

Amanda felt a little of her confidence go with them.

A moment later, though, she heard noises downstairs.

Evan heard them, too, and stepped into the hall and shut the light off. While he was distracted, she used her free hand to reach for Tyler's cell phone and, without holding it up to her face, pressed redial.

Evan heard the sound of Alex's voice answering hello on the other end, though, and turned back toward Amanda in a fury, snatching the phone from her and ending the call. He stepped back, then threw it hard at her, and although she tried to shield her face, it clipped her near the eye, then it slid under the bed, out of reach.

One of the stairs creaked.

Evan stepped out into the hallway, gun held nervously before him. He started to walk toward the stairway. Amanda gently left Rebecca's side, ignoring her soft sounds of panic. She looked for something to use as a weapon and saw a large vase filled with dried flowers on top of the dresser. Taking hold of it, she crept out of the bedroom.

Evan was just ahead of her, standing at the top of the stairs. If she aimed it just right . . .

Amanda heard a low growl.

"Shade, no, he's got a gun!" she shouted, throwing the vase at Evan, which clipped him on the side of the head before it shattered somewhere below.

She turned on the hall light, hoping to help the dog see the gun.

But Evan was already firing at the dog. Shade kept coming. Evan turned the gun on Amanda.

Shade leaped, knocking him to the floor, then, moving between her and Evan, stood bristling, growling at him.

Evan hurriedly came to his feet. He raised the gun again.

Shade leaped again and sank his fangs into Evan's throat.

The man burst into flames. His body, his arms, his legs, his face—all afire. His mouth opened as if to scream, and then he vanished.

Amanda stood frozen in shock.

The stairs showed no sign of burning. There were no ashes anywhere. Had she really seen . . . ? Yes, there was Shade.

Shade looked up at her. For a brief moment she wondered if he was going to attack her next, but there was nothing fierce in his gaze. He sat calmly, as if he knew she was not ready to be approached.

"Don't think me ungrateful," she said, hearing her voice tremble, "but that scared the hell out of me."

47

S hade cocked his head, then rolled over, exposing his belly. Tyler had said that until that night in the desert, Shade had never struck this submissive pose for anyone but Tyler.

She moved cautiously down the hall and reached out a shaking hand to stroke his fur. It had a calming effect on her. She tried to discover if he had been hit anywhere, but he seemed unharmed. He came to his feet, and she buried her face in his soft fur. "Shade, help me. I know you know what to do. I'm so new to this, and I'm so scared."

He softly nestled the crest of his head against her cheek, and made a kind of sighing sound. His breath was sweet and warm.

She again felt a sense of calm, one that allowed her to think more clearly. She reexamined Shade for any sign of injury, but although she could see places where bullets had struck the woodwork on the stairs and banister, he bore no wounds. She didn't understand what had happened to Evan, but she had no time to worry about that now.

"Rebecca!" she said suddenly, and ran back down the hall. Shade followed at a more stately pace.

She entered the room to see her cousin cowering in fright.

"I know, I know," Amanda said. "But he's gone now. Shade . . . got rid of him for us."

Rebecca looked gratefully at the dog.

"Hang on, let me find something to cut you loose."

Amanda ignored the ringing of Tyler's cell phone, somewhere under the bed, as she rummaged through a drawer and found a pair of scissors. She cut Rebecca's hands and feet free of duct tape, then gently worked to pull it off her face. She had nearly completed this process when Shade came to his feet and went to the door.

Amanda tried not to be alarmed by this.

She let Rebecca manage the last of the tape. Rebecca drew a few deep breaths, then reached for Amanda and began to sob in her arms.

Even over these sounds, they both heard Shade growl.

Rebecca whispered, "He's back!"

"No, no, he's not."

"How can you be sure?"

"I'm sure," she said with a shudder.

"Amanda?" a familiar voice called.

"Alex! Yes, I'm here! Rebecca, too—we're up here."

"Umm, could you call Shade off?"

"Shade!" Amanda said, moving to the doorway. "You know Alex!"

Shade remained in a warning stance—high on his toes, back bristling, ears pitched forward.

"Oh!" Amanda said, seeing that Alex had her gun drawn. "It's probably the gun. Put it away and I think he'll let you up here."

The moment Alex holstered the gun, the dog came forward to greet her in a friendly manner.

"What's going on here?" Alex asked, seeing the bullet holes in the staircase.

"Long story, and we don't have time for all of it now." Out of immediate danger, all her fears for Tyler came rushing back. "Alex, they've taken Tyler. We need to get out of here and . . ."

"And what?"

Amanda looked in panic to Shade, who stared back at her. Never had she wished so much that he could talk. She tried to calm down.

"We need to get back to Tyler's house," she said, and the dog wagged his tail. "We'll all be safer, and I—I can figure things out once we're there."

Rebecca hobbled out of the bedroom. She had Tyler's cell phone in her hand. "Yes. Let's get out of here. Please." She began to gingerly make her way down the hall.

Alex lifted her brows in surprise. "You're hurt! Let me help you."

"Just twisted my ankle when I was—" She drew in a sharp breath. "I'll be okay," she said, then burst into tears again.

"Come on," Amanda said as she and Alex each put an arm around her cousin's shoulders and helped her down the stairs. "Let's get you back to your brother."

Alex drove them back in the van. She had brought several guards with her. Rebecca and Amanda sat in the far back, on the mattress, Shade nearby.

Rebecca gave Amanda Tyler's phone. "Does your eye hurt?"

Amanda reached up to where the phone had struck her eyebrow ridge. "It's a little bruised, that's all."

Rebecca's voice dropped to a whisper as she said to Amanda, "You really saw them, didn't you?"

"Your parents?" she whispered back. "Yes. I realize it's a shock at first, but you'll get used to it."

"I remember when you told Brad and me that you had seen them. We ridiculed you."

"Well, of course you did."

Rebecca ducked her head. "Yes, 'of course.' That's what I do best, isn't it? Make fun of you."

Amanda felt a brief temptation to milk these feelings of guilt for all they were worth, then decided against it. "I'm kind of amazed that you're seeing them now, too, but it's also something of a relief, if you know what I mean?"

"I thought I was going crazy."

"Oh, I've been thinking that about myself for years. I have to know— are they wearing evening clothes?"

"No. Tennis whites." She shivered. "The last thing I saw them wearing."

"What do you know . . ." On the whole, Amanda thought, she was glad she saw them looking more elegant.

"This can't be happening," Rebecca said.

"You need some rest. I'm sure it's all been horrible for you. I'm so sorry it took so long to free you."

"You were . . . you were really brave."

"I'm used to the ghosts," she said.

"Not used to men with guns."

"No," Amanda admitted. "But don't think I wasn't scared, too."

By the end of even the short ride back up the hill, Amanda was glad that she could hand Rebecca off to Brad and Ron. She found it unsettling to be around her cousin while she was in this mood. She thought of Rebecca as bold and daring—if often without regard for other people's feelings. Seeing Rebecca scared and repentant was hard to take in.

"I'll be up in Tyler's rooms," she told Ron and Alex. "Come and see me once you and Brad calm her down and take care of her cuts and bruises, okay?"

As she passed the library, she heard a dog pawing frantically at the doors. She took pity on Wraith and opened them. The dog bounded out of the room but went straight to Amanda, exuberantly circling her, wagging her tail and giving joyful barks. Shade joined in the celebration.

Amanda stood stock-still, momentarily paralyzed with fear—then told herself to relax. These were cemetery dogs. She must think of Wraith in the same way she thought of Shade.

"Well, yes," she said over the din. "I'm glad to meet you, too. But we have work to do."

Both dogs immediately grew quiet and stared at her.

She reached out carefully to touch Wraith. The dog's fur was silky. Shade's fur was pleasant to touch, but this dog—this dog's fur was amazing. She felt suddenly that she would never have anything to fear from this dog. She wanted this dog, and if Tyler thought they weren't going to keep it—why, she'd keep it herself.

She knelt beside Wraith, and the dog breathed softly onto her cheek. Like Shade's, Wraith's breath was warm and sweet, a scent that calmed her.

She found an unexpected sense of confidence. She could help Tyler. She wasn't sure exactly how, but she would find him. Now—how to begin?

To her relief, her aunt and uncle appeared. Both dogs growled but ceased when she ordered them to be quiet. "Thank goodness you're here," she told the ghosts. "I'm trying to figure out what to do next. Can you help me?"

Her aunt and uncle both pointed to their wedding rings.

"I need to find the ring?"

Her aunt and uncle nodded.

"Shade," Amanda said, "I could search the whole house and never find it. You've been at his side almost constantly. Do you know where the ring is?"

He immediately trotted into the library. Amanda and Wraith followed. Her aunt Catherine and uncle Jordan disappeared.

Once there, Shade became less helpful. He sat down on a rug in front of the hearth and stared at the fireplace. There was no fire burning now, so she bent to examine the grate. It was solid. None of the bricks was loose. She sighed and decided not to waste time trying to coax him. Feeling like a snoop, she began opening desk drawers. She found the pages Tyler had given her to read, and quickly reread the section in which Adrian had given Tyler the ring.

Adrian had told Tyler that if he accepted the bargain, the dog would always find him.

She looked up at Shade. "You can find Tyler?"

He barked.

"I'll take that to be a yes."

She frowned. The ghosts had been clear about needing to take the ring, or she'd urge Shade to take her to him now.

Wraith was staring at Shade.

No, she realized. Wraith was staring at something above Shade.

The mantelpiece.

She moved back to the fireplace. The front piece was a dark wood, carved in an intricate design, a series of Celtic knots into which a dragon was interwoven. She felt along it, looking for a secret latch or other mechanism. She found none.

Then she looked at the left side of the mantel, which faced a wall of books. Normally, no one would see it without coming around to this side and standing in a narrow space between the mantel and the shelves.

The end of the mantel was carved with a winged death's-head.

"*Memento mori*," she said.

The dogs were now looking at her expectantly.

She studied the figure and realized that one of the eyes of the skull looked a little different from the other. Its surface was slightly smoother.

She pressed it, and a drawer slid forward.

She pulled, and it came free, spilling its contents at her feet.

More than one hundred silver mourning rings rolled across the hardwood floor.

48

Y ou don't need to tell me," Adrian said angrily as Daniel entered the basement. "Evan is dead."

"Dead! No—"

"Ah. You didn't know." The shell eyelids blinked with a little clicking noise. "And yet you arrive here without him."

"He wanted to go back to the house and shoot the girl—not the girl you wanted, this one was Brad's sister. I wanted to hurry up and bring Hawthorne to you."

"Hawthorne?" Adrian said sharply. "You've brought him here?"

"Yes, my lord—I mean, sir." Daniel winced at this slipup, but Adrian seemed not to notice. "I hope I did the right thing."

"The right thing? My boy, you have exceeded my expectations! Bring him down here at once."

Daniel hurried up the stairs, and cautiously approached the man he had left tied up on the kitchen floor. Hawthorne hadn't moved. His eyes were still closed, his face gray. His clothing was drenched in blood. Daniel almost expected his skin to be cold as he picked him up again, but instead the man burned with fever, a warmth Daniel felt even through the layers of Hawthorne's clothing. He had never known anyone to get such a high fever so soon after an injury.

Adrian had told them that they would not be able to kill this man, only to injure him so badly they would have time to search his clothing for the ring. But maybe Evan's bullets had done the job. It was hard to believe a man in this condition could live much longer without medical attention. Daniel found himself feeling itchy wherever his skin had come in contact with Hawthorne's blood. He told himself to stop being such a wuss.

He could not help but look at Hawthorne's fingers, double-checking them. He wore no ring. Eduardo had told Adrian that the man did not wear the ring, something Eduardo had known first because Brad and others who came in contact with Hawthorne had said he wore no jewelry, and second because he had checked this for himself, using a telescope to spy on Hawthorne when he walked from his car to the hospice or stood on his balcony. He dared not come closer, Eduardo said, because of the dog.

And now Eduardo was dead, and the only other time Hawthorne had been at their mercy, out in the desert, they had been worried about a witness—this woman who was his lover, as it turned out. And then the dog had arrived, and they had had to leave before they met Eduardo's fate.

How had Evan died? he wondered. Probably the dog. Despite the heat emanating from Hawthorne's body, Daniel suddenly felt cold with dread. That dog had jumped right into the truck. He had been inches from meeting Evan's fate.

It was difficult to negotiate the narrow stairs while carrying Hawthorne, but he managed it.

Adrian motioned with his clawlike hands. "Here, here, on the table!"

As Daniel complied, Adrian went down on all fours—his only means of moving around now—and scuttled to Daniel's side. Daniel could not help giving a small cry of pain as Adrian used his pincer hands—which he saw now had grown stronger and larger—to grasp Daniel's leg and arm, slowly pulling himself up in this manner until he stood.

"Ah, yes!" Adrian said. "Hawthorne! My dear Daniel, you do not know—cannot conceive of—how long I have waited for this encounter!" He laughed. "Oh, this is excellent."

Hawthorne moaned.

"Quickly! Chain him!" Adrian ordered. As Daniel obeyed, Adrian studied him, then said, "Do you think he is harmless?"

"Evan shot him, sir, I don't know how many times. He's got a high fever."

"Do you see these three bullet holes in his clothing, these two through the chest? And this one, in the stomach area?"

"Yes, sir."

"And all this blood?"

"Yes, sir."

"Tear open the shirt. Look at the wounds."

Daniel did as he was told and then stared in disbelief—though Hawthorne's torso was covered with drying blood, his wounds were nothing more than red marks. A glance at his face showed color returning to it.

"I warn you, Daniel, he is far from harmless. He could easily kill us both, without experiencing anything more than temporary discomfort."

"Yes, sir."

"Search him for the ring. Search thoroughly. Then bring me a sharp knife."

Daniel did as he was asked, all the while thinking of Adrian's caution. He had never seen Adrian respond to anyone as if he were afraid—but clearly, he was afraid of this man. Even his previous warnings about Hawthorne had not prepared Daniel to see such a reaction.

He scratched at his hands.

By the time he returned from the kitchen with the knife, all signs of the bullet wounds had disappeared. Daniel reached Adrian's side just as Hawthorne's eyes opened. For a moment Hawthorne seemed utterly confused, pulling weakly at the manacles, frowning as he looked about the room.

Adrian took his face between the powerful pincers that served as his right hand, forcing Hawthorne to look up at him.

At first sight of the fleshless face, Hawthorne attempted to turn away, but Adrian held him fast.

"Do you not recognize the man who gave you your very life, Captain Hawthorne?"

There was a flash in the dark eyes, then Hawthorne said, "I thought the fever was giving me a nightmare, but I should have known you by the stink, Adrian."

For that little joke, Adrian pressed the pincers closed until Hawthorne's jaw broke.

Daniel saw the agony of this injury written on the man's face, although Hawthorne did no more than grunt at the moment the bone audibly cracked.

"Now, while you are healing, I shall ask Daniel to note that your powers of recovery do not exclude you from the experience of pain. If you do not want to live out eternity in this cellar, experiencing more pain, you will tell me what you have done with my ring."

After a moment, Adrian said, "Yes, now I think you are well enough to speak. Where is the ring?"

"Shade will find me, you know," Hawthorne whispered.

Adrian laughed. "Dear me. Do you think that dog will be of any help to you? You forget that he and I share a bond as well. He cannot attack me."

Hawthorne looked to Daniel. "What a comfort to you. If you are Adrian's creature, you are in danger from that dog."

"Don't worry, Daniel," Adrian said quickly.

"But, sir—what he did to Eduardo, and probably to Evan—"

"You will not share their fates," Adrian said distractedly. "Tyler!"

Hawthorne's eyes were drifting closed. Adrian pinched his face again, and Hawthorne looked up at him but seemed unable to focus. Adrian let go of him.

"Tyler," he said in a coaxing voice, "where is my ring?"

"What ring?" Hawthorne murmured and closed his eyes.

"Daniel, feel his face. Is he warm?"

Daniel obeyed. "Still burning up, sir."

Adrian sighed. "Damn. I should have let that little demonstration wait."

"What shall I do with the knife, sir?"

Adrian looked thoughtful for a moment, then said, "Set it on the desk for now. We must make an elixir that will shorten the time of his fever . . . if I can remember how to make it." He laughed. "However, if I concoct a poison by mistake, it will simply give me something else to use to persuade him."

Daniel said nothing.

"Now, listen carefully, Daniel. In the cupboard to the right of the desk, you will find a bottle labeled *Tanacetum parthenium* . . ."

"Sir, may I please wash first? My skin—it itches."

Adrian stared at him. "Does it? Yes. Shower and change your clothes. You may have something of a reaction to his blood. When you come back down here, bring a pair of gloves with you. Oh—and that item I had you purchase at . . . what is it called again?"

"The hardware store, sir."

"Yes. I think we should have that on hand."

Daniel went upstairs and showered for as long as he dared.

49

Amanda stood watching in dismay as the rings rolled in every direction.

"Can you help me out here?" she asked the dogs.

They sat staring at her.

"Let's forget about the ring. Let's just find Tyler."

When she headed toward the door, Shade blocked her way.

I don't have time for this!

But each time she tried to dodge around him, he stepped in front of her.

She felt her fears rise, but she quickly tamped them down. Shade wasn't growling or trying to bite her. "Are you herding me?"

He wagged his tail.

"All right, all right!" She decided to do as he clearly wanted her to— after all, he had been with Tyler for a couple of centuries, and she had little hope of finding Tyler without him.

She scooped up the rings she could easily find, and placed them on the table. She then got down on her hands and knees to recover as many of them as she could. It was in this position that Ron and Alex found her a few moments later.

"What are you doing?" Ron asked.

"Help me gather these rings."

"Tyler has been shot and kidnapped, and you're looking at jewelry?" Alex asked angrily.

"Believe me," Amanda said, not looking up from her task, "we have to find his ring before we find him."

"You're crazy!"

"Alex . . . ," Ron began.

"I'm sure it looks that way, but, Alex, you must already know that Tyler . . . isn't like other men. He has gifts, and . . . he's different in other ways. He needs this ring. I wish I could tell you more, but it's up to him to do that."

"I don't understand—" Alex began.

"We don't need to understand," Ron said, interrupting her. "Amanda knows things about this situation that we don't, and if she could tell us about them, she would. If she says this will help him, it will. Let's help her."

He got down on the floor and began retrieving the rings that had rolled under the far couch.

After a moment, Alex said, "Right," and did the same.

Amanda sat back on her heels, momentarily overcome.

"Thank you . . . thank you both."

Ron passed by her to place the rings he had found on the table, and gave her a reassuring squeeze on the shoulder.

When they were sure they had gathered all of the rings, Amanda waited to see if some sort of feeling came over her. None did. The ghosts were nowhere in sight.

Great, now that I wish you'd appear, where are you?

The rings were varied, both in style and in the materials from which they were made. Some were fashioned from gold, others from silver, some were oval, others were square, some swiveled on hinges set at each end of their shanks. Ivory, enamel, and even braided hair were worked into their designs. Some held miniatures of the departed—several were of children. Others were designed with willows, forget-me-nots, or memorial urns. One was of a skeleton holding an hourglass, in which all the sand had run to the bottom. Others seemed to be small portions of portraits, one an eye and cheekbone, made to look as if the beloved deceased were watching the bearer. Most, though, were a variation of the winged death's-head.

"They're sad, aren't they?" Alex said.

"Amanda," Ron said, "you do realize these are worth a fortune?"

"That's not really important to me right now. I need to find a particular ring."

"Can I help? I know a little something about mourning rings."

"You do?" Alex said in surprise.

"Well, yes," he said, almost apologetically. "Derek, my grandfather, was a collector of antiques, and I helped him catalog most of his belongings. He wasn't so great with computers, so it was a way I could help him out. He liked mourning rings and memento mori in general."

Amanda said, "Can you tell how old they are? I'm looking for one that's older than the time of Napoleon."

"Can any of these be that old?" Alex asked.

"Oh, sure," he said, starting to sort through them. "The practice of making them goes back to ancient times. Most of these are Victorian, probably made late in the nineteenth century. Queen Victoria brought them into fashion when she mourned the loss of her husband."

He quickly sorted a large number of rings out of the mix. "These are probably Victorian."

About twenty rings remained. Most were similar in design.

"Okay, that helps. Tyler will immediately recognize the one he needs." *I hope.* "I'm taking all of these." She put one on the ring finger of her right hand. No special feeling came over her.

"One for every finger and toe?" Alex asked.

Amanda thought for a moment, her hand going unconsciously to the simple chain necklace she was wearing. As her fingers closed around it, she said, "On this."

She unfastened the chain, laced it through the remaining rings, and fastened it again.

She no sooner had this around her neck than Wraith came to her side, leaning against her, then went with Shade to the library door.

"Now what?" Alex asked.

"Follow the dogs."

They didn't have far to go—the dogs hurried into Tyler's room. Shade scratched at a desk drawer. Amanda opened it to find a set of keys to the van. "I guess we're going in the van," she said, following them downstairs. The ghosts of her aunt and uncle were waiting for her. So were Brad and Rebecca.

"We're going to be a little crowded," Alex said.

The ghosts shook their heads.

Forty-five minutes later, she was driving down the canyon road in Tyler's van, only the dogs with her. Most of those forty-five minutes had been spent convincing the other humans to stay behind. She got the clear message from her aunt and uncle that she should go alone. Rebecca got the message, too, and quickly became her ally, although the others saw this as more mistreatment of Amanda by Rebecca.

"Really, it's not," Amanda had said. "Alex, please, we need someone to keep the house and everyone in it safe." She handed her Tyler's cell phone. "Keep this. Start writing down the numbers he has stored in it—we may need reinforcements."

It was a nice try, but Alex told her to keep it, and didn't give up on insisting that she should go with her. She believed Alex would have forced her way into the passenger seat of the van, but when she opened the door, Shade bared his teeth and barked fiercely at her. Alex was clearly taken aback but offered no protest as she shut the door and let them go.

The dogs were crowded at the front of the van, Shade on the passenger seat, sticking his head out the open window, Wraith staying close to her. Wraith had hardly left her side since she had put on the necklace of rings. It made her feel sure that at least one of these rings was the one Adrian had given to Tyler.

"I'm almost at the end of the canyon road here," she said, glancing at Shade. "I take it you'll tell me which way to turn?" Both dogs suddenly looked straight ahead, ears pitched forward.

She looked back at the road and slammed on the brakes to avoid hitting a man who stood in the middle of her lane.

She drew in a sharp breath. "Colby!"

He sauntered over to the passenger door, opened it, and politely requested of Shade that he get in the back.

Shade cocked his head, then moved off the seat.

Colby looked at the back of the van and laughed. "A bed! How very convenient."

"Look, Colby—"

"Yes, I know—you're in a mad panic to get to Tyler, completely understandable, but let's say I may be able to help you get there faster than even these two dogs can do the trick. Shade will have to hunt him out, you know, and it could take days. Tyler might still be alive but—" He paused and watched Wraith, then looked at Amanda. "Good God."

"What?"

"She's bonding with you. Nothing complete yet, but—well, forgive me. This isn't to the point."

"So tell me! Which way do I turn?"

He smiled. "Oh, there's a small price for me to serve as your personal GPS."

"What?" she said warily.

"Let me make love to you."

She felt a little rise of hysteria and clamped down on it. "I'm sorry—I don't mean to insult you, but really, I've never been further from being in the mood. If you can't help me, please just go."

"He's torturing him, you know. Constantly. Tyler recovers and Adrian inflicts another painful injury."

She felt herself grow light-headed. *I will not faint.* Wraith moved closer, and she petted her and felt calmer. "He's your friend. Help me save him."

"Is he my friend? You know, really, I don't have friends. Tyler said as much to me not long ago."

"He did mention that you go out of your way to provoke him, but he is concerned about you."

Colby smiled. "I could almost be touched by that. But I'd really rather be touched by you. And that I touch you back. I can promise you that it will be incredibly pleasant for you."

"Why are you asking this of me? You aren't going to convince me that you're really interested in me."

"But I am."

"Colby, that is such—"

"I am. But as for why—oh, let's say that Tyler was right. I go out of my way to provoke him. There! How honest of me! But I really don't want him to suffer too much pain at Adrian's hands—such as they are."

"What does that mean?"

"You'll see, I'm sorry to say."

She stared out at the road, wondering what she should do. She stroked Wraith's fur. Every second that went by, Tyler was suffering. But she couldn't bring herself to be with anyone other than Tyler—and even if she hadn't cared so much about Tyler, she could not make love to someone who would make a weapon out of intimacy. She'd already been there, done that.

He's in trouble.

Tyler's words came back to her. She was quite sure that Colby would never divulge his problems to her, but she said, "You don't really want to be with me at all."

"Don't I?"

"No. And you know what? I don't think you want to be dealing with Adrian for the rest of eternity either."

"Adrian," he scoffed. "I knew him before he called himself that. He is incredibly boring, you know. Really, nothing is more boring than purity—whether it is pure evil or pure good. Adrian and Tyler deserve each other."

"Tyler isn't pure good."

He raised his eyebrows.

"He's not. The perfect have nothing to regret. He regrets losing his temper with you."

"He always was more human than not. Please don't think I'm praising him by saying that."

"You're human, too. Or you'd like to be. You still have empathy, I think. You really do want to care about someone other than yourself."

"Don't kid yourself."

"I don't think I'm the one kidding myself right now."

He said nothing, and she sighed. "Shade, which way do I turn?"

"Oh, for God's sake. I really don't want to be stuck with Adrian. Turn right."

She hesitated.

"I know Tyler told you I'm a liar. And I am. So—Shade, if I lie, you may bite me."

"No! That would mean—no, Shade. Not that."

"You've seen what happens?"

"Yes."

"And even if I might give you false directions, you'd keep me from going up in flames?"

"Yes."

"Too bad. If I thought I could get that result, I'd lie my ass off. Now turn right."

50

Tyler opened his eyes to see a beautiful woman in an evening gown holding his hand. Why was she so sad?

He was cold. He looked down at his blood-soaked, nearly naked form, and felt shame that this woman was seeing him in this state. Her gaze never left his face, though, and he began to feel certain that she was trying to convey some message to him. The memory of the photo at Amanda's house came back to him. This was Amanda's mother. What did she so urgently need him to know?

A moment later, the knife sliced through him again—between his ribs, this time—and the woman disappeared. He strained against the manacles, the searing pain bringing him back to full awareness of his situation.

"Why are you being so stubborn?" Adrian asked. "It's not as if I'm asking you to return my money. You can have it and keep all your powers. It's selfish of you to try to deny me this one request, when I've done so much for you. Just give me the ring."

Tyler wanted to scream, knew Adrian wanted to hear him do just that, and concentrated all his efforts on riding out the next few agonizing moments.

Not that Adrian had been denied the sound of his screams. The pincers had been at work, breaking his bones, tearing at his skin, crushing his testicles. That he rapidly healed only gave Adrian another opportunity to torture him when he regained consciousness moments later.

Even Adrian had tired of this, though, and apparently realized that the potion he had forced Tyler to drink—designed to reduce the fevers and further speed his ability to heal—was only going to be of limited use against such harm to Tyler's body. So Adrian chose to go about it more methodically, and ordered his assistant to take over the job.

That he had coerced his assistant into obedience was not lost on Tyler. There was reluctance in this man Daniel. Reluctance that even Adrian was aware of—no, Tyler realized, that Adrian enjoyed. Daniel's evident disgust with the role of torturer made his submission all the more delightful to Adrian.

What plans did Adrian have for Daniel? He looked at the skinless form, the pincers, the thin legs, much of which appeared to be borrowed from other creatures, mostly insects and arachnids. Like a self-assembled Frankenstein, although clearly not all the parts had been taken from humans. He suddenly had no doubt that Adrian would make similar use of Daniel.

Despite the fact that Daniel inflicted pain on him again and again, Tyler began to pity the man. Daniel was doomed.

"Is there anyone in your family you'd like me to contact after you die?" Tyler asked him. "Any message for them?"

Daniel looked startled, then afraid.

Adrian began to laugh. He laughed and laughed.

Daniel turned away, but Tyler had seen a look of resentment briefly cross his face.

Adrian moved closer. "What makes you think you will get out of here to deliver any more of your precious messages, Tyler? Didn't they teach you the story of Prometheus at Eton? Surely some tutor taught it to you even before then." He laughed again. "But Daniel has no idea what I'm talking about."

"He gave men the gift of fire," Daniel said quietly. "He made Zeus angry."

"Yes," Adrian said, clicking his eyelids as he blinked in surprise. "And was chained to a rock and had his liver eaten by an eagle every day, and had it grow back in time for the next round—not so unlike our friend Tyler here. But tell me, who taught you anything about Prometheus?"

"We have schools here, too . . . sir."

Adrian stared at him for a long moment, then smiled. "Quite. Now, Tyler, you really mustn't try to tempt dear Daniel into being your ally, because that will make me extremely angry, and Daniel knows more about that than he knows about Greek mythology. Am I right, Daniel?"

"Yes, sir."

"You see, Tyler, you will make things easier for me and for Daniel and for your beloved Amanda and yourself as well if you simply tell me where the ring is."

Tyler felt his stomach turn to ice when he heard Adrian say Amanda's name, but made no response.

"I know all about her," Adrian said. "I am a little surprised that you chose someone so—what was the phrase her cousin used to describe her, Daniel?"

"Clumsy and unsophisticated, sir."

Tyler watched in fascination as the ghost of Thelia Clarke reappeared and moved toward Adrian. Her face bore a regal look of disdain, and she swatted at him, almost as if he were one of the insects he half resembled.

Her hand swept through him, and Tyler would have thought her blow had had no effect if he had not seen Adrian's face change. Adrian turned and stared in the direction from which the ghost stood eyeing him with disfavor. His eyelids clicked rapidly, but it was plain to Tyler that he could not see Thelia Clarke.

Adrian loomed over Tyler. "What damned creature have you summoned here, fool?"

"I've summoned no one into your stinking presence. And really, you know far more about damnation than I do, Adrian. If for nothing more than what you've done to Daniel, I have no doubt you'll soon be shaking hands with the devil himself."

"I ask you who is here!"

"Afraid, Adrian? You should be."

"Really? I might say the same of you. I don't suppose that—given your limited view of the room—you can see the bag of quick-setting cement next to this table. I had Daniel fetch it for me from the garage during one of your unfortunate periods of unconsciousness. Isn't this a wondrous age? Quick-setting cement." He smiled. "I'm sure you don't need to see it to imagine what it will be like to be encased in concrete for a time. I promise to leave breathing tubes to ensure that you have plenty of time to enjoy the experience."

For a moment the image Adrian presented had its intended effect, and he felt fear, cold and unrelenting. It was all too easy to imagine end-less decades entombed alive in silence and darkness, unable to move—and unable to die.

Then a hand took his own, and he looked up to see Thelia, smiling and shaking her head, as if to tell him that he should not let Adrian frighten him. Gradually her presence calmed him, and he began to con-sider the implications of being able to see her, when Adrian could not. He returned her smile and saw Adrian's displeasure at his smile.

"Did it never occur to you, Adrian, that the rules of the game might not be the same for the two of us? That the way you choose to live affects all else? You've always been your own poisoner, Adrian."

"Cut his throat!" Adrian ordered Daniel.

Daniel approached the table, but he was shaking and seemed unable to bring himself to obey Adrian's command.

As if forgetting that he did not have hands, Adrian reached out with a claw to grab the knife, but only managed to knock the blade from Dan-iel's hand. It skittered across the floor and came to rest beneath a desk.

Adrian turned in fury and grabbed Tyler's throat with his sharp claw.

Tyler felt the claw pierce his artery, saw the warm blood spray from his own neck, and lost consciousness.

He awoke to hear Daniel screaming pitifully, although Adrian did not appear to be touching him. The sound was horrible, and Tyler began to pray for some way to relieve the man's agony.

Thelia was still at his side. He saw her cock her head to one side and look up, as if she heard something outside.

In the space it took Daniel to draw a breath, Tyler heard it, too, and eventually, so did Adrian.

"Shut up!" Adrian snapped at Daniel. "Listen!"

The sound was unmistakable, one Tyler would have known anywhere.

The howling of a cemetery dog.

51

H ere we are," Colby said.

"There isn't anything here," Amanda said, suddenly fearing that she had been dealing with a creature who was in league with Adrian, who had guided her through the winding curves of a neighboring canyon and was now leaving her in the middle of nowhere.

Colby smiled. "I haven't led you astray. Adrian's up to some old tricks and has shielded this place from prying eyes and ears. Now, I really do wish I could be of more assistance, but you've got the ring and the dogs, after all. This is where I must take my leave of you."

"You're going?"

This time, when he smiled at her, it seemed to be with genuine tenderness. Before she knew what he was doing, he took her hand and kissed it in a courtly manner. "I hope we meet again, Amanda Clarke. I do mean that." He let go of her hand and laughed. "And won't that irritate the hell out of Tyler!"

He vanished.

Even though Tyler had warned her that this was among Colby's powers, she gasped in surprise. And felt a little bereft.

They had stopped at what appeared to be a rough asphalt driveway leading to a lot that had nothing more than shrubbery and a few trees on it. There was no other turn to make, but they also hadn't reached any real destination.

She took a deep breath and turned into the driveway.

An instant later, she saw her father's ghost. Her hopes soared, and she swore that if she and Tyler escaped with their lives, she'd beg Tyler to help Colby in return for his kindness.

Her father was beckoning her to get out of the van. She did, bringing the dogs and her flashlight with her. The dogs watched him but did not seem to be as hostile toward him as usual.

The moment she stepped onto the driveway, she saw the house behind the trees and shrubs. She was startled and wondered how she could have missed seeing it from the road.

The two-story house was old for this part of Los Angeles, probably built in the 1920s, judging by its style. The windows were darkened by heavy curtains, but she saw no sign that anyone was at home.

"Is this where Tyler is?" she whispered to her father.

He nodded and pointed toward a narrow garage, one with hinged double doors. She crept toward it. The doors were not latched, and when she swung one open, she saw the truck in which Tyler had been taken. She glanced toward the house, then dared to turn on the flashlight. She aimed its light into the back of the truck, already sensing he would not be there, and cringed at the sight of the darkened bloodstains on the truck bed.

She saw a tool bench and looked it over. It didn't have much to offer—mostly odds and ends of small hardware, greasy nuts and bolts that appeared to be left over from a previous tenant. "No ax, not even a crowbar," she said wistfully. "I wish I had thought to bring one."

She crept back toward the house and looked for a house number. There was none to be seen. She took out Tyler's cell phone, thought of calling Alex, and changed her mind. Better to keep the others safe. She had a plan, one she was sure would not meet with their approval, but which was the only way out of this she could think of. A possible fault in her strategy occurred to her, though.

She knelt beside Shade and Wraith and said, "Tyler needs the ring, right?"

The dogs wagged their tails.

"I've been thinking about what happened when Tyler became . . . as he is. You chose him, didn't you, Shade?"

The dog looked toward Amanda's father, who nodded his head. The answer was yes.

To be certain, she said, "If he doesn't have the ring, can Adrian force Shade or Wraith to serve him?"

Some communication seemed to take place again, and her father shook his head.

The last question was the hardest. "Wraith seems to like me, so, since I have the ring right now, should I—well, if it looks as if Adrian is going to take her or the ring before I can give the ring to Tyler, should I—should I try to kill myself so that Wraith becomes my dog instead of Adrian's?"

Her father shook his head vehemently. He came closer to her, placing his hands on either side of her face, though all she felt was a slight chill. She could read the message in his eyes.

"No, it seemed wrong to me, too. But I had to ask, given what's at stake here." She sighed. "Thanks for helping me out, Dad. I just wish there was an army of you at my back."

He smiled and gave her a cold kiss on the forehead before releasing her and stepping back.

"Where's Mom?"

He pointed to the house, then hesitated, then touched the ring on her finger.

"In there with Tyler?"

He nodded.

"Well, I'm glad of that. At least he's not alone." She made sure the necklace of rings was hidden beneath her clothes, and found herself calming as she touched them. She took a deep breath. "Let's get on with it, then."

The dogs seemed to take this for a command and herded her toward a back door.

She reached a shaking hand to the doorknob and tried turning it.

The door was locked. She was considering breaking the window in the door when the dogs threw back their heads and began to howl.

The moment they did so, she also heard screaming—horrific, pain-filled screams that at first frightened her, then quickly made her fear turn to anger.

52

Get my cloak!" Adrian snapped. "Hurry! She'll find a way in any moment now!"

Amanda was here. Tyler knew it as surely as he knew that Shade and Wraith were with her. He ignored the sounds of Daniel scrambling to obey Adrian, ignored Adrian's furious criticisms of his servant, and strained against the manacles. The intense pain in his wrists and hands told him to stop, but he pulled harder, until the skin near the manacles was torn away and the cuffs were slick with blood.

His shoulders and elbows were on fire, but he forced himself to keep pulling, hoping to break his own bones if that was what it would take to free his hands. His earlier injuries had weakened him, and with growing frustration he realized that until his strength was fully recovered, he was unlikely to succeed. Still, he tried, wanting desperately to be free to protect Amanda from Adrian.

"Stop him from doing that!" Adrian shouted.

Daniel moved over to Tyler, looked frantically about him, and grabbed a rag that he tore into strips. With these, he began to wrap Tyler's left hand and wrist. "No," Tyler protested. "Please . . ."

Daniel met his eyes, looking scared, but continued working. Both hands were throbbing with pain, but Tyler sensed that the big man was trying to be gentle. He finished tying up the ends of the makeshift bandage and moved to Tyler's right hand. The left was now so thickly covered there was no question of pulling it free.

Tyler could have wept with frustration. He tried to calm himself, to keep his head clear. Amanda would need him to have his wits about him, however little use he might be in physically aiding her. He felt Daniel give his shoulder a quick, awkward pat.

Daniel had already stepped away to obey Adrian's next imperious summons when Tyler realized that something cold and hard had been bound into his right hand, almost completely covered by the bandages. He folded his fingers over the end of a small metal object.

A key.

53

The screaming stopped.

Amanda glanced around the back porch. She saw a clay flowerpot, filled with dirt, all plant life long gone. She grabbed it and ordered the dogs back, then launched it through the door's glass pane.

She hid to one side of the small porch, expecting that the noise of the glass breaking would bring someone up to investigate. She heard a voice, indistinct but with a strident quality, as if issuing commands. She strained to hear what was said but could not make out the words.

She continued to wait and listen hard for long moments, but heard no sounds other than her own pounding heartbeat and the soft panting of the dogs, just behind her. She took a steadying breath and reached inside the door and unlatched it, then opened it cautiously.

She stood aside, again uncertain. The dogs came up beside her and leaped over the broken glass and into the kitchen. They looked back at her, waiting. Once she entered, they quickly moved to a closed door and scratched at it. She opened it, and was immediately taken aback by a strong odor of mustard and an underlying scent of decay. The dogs seemed unaware of this—no sooner was the door open than they ran down the stairs.

She heard Tyler's voice shouting hoarsely, "No! Shade, Wraith, no!"

This was followed by the sound of a blow and a groan.

She hurried down the stairs after the dogs.

First she saw the dogs growling at a man who cowered in a shadowed corner. Her mind went back to her own experience of being attacked, then to what she had witnessed not long ago on the staircase of her home. Although they bared their teeth at the man, she sensed that they hesitated to attack. "Come to me," she said to the dogs, not quite steadily.

They quickly retreated to her side, although almost immediately Shade began to whine, focused toward her right. She turned to see what held his interest and received a shock that made her sway on her feet.

Tyler lay on a table, his face and body covered with blood, some of it drying. She could see a red slash on his throat. His hands were wrapped in rough bandages, his face etched with pain. She hurried to his side, the dogs with her. "Tyler—"

"Amanda, I'm so very sorry," he said, in little more than a whisper. He made a motion as if to reach across his body with his right hand, but the chains brought him up short. She gently took the hand in hers, flinching at the touch of cold iron. "Loosen that bandage a little, will you, love? I can hardly feel your touch."

She read the message in his eyes and carefully extracted the key. His hand felt warm—too warm—he was feverish. He pulled her closer to him.

"Hears everything. It's not safe . . . to talk now," he said in a whisper, and she did not miss the slight pause. Not safe to use the key, then. She slipped it into her pocket, and she saw that he was pleased that she had understood him. He reached up again, and she bent nearer. He brushed the backs of his fingers against the thick sweater she wore, near her collarbone, moving exactly to the necklace of rings before he let his hand drop.

"Shade should not have shown you . . ."

"Where to find you?" a voice said from behind her. "You're wrong about that. Delirious, no doubt."

She turned around. On the far side of the room, a hooded and cloaked figure, looking something like a black-robed monk—no, she thought, like Death—stood behind a large desk.

"Please allow me to introduce myself," the man said. "Adrian, Lord Varre. Daniel, come here. Give me your arm."

Daniel moved to his side and supported him as he walked toward the table. He had difficulty moving, and she heard him muttering as they crossed the room.

Is Adrian injured? Amanda wondered.

As they drew nearer the table, Shade jumped up on it, standing protectively over Tyler. Daniel came to a halt.

"Forward, you fool. The dog has been told not to harm you or you'd be dead already."

Shade curled his lip but didn't snap. He settled alongside Tyler, and for a moment she wondered if his weight would cause Tyler discomfort, but it seemed to Amanda that as soon as Shade was beside him, Tyler's face grew less pale and drawn.

Unnerved by Adrian's approach, she released Tyler's hand to move around the table, positioning herself so that the table stood between her and the cloaked figure. Wraith followed her.

"It's no use!" Adrian said testily to Daniel as they neared. "I can't move or breathe." He turned to Amanda. "I apologize, Miss Clarke. I had hoped to spare you my . . . temporary hideous appearance by wearing these robes. You will doubtless find the way I look now rather horrifying, but I am told you are one who can see beyond the mere physical."

"I'm here for one reason—to get you to release Tyler. Do that and I'll look at anything."

"Oh, eventually, I'm sure he'll find a way out of here." He tore impatiently at the robe, which fell in a heap at his feet. When she saw the glistening, skinless face, the insectlike body and arms and legs, she could not suppress a small sound of revulsion, or prevent herself from leaning back.

"I know. I know," he said consolingly. "I'm sorry you did not have the opportunity to see me in my original state. I was quite handsome." He gave a little creaking bow. "I am working my way back to a . . . more presentable form."

She couldn't bear to keep looking at him. She turned her gaze back to Tyler.

"Daniel," Adrian said, "lower the lights. Yes, that's it. Miss Clarke needs a bit of time to grow accustomed to me."

"Don't be worried about that," she said, not liking to think much about what might now be hidden in the shadows. "I won't be here that long. Just release Tyler and I'll go." She saw Shade softly exhaling on Tyler's wounds. Relieving pain, she hoped.

"I know quite a bit about you, you know," Adrian said. "Even rather intimate information, Miss Clarke. It is still *Miss* Clarke, isn't it?"

Amanda ignored him. She turned to the cowering man, who had retreated to a far corner. "Are you the one who shot Tyler?"

"No," he said, eyeing her fearfully, then confessed, "I brought him here."

"Brought him here! So he could be tortured!"

"Amanda, it's all right," Tyler said. "Don't blame Daniel for following Adrian's orders. You heard his screams a moment ago."

"Oh . . . I thought that was you."

"I've had plenty of screams out of your lover," Adrian said. "There's no need for that to continue, though."

"I agree. Release him."

"Perhaps I will, but you really aren't in control of what takes place here, you know. If you want Tyler to be freed—well, that depends on you, of course. I asked you if you were still Miss Clarke because it's clear that even though Tyler has taken your virginity—"

"You have no right—," Tyler began angrily, but Adrian merely reached over and slit his throat with a claw.

54

Amanda screamed and tried to staunch the flow of blood with her hands. Within seconds, the wound had stopped bleeding, but Tyler lay unmoving, his skin cold and gray. Amanda's mind was in a whirl, mostly from the shock of seeing Tyler attacked. Why hadn't Shade or Wraith defended him?

As if reading her mind, Adrian said, "Shade recognizes me as a former master, even if not a current one." He sighed. "There's so much Tyler is unaware of. He doesn't realize how special you are. For example, you bear a scar on your face—an attack by a dog?"

"So what?" She was relieved to see Tyler's chest begin to rise and fall. He was breathing again.

"There are stories," Adrian said. "Stories of a rare set of women with such a scar, women who have the gift that Tyler has now. I searched all my long life for such a woman." He paused. "Once, I thought I had found one, but I was wrong. I would wed such a woman. She would then live with me forever."

She looked back up at him at last. "Do you expect me to believe *anything* you say to me?" She moved so that Adrian couldn't reach across the table with that claw of his. Wraith followed her. She noticed that Adrian took a moment to track her movements. Perhaps he was having trouble seeing in this low light.

"You have been marked with a particular sign," Adrian said. "Tyler cannot avoid a woman like you any more than he can avoid the dying and the undead. Shade recognized you, you see. He became quickly attached to you, didn't he? And this other one—Wraith, you called her? Every sign shows she's ready to become your own. The difficulty, alas, is that Tyler made you his."

"You're saying Wraith won't defend me because—because—" She broke off, revolted by the idea of speaking to Adrian on the subject of making love with Tyler, even to mislead him about what had actually taken place—or not taken place—between them.

"If Tyler had not taken . . . liberties, shall we say? . . . with you until *after* you had taken on your destiny, I would be a bit more vulnerable to you than I am now. But because he couldn't control his lust, happily that problem doesn't arise. In that act of lust, he bound you to both himself and to me. You might say we are relatives of a sort, and I'm protected from you. And vice versa."

Mentally she thanked Tyler and the ghosts with all her heart. To make certain she understood these ground rules, though, she said, "Explain that further, please."

"Tyler and I have a sort of blood relation, one might say. And so as much as Shade might be tempted to attack me, he won't. Tyler himself can only do limited harm to me—as I can only do limited harm to him."

She looked at Tyler's still and bloodied form. "You call that limited?"

"He isn't dead, is he? You are as unfinished, my dear, as . . . well, as I am at present," he said, holding up his claws. "Your incomplete nature is simply less visible than mine."

"Let me guess," Amanda said. "You've got a plan for you and me to complete each other?"

The insect eyes blinked with a clicking sound. "Tell me, Amanda, how would you like to be very, very wealthy?"

"I already am."

"Oh, but you're a pauper compared with me." When she said nothing, he went on. "Let me put it to you another way. You have something of mine, and I want it back."

"You gave it away at Waterloo."

"So he told you that tale, did he?"

"And more."

He considered her for a long moment, his eyelids clicking again as he blinked. The sound unnerved her. She had edged even farther along the table, nearly to Tyler's feet, when suddenly her own foot struck some sort of metal object. She glanced down and saw that stacks of metal cans and jars—potions of some kind, no doubt—were stored beneath the table.

She looked at Wraith, who was watching her intently, and in that moment Amanda felt as if she and the dog were in perfect communion. Wraith's face opened in a doggy grin, and seconds later, just long enough for Amanda to grasp the manacle on Tyler's right ankle, the dog crashed into a stack of cans.

The noise startled Adrian, who tottered back on his thin legs, nearly losing his balance.

"Stop it! Stop that dog!" he shouted, all his attention on Wraith.

Amanda stuck the key in the lock and turned it, even as she shouted to Wraith to come to her. She left the manacle in place, hoping Adrian would not immediately notice that it was now loose.

She moved to Tyler's other ankle, bending down as if to try to catch the dog, and Wraith, with beautiful timing, covered the sound of the second lock giving way by crashing into a stack of jars, shattering them.

"No! No!" Adrian cried. "Damn that dog! My herbs! My potions! Daniel, get over here!"

But Daniel was having nothing to do with dogs. Shade stood and leaped from the table, eager to join in the game. Amanda began shouting would-be commands, relieved to see that the dogs knew to ignore her. Daniel's fearful cries were added to Adrian's angry ones.

She couldn't have asked for a better distraction. The two large dogs—chasing each other in and out from under the table and around the cellar, knocking into metal cans, breaking glass, and barking sharply—provided enough mayhem to prevent Adrian from being aware of Amanda's work on the manacles.

When she finished, she managed to get the dogs' attention and brought them to her side. She then began apologizing to Adrian, and under the guise of trying to clean up the mess, attempted to distract him from Tyler.

He had no reason to suspect she had a key, she realized. Where had it come from? She glanced at Daniel, but he studiously avoided looking at her.

Adrian was in a towering rage. She suddenly realized that despite his fury, he had never aimed his deadly claws at the dogs. Just as the dogs were prevented from attacking him, perhaps he was prevented from attacking the dogs.

Shade returned to Tyler's side, but Wraith stayed with her. The items that had spilled from the canisters and jars were a mixture of pleasant (herbs and dried flowers) and disgusting (dried insects and amphibians, as well as some items she'd just as soon not identify).

But in this mood, Adrian was all the more dangerous to Tyler. Years of dealing with Rebecca's temper had taught Amanda the trick of distraction. As soon as he took a breath to continue his tirade, she asked, "Do you have a broom?"

He fell silent, eyelids clicking.

"I'll not have my future wife sweeping floors! Daniel! Come here and clean up. For the last time, the dogs have been commanded not to harm you. Quit acting the coward or I'll give you something to fear!"

Daniel sidled over, then said meekly, "Your lordship, you've never asked me to clean in here before . . ."

"You'll find a broom and dustpan in the corner closet, behind my desk. Be quick about it."

Amanda heard Tyler moan, and sought a new distraction. "You store some weird—um, unusual things in here. And what's this?"

Adrian moved awkwardly to the end of the table. "Cement."

"What a shame the bag broke open."

"All the easier to use it," Adrian said. "Now, let's talk about that ring."

55

L et me walk out of here with Tyler, and it's all yours."

He stared, eyes clicking. "No."

"Why not? The ring is what you've wanted, right?"

"Yes, but you see, what I plan to do with the ring is to—how can I put this delicately?—take back certain powers I loaned to Tyler. He'll be just like any other man then. Do you see the problem?"

He's not like any other man, immortal or not, she thought. But aloud she said, "Not exactly. Explain it to me."

"You, my dear, will stay young, and he'll age and die. You may tell yourself that you'll love him no matter what, but believe me, there are few things less attractive to a young woman than an amorous old man."

"But I won't really be young, will I?"

"You'll find a man who can retain his youthful appearance to be of greater interest. I will become that man."

"I can't imagine that, just now. I mean—I can't even figure out how you breathe without a nose."

"Can't you?" he asked, staring at her in his unnerving way.

"Well, I suppose you breathe the way an insect does, perhaps through some sort of openings in your torso?"

"Yes, although I have the ability to breathe through my mouth as well. A dual system, for the moment. And you've confirmed, Amanda, that you are not as stupid as you seem to try to make me believe you are."

She gave a start, because her parents suddenly appeared on either side of him. Shade growled, but to Amanda's ears, it was a rather half-hearted growl.

"What is it?" Adrian asked nervously.

He's an insect, she told herself. Think of him as an insect. Aloud she said, "It's cold in here—don't you think? Doesn't the cold slow insects down?"

An instant later, the temperature of the basement dropped.

"You—you've summoned spirits of some sort!"

"Really, it has never been a matter of *summoning* my parents."

"Ghosts—!" Daniel said, dropping the broom and backing away.

Adrian straightened. "Pay them no heed, Daniel. The dead can't harm the living, for all they enjoy frightening them."

Amanda said, "They can harm your kind, I'm told."

"I advise you to take care, young lady. I would prefer a long-term companion in the years to come, but not at any price. Believe me, I've made do with temporary company from women. That would be preferable to living with a shrew."

His stare was so hostile this time, she found herself taking another step back.

Amanda saw her father move to Tyler's side, and saw that Tyler's eyes were open. Her father gestured silence, and to her surprise Tyler seemed to be able to see him. Tyler glanced at Amanda, then as Adrian turned toward him, feigned unconsciousness.

Her mother, she saw, was pointing to a desk behind Adrian. No—to an object below the desk. A knife.

"Now," Adrian said, unaware of the movements of the ghosts, "I believe I shall have that ring, and leave our courtship for a later hour."

Suddenly he dropped to the floor, and she discovered that cold or no, Adrian down on all fours could move much faster than Adrian tottering upright. She screamed and tried to run, but took no more than two strides before he grabbed hold of her ankle. Horrified, she tried to kick him away, but he knocked her down. She fell hard, hitting her head as she hit the ground, and lay stunned for a moment as he crawled up over her.

He pinned her beneath his weight, holding her arms in his sharp claws, and she turned her face aside just in time to avoid his slime-covered lips from descending on hers. His kiss landed on her cheek instead, and he laughed as she tried uselessly to throw him off. She heard the sound of chains giving way across the room. Wraith circled them fretfully but did not attack Adrian. Beneath her, shards of pottery cut through her clothes and pierced her skin, and all around her desiccated frogs and salamanders covered the floor.

They were nothing to the horror above her, though. Adrian's torso, covered in hard shell-like segments, like those of a lobster, cut into her as he pressed her against the floor.

She became aware of a movement above her—Tyler had risen from the table. His arms locked around Adrian's throat. He pulled mercilessly, trying to force Adrian to free her.

Adrian growled in anger, but she could feel no lessening of his strength.

"He doesn't breathe through his throat!" she shouted, realizing Tyler would never choke him in this way. Adrian rewarded her by pulling her right hand up and biting the ring off her hand, finger and all.

She screamed, even as Adrian released her. Tyler let go of Adrian's throat, grabbed Daniel's fallen broom, and used the broomstick to deliver a series of powerful blows to Adrian's head. Dazed, Adrian turned his attention to Tyler.

Amanda cradled her injured hand and ran toward the desk, where her mother's ghost waited. Daniel came rushing toward her, and she shrank back, then saw that he was standing guard over her, ready to use himself as a shield between Adrian and her.

She scrambled beneath the desk and felt for the knife with her left hand, her fingers curling around the handle just as Adrian grabbed the broomstick in a claw and broke it into splinters. He lunged after Tyler, but Shade caused him to stumble, allowing Tyler to dodge just in time to avoid the snapping claws.

Adrian cursed the dog, then said, "I've got the ring, Tyler! And your lover's finger as well. Delicious!"

"Amanda, Daniel, leave while you can!" Tyler said.

"Utterly useless to think you can protect them, or that I won't find them if they run," Adrian said, grinning in delight. "You know that in a matter of moments, I'll be able to kill you once and for all."

"You're still mortal, Adrian. The ring was false. Can't you feel the truth of what I say to you?"

Adrian's smile faltered. "It can't be true," he said. "I felt its power!"

"Really? Do you feel that power within yourself now?"

As he asked this, Tyler reached for a chair and threw it at Adrian. Adrian turned to the side to deflect the blow, and the chair smashed into the shell-like segments that made up his torso. Adrian screamed as one of the segments cracked, revealing a set of openings in his side.

Spiracles—the openings insects need to breathe, Amanda thought. Adrian was neither fully human nor insect, but— She saw a bag of cement, and whispered to Daniel, "Help me," and gave him brief instructions. She discovered, to her surprise, that her right hand was no longer bleeding, and that it was not painful to hold the weapon with her remaining fingers.

Adrian rushed toward Tyler. Tyler fended him off with the fallen chair, using it to shield himself from Adrian's claws. But Adrian was succeeding in breaking off pieces of the chair with each new onslaught.

Amanda slit the bag of cement with the knife, and Daniel lifted it. She could see he had little confidence in her plan, and she didn't blame him.

"Now!" she shouted, and they rushed toward Adrian.

Adrian, all his attention on Tyler, didn't see them approach. Amanda carefully aimed the knife and stabbed into one of the spiracles even as Daniel dumped the cement over Adrian, aiming it for his torso.

It raised a dust cloud in the confined space that caused them all to cough. Adrian got the worst of it, though. As the dust entered the openings through which he breathed, Adrian began trying to draw breath through his mouth, wheezing and choking. Amanda used the knife again—this time to cut off one of his claws.

Again he screamed and turned on her.

Aiming to stab her throat, his remaining claw hooked on the chain around her neck and, as he tried to pull free, broke it.

Rings spilled free.

"You! You bitch from hell!" In a fury, he stabbed his remaining claw through her chest, then turned to chase down the rings, which were rolling in every direction.

The knife fell to the floor as she reached over her heart. She felt warm blood streaming over her hand just before she collapsed. Wraith quickly lay beside her.

With a cry of anguish Tyler picked up the knife, turned, and slashed the blade across Adrian's neck, nearly cutting his head off. Adrian rolled onto his back, his remaining legs and arm waving weakly before he fell still.

Tyler ran to Amanda and lifted her into his arms.

"No," he said. "Please, God, no—"

I'm dying. Tyler.

"Amanda, no—" He began to weep.

Sorry, my love, at this point it's not up to me.

"Oh, God, no. Please don't die. Please don't."

I'd rather not go, if you want the truth. Not just yet. I want a life with you. I can have one, you know, if you don't mind sharing yours.

"Then take my life. I'll gladly give mine in exchange!"

No good. If you want me around, you've got to stay around, too, I'm afraid. At least that's the way they've explained it to me.

"They?"

Look around the room. It's getting crowded in here.

He looked up to see Amanda's parents and another couple from the photo he had seen—her aunt and uncle. They were joined by others—Harry Williams, Benecia Wright, Horace Dillon, and the ghosts of a dozen more began drawing closer. Familiar faces—some recent, some from long ago—appeared. It was Private Makin who stepped forward.

Hallo, there, Captain! We'd have brought the others, but it was decided a delegation would be best, given the limited space and all. I'm going to be brief, on account of—well, time being what it is for the living.

You passed a little test, you might say, by not being selfish about hand-ing off your duties to Amanda. Showed you loved her. That's a good thing. That said, your time's actually not quite up yet. You want to live it alone, no problem. You want her to wander the earth waiting for you to show up—'cause that's what will happen to her—no problem. But if you don't mind having a partner—we've asked her, and she'd like to stay with you, for however long your lives last, and how long that may be is nothing we have any say over.

As for all of us, we're just here to tell you to trust yourself. You've always done right by us, and we know you'll do right by her. Oh, and—every last one of us thanks you, whatever you decide.

In the next instant, they were gone.

"Do you—do you truly want to stay with me, Amanda?"

Without a doubt.

"Then, oh yes, I want you at my side." He paused, looking slightly panic-stricken. "I've never, um . . . saved anyone. I don't know what to do next."

If you don't mind, ask Wraith to stand up—she's been protecting the ring by lying on it. And, Tyler? Better hurry.

Her skin was cold and her breathing had stopped. He turned to the dog, but Wraith was already coming to her feet, and Tyler saw the ring—the ring he knew to be the true ring. He picked it up and carefully placed it on Amanda's left ring finger.

Wraith exhaled softly on her face, and Tyler felt her warm beneath his hands. She was breathing again, and he could feel her pulse. A mo-ment later, her eyes fluttered open, and she smiled sleepily at him. He could feel the fever just starting to take hold of her.

He was about to kiss her and tell her that he was going to take her home, when Daniel said, "Captain Hawthorne, sir—help."

They looked over to see him doubled over in pain—and a legion of spiders coming down the stairs.

56

"A drian is causing this," Tyler said. "He's trying to revive. He must be trying to control Daniel as well."

Amanda looked up at him and smiled. "Here's where all that sleeping on the floor is going to pay off."

He thought the fever must have her further in its grip than he imagined, but she turned to Wraith and said, "Now."

Wraith eagerly leaped onto Adrian's carcass and bit into what remained of his neck. Adrian burst into fire, although the dog was untouched by the flames. A moment later, Adrian disintegrated without a trace.

The spiders on the staircase halted their march, bumped into one another in confusion, then began to scurry back up the stairs as if they couldn't wait to be away from the place.

Daniel remained curled up in a ball, shaking as both Shade and Wraith approached him next. The dogs merely breathed on him, then went back to their masters.

Daniel gradually looked up at them.

"Feeling better?" Tyler asked.

"Yes, sir." His face clouded. "I've no right to ask it, but what's to become of me?"

Tyler looked to Amanda, who read the question in his eyes, and nodded.

"Would you like to live with us?" he asked. "We can always use—er, discreet staff."

"You'd allow that? After all I've done to you?"

"You gave him the key to the manacles, didn't you, Daniel?" Amanda asked.

"Yes, ma'am, but I also robbed his place, and nearly killed him on a road, and delivered him to Adrian, and what I've done since—"

"We know," Tyler said. "Now, if you'll lock up here, we'll wait for you outside."

"In the van at the end of the drive," Amanda said. Tyler felt her skin growing warmer with the rising fever and watched her struggling to stay awake. She reached to touch Tyler's face and halted in amazement. "Oh, look! My finger! It's back."

"Yes, you'll get used to such things. Eventually. Now about the van—" Tyler's eyebrows drew together. "How did you find this place?"

"Colby helped me," she said drowsily.

"Colby *helped*—"

"Yes. I think we need to try to help him one day soon. Whose fever am I feeling against my skin, yours or mine?"

"Both, I'm afraid," Tyler said. "Although Adrian gave me a potion to reduce the effects of mine. I'll be able to guide Daniel home."

"Oh, good," she said, and fell into a deep and healing sleep.

57

T yler Hawthorne put his arm around his wife. Amanda, far from fearing the dogs, now enjoyed sitting on the floor with them, or in this case, the deck outside the bedroom. So the Hawthornes, barefoot and in bathrobes, leaned their backs against the wall, a dog at each side. The sun had set an hour ago, but the night was warm, and no one was in a rush to go inside.

Amanda, nestled close to him, looked down at her house below. Brad and Rebecca were still staying at Amanda's house, but had gone out to a concert this evening with some friends.

Colby had stayed at the wedding only long enough to claim a kiss from the bride, and seemed disappointed when Tyler had not responded jealously. He had given Amanda a chaste kiss on the cheek, shrugged when Tyler asked him not to be a stranger, and disappeared.

Ben and Daniel had the night off. Alex, who had sent the rest of her team on to other assignments, was on a first date with Ron. He smiled, thinking of how hard it had been for Ron to work up the nerve to ask her out, when she had wanted nothing more for weeks.

The ghosts were about their business elsewhere.

What the future held for them, he hardly knew. But he looked forward to it, content, as he had not been in a long, long time.

"Listen," Amanda said, sitting up a little straighter.

He did, on the alert for any disturbance. But the dogs were relaxed.

She smiled slowly and said, "They're back."

He listened more closely and returned the smile.

A soft rhythmic song carried on the breeze.

Crickets.

ABOUT THE AUTHOR

Nationally bestselling author Jan Burke has written twelve novels and a collection of short stories. Among the awards her work has garnered are the Mystery Writers of America's Edgar® for Best Novel, Malice Domestic's Agatha Award, Mystery Readers International's Macavity, and the RT Book Club's Best Contemporary Mystery.

She is the founder of the Crime Lab Project (www.crimelabproject .com) and is a member of the honorary board of the California Forensic Science Institute. She lives in Southern California with her husband and two dogs. She is currently at work on the next novel in the Irene Kelly series. Learn more about her at www.janburke.com.